Lessons in Faking

Selina Mae

ISBN: 9798893310696
Specs: Paperback with flaps and stenciled edges, 5 ½″ × 8 ½″
Price: $18.99 US / $25.99 CAN
Publication Date: 11/11/25

This is an uncorrected proof.
Please do not quote for publication until you check your copy against the finished book.

uncorrected proof

Lessons in Faking

uncorrected proof

Hall Beck University

Lessons in Faking

Selina Mae

uncorrected proof

This is an uncorrected proof. Please do not quote for publication until you check your copy against the finished book.

LYX

An imprint of Authors Equity
1123 Broadway, Suite 1008
New York, New York 10010

Authors Equity
1123 Broadway, Suite 1008
New York, New York 10010

Copyright © 2025 by Bastei Lübbe AG
All rights reserved.

Cover design by © Jeannine Schmelzer, Bastei Lübbe AG, and © Guter Punkt, Munich
Cover art by © fjordwind and motifs from Shutterstock (© Bobnevv; © Giuseppe_R; Platon Anton; Miloje)
Book design by Scribe Inc.

This is a work of fiction. Names, characters, places and incidents either are products of the author's imagination or are used fictitiously.

Most Authors Equity books are available at a discount when purchased in quantity for sales promotions or corporate use. Special editions, which include personalized covers, excerpts, and corporate imprints, can be created when purchased in large quantities. For more information, please email info@authorsequity.com.

First published in Germany in 3035 by LYX, an Imprint of Bastei Lübbe

Library of Congress Control Number: {to come}
Print ISBN 9798893310696
Ebook ISBN 9798893310801

Printed in Canada
First printing

www.lyxbooks.com
www.authorsequity.com

uncorrected proof

This book contains explicit content.

For more detailed information, please see the last page.

Disclaimer: The content warning includes spoilers for the entire book!

We wish you the best possible reading experience.

Love,
Selina & LYX

Chapter 1

I was sure of exactly three things.

1. Revenge is just another word for justice.
2. Money does buy happiness.
3. Stay away from Dylan McCarthy Williams or my brother will have me murdered in my sleep.

And how badly did I need this, really?

Technically, I was failing Statistics II—yes. And sure, Professor Shaw said this weekly tutoring thing would be the only way to get through his class, after the midterm I had "completely violated" (his words, not mine).

But let's face it. Perhaps college just wasn't my thing. Despite my mother's reputation, statistics certainly wasn't. And McCarthy certainly wasn't, either.

His tall frame hovered over a stack of papers, dark brows drawn together as he assessed one of them. Sitting in the small office chair, coffee-colored hair falling into his features, he hadn't acknowledged my presence in the doorway. Not after I'd knocked. Not after I'd opened the door. Not after I'd—

"Athalia Payton Pressley," he drawled, not looking up. My body deflated in sync with the sound of his voice, and he dropped the red pen used to scribble into his notes. Somehow, the gesture felt intentionally passive-aggressive. Like he was saying *How dare you interrupt my work?* without ever opening his mouth.

"Would you just sit?" he continued. "Or were you planning on staring at me for the entire hour?" His eyes found mine and his brows rose, with a prompting look on his face that made me want to run the other way, but instead, forced me into the chair opposite his. I crossed one leg over the other, holding the hem of my skirt in place, smoothing a hand down the wool fabric of my long sleeve.

Innocently, I blinked at him. "I was promised Shaw's best and brightest," I said, pulling a stack of notes out of my bag. "Have you seen them, by any chance?" With a loud thud, I maneuvered my papers onto the desk, and ignored that I had barely half as many as he did.

An unamused huff escaped him, and he reached for the passive-aggressive pen again. The smile on his face clearly said: *I'm not here to bullshit back and forth with you, I'm here to ass-kiss for extra credit and a good reputation.* It also said: *I'd much rather kill you now and live with the consequences than do this.* But any threat was hidden behind deep dimples and the words "You can't really be surprised, can you?"

He gestured to his own frame, down the plain black t-shirt, silver chain disappearing under its neckline. His outfit didn't necessarily scream *Straight A Student!* but McCarthy's reputation preceded him, and no, I *wasn't* surprised. He just didn't need to know that.

McCarthy was, if nothing else, what my brother hated most in this world. More than strawberry ice cream ("It's a sorry excuse of a flavor, Athalia! No, I'm not debating you on this.")

More than Eric (my first boyfriend). More than our dead parents (for . . . dying?). There were a few noteworthy reasons, and a couple of hundred less so.

1. McCarthy stole his jersey number.
2. McCarthy stole his spot as team captain.
3. McCarthy stole his girlfriend, Paula, three days after their break up.

Of course, it was pure coincidence McCarthy ended up with the number seven on his jersey, and in the end, their bickering had cost both of them their chance at captaining the Hall Beck soccer team. But Henry Parker Pressley was of the firm belief that McCarthy had been out to get him, from the moment they met three years ago.

I didn't know why, and I didn't particularly care, either. To Henry, all that mattered was that I stood in solidarity with him. So McCarthy was high up on my own metaphorical hit list simply because he was #1 on Henry's.

There wasn't much history between McCarthy and me. Although my brother didn't care about much regarding my life, he'd obviously made sure of that. Given what I knew of McCarthy, though—the arrogance, the sarcasm, the general attitude—it seemed Henry had done me a solid. One that didn't change anything about the fact I was still sitting across from his apparent arch-nemesis now.

While I usually didn't mind facing conflict head-on, the thought of asking Professor Shaw for a different tutor was appealing. His office was just next door. I could knock, apologize (for . . . failing his class?) and promise to get to a passing grade by the end of the semester.

And with anyone else, that might've worked, but that man hated me. Shaw wouldn't be an escape, so my eyes scanned the room for another out. Honestly, whoever had chosen it couldn't have found a smaller one if they'd tried *really, really hard*. Compared to the vast dining halls of Hall Beck University (in which I'd eaten a total of four times), the massive library on the main campus (that I'd been forced into more often than I would've liked) and lecture halls with hundreds of seats (that still ended up completely packed whenever I'd get there, two minutes before a lecture began), this was a broom closet. Crammed into it a wooden desk full of loose papers, a bookshelf filled with folders of various colors, and a man too large for the chair he sat in.

Behind McCarthy, a window looked out onto one of the courtyards of the university, showing the mild fall weather of the East Coast. Dust collected in the corners of the glass. The space was too small, too packed for this to end well.

"What makes you think this is a good idea?" I asked.

"It's not." McCarthy shrugged, technically agreeing with me.

The thought of the both of us agreeing on *anything*—even if it was the mere fact that we wouldn't get along—struck me as odd.

Odd enough, that I must've made a face, because he went on to say, "Poor Princess Pressley." A note of amusement lingered within his otherwise dismissive tone. "Can't believe someone wouldn't be thrilled to spend time with her."

My last attempt at civility was letting that comment slide. By now, I'd been called far worse than princess. He scanned through the few notes I'd collected in the first weeks of the semester, and I glared at him regardless of the fact he wasn't looking at me.

"Jesus Christ." His silence had been far too short. "How did you pass *Statistics I* like this?"

I didn't need confirmation to know he'd found the midterm that had gotten me into this predicament in the first place.

Passing the Statistics final last semester hadn't been as hard as taking the class. Blind as a bat, and with his long, greasy hair hanging into his face at every given opportunity, how would Professor Shaw have noticed little old me—with my phone under the table—snapping photos of the questions and sending them to someone who *did* know the answers? Exactly.

My brother, uptight and smart enough for the both of us, would probably call that cheating. I'd call it being resourceful. She'd been paid handsomely, and I'd passed my class. A win-win.

The problem: my performance in the last class and my final, acceptable grade, didn't correlate. *Hah, statistics.* And though Shaw hadn't had any proof of my cheating last semester, he sure had been determined to catch it this time around. Hence the seating chart he'd introduced in our first lecture of *Statistics II*, and why I was seated in the front row. It forced me to take my midterm fair and square, and, well, here we were.

With a D.

McCarthy snorted with amusement, as if he'd heard my inner monologue and knew my answer to his question, even before it formed on my tongue. "Of course." He nodded knowingly. Rolled his eyes. "When do the Pressleys not throw Daddy's money at their problems?"

"It's Mommy's, actually." I ignored the way my insides clenched at the mention of my parents and smiled innocently, watching him place my notes on the desk between us so we could see them from either side. "And clearly," I continued, "this is me not throwing it at my problems, or you'd have noticed by now."

"That's funny." He didn't laugh.

And after he didn't laugh, he cleared his throat like we were really doing this. Like he would really teach me 'A-B tests' and 'bandit algorithms'. And like he really expected me to get it.

"Why would you want to torture us like this?" I hoped my words would divert us from the path toward hypotheses and variables. "You're out of your mind if you think—"

"—It's my job, Pressley," he said, face straight. Then, the right corner of his lip twisted, just the tiniest bit, in a cruel, yet irritatingly intriguing way. "You know," he teased. "That thing where you show up, do what you're told, and get money for it at the end of the month? With your background, I don't know if you're familiar—"

"Wait." I was just beginning to get it. "You're TA-ing for Shaw? Why?"

"Why not?"

"You don't need the money," I assessed, green eyes narrowing slightly. Very quickly, they flicked to the watch on his wrist that had probably cost as much as the pair of Miu Miu's in my closet. *More.* "You definitely don't need the money."

"And yet here I am."

And yet here he was.

So, on I went. "What happened to the cute senior from last year? I liked him."

"Believe it or not—he *graduated*."

"And you just had to be the one to replace him?" The smug smile on my lips was a complete lie. A front that kept the realization from manifesting on my face. My chances of getting another tutor had been slim before, but knowing McCarthy was TA-ing for Shaw had just reduced them to zero, and I was dying inside.

There was no way he'd bother assigning me another tutor, when he had McCarthy—his *TA* to do it. "No one else up to the task?"

"They dodged a bullet." He was beginning to get annoyed. I could feel it. In the way he impatiently drummed his fingers on the wooden desk and the way he fumbled with the papers between us, to steer my attention onto them. "Now, if you don't mind—"

I leaned back into the uncomfortable chair, and his exasperated groan almost made me laugh. "TA'ing for Shaw, huh?" I sighed. "Must be the worst." The bags under his eyes told me he couldn't have slept more than a few hours last night. Still, somehow he looked more put together than I did after a full night's rest. "Do you get in trouble if you can't get the job done?"

He leaned his forearms onto the desk. His dark hair fell into his face, and the glimpse of a smile played on his lips—not an amused or happy one. Challenging. "That depends," he said softly. "Will you get in trouble if you fail his class?"

"Do you get your pay cut? Overtime?" I swallowed hard; smile still on my lips when my head tilted. "Could I get you fired, McCarthy?"

I could see the gears in his head turning. Crossing his arms in front of his chest, he shrugged as he leaned back into his chair. "I always get the job done." His gaze cut to a door I hadn't previously noticed. Just for a second. "And just so you know, that door connects to Shaw's office. In case you want to make sure he can hear your insults, speak up just a little more next time. You can guess how thin these walls are."

I tried to prevent the panic currently seeping through every fiber of my being from showing on my face. I shifted my eyes from the *alleged* connecting door.

"Right," I said. "You were saying? About..." My voice trailed off, reading the half-hearted notes I took in the last lecture. "About 'two-sample comparison'?" When I looked up, I saw the victorious smile I'd expected, and I almost regretted caving.

If there was one thing worse than McCarthy's presence, though, it was the wrath of a certain Professor Simon Shaw.

My brother would understand. He'd have to.

Chapter 2

I heard my best friend before I saw her.

The rattling of her crowded keychain when she opened the door to our shared loft on the edge of campus. The thudding of her rushed steps, only briefly interrupted as she kicked off her shoes by the door. And finally, "You can't be serious." Her tone clipped and annoyed as she rounded the corner into the open kitchen.

"Dead serious."

Wren frowned, and the grocery-filled tote bag slipped out of her hand.

"No," she insisted, even though the string of text messages she'd received as soon as I left McCarthy's office were quite clear.

"Yes."

"McCarthy?"

I nodded again.

She let go of the deep breath she must've been holding for a while, blowing strands of short, split-dyed hair out of her face in the process. The black and white of either side of her hair parted in the middle and barely reached her shoulders; the color was a DIY project from way before we'd known each other.

"You should've seen his face," I groaned, jumping of the stool to help her put the groceries away.

"I'd rather not."

"It was just *so*—" I struggled to find words that would describe the mix of arrogance, confidence, and smugness. "As if his ego isn't big enough as it is," I continued, opening the fridge a little too forcefully. "Now I'm stroking it every time I accidentally learn something from him, which is supposed to be the point of the whole thing, right? Thanks to him, it's the only thing I don't want to do now." I closed the fridge with a thud.

Wren gave me her best attempt at a sympathetic smile, which meant her nose twitched and she grimaced more than smiled. But I got the message, and slumped back onto the stool.

"I doubt he'd be able to teach you anything to begin with," Wren muttered. There was another twitch of her nose, then a sigh—a sound filled with both pity and determination. She turned toward me again. "I'm sure I could pick up Statistics in a heartbeat," she said. "I'll be your tutor. Fuck McCarthy."

A low, almost defeated laugh rattled through me.

"I'm serious," she added, sounding convinced.

For a second, I let myself imagine it. Wren in that office chair opposite me. Wren asking me questions I didn't know the answers to. And asking me again and again, until I eventually did. No McCarthy in sight. It was beautiful, almost utopian.

"I know." I dragged the last word out, sounding almost whiny. "Which is why the offer is so terribly inviting." She crossed her arms, revealing the stick and poke tattoo of a knife along the side of her hand—the result of our procrastination, during summer exams last year.

Okay so? her expression asked, and prompted me to go on.

"But I cannot possibly in good conscience steal that much

of your time. Again."

Wren Inkwood was the kind of friend who accompanied you to every party, despite the fact she didn't like to drink and she did not like people. She was the kind to beat up your boyfriend when she'd found him cheating on you—before she even told you he had. The kind to take you home for Thanksgiving, despite only knowing you for ten weeks.

And because she was clearly the 'above-and-beyond' kind of friend, and I was the 'average-at-best' kind, I wanted to take less and give more. I wanted to be there for her, instead of the other way around. Which is why I was persistent in my stance.

"You can't be serious, Athalia."

"I am."

"Don't be ridiculous."

"I'm not."

The knock on our front door felt like my saving grace—a way to get out of an argument before it had really even started. Though, once I was greeted by the less-than-pleased expression on my twin's face, I immediately missed the childish back and forth with Wren, who disappeared into her room.

I wanted to see him more often, yes. But never when he was in a bad mood.

"Henry." My brows rose as he slipped inside and headed straight for the kitchen. "Why don't you come in?" I muttered, waving him in with an unnecessary swat: I could hear him rummaging through the cabinets already.

I followed. "You know I love your annual visits, but a bit of a heads-up would be . . . great."

Henry was still in his jersey, crimson shorts on full display, a little eight stitched onto them, and a black hoodie thrown over the matching shirt. His light brown hair parted neatly in the middle, as always.

"They're not *annual*," he finally acknowledged. His snack search ended with a half-brown banana from the otherwise empty fruit basket, but taking it forced him to first place the stack of papers in his hand onto the island.

I stiffened. "Where did you get those?"

The question was unnecessary.

"Oh, these?" He shrugged, using the banana as an extension of his finger to half-heartedly point at my statistics notes.

He took a bite, then with a full mouth went on to say, "Funny story, actually." The expression on his face told me it wasn't—or at the very least *he* didn't think it was. "McCarthy gave them to me after practice." Disdain spread across his face as soon as he said his name. "Told me my *sister* must have left them at his office, and if I was already stopping by anyway—"

"Not that you were going to," I reminded him. "Stop by, that is."

Henry ignored the dig. I wasn't surprised. "He wants me to let you know that, apparently—" My brother was nothing if not dramatic, and he paused like he needed the moment to collect himself. I braced myself for impact—for whatever message McCarthy had left my brother.

"Apparently," Henry repeated, waiting until I looked back at him. "He really enjoyed himself today. Is looking forward to *next time*, even." And as if it couldn't get any worse: "'But remind her how thin the walls are,' he said. 'I won't go as easy on her again.'"

We stared at each other in very different kinds of disbelief. Mine was: *I cannot believe McCarthy would feed my brother this bullshit.*

His was: *I cannot believe my sister is hooking up with my arch-nemesis.* (Like I said, he's dramatic.)

And when I didn't say anything in my defense—because I was still too stunned to say anything at all—the accusation shot out of him. "You're sleeping with McCarthy!"

That snapped me out of my silence. "Good God," I gasped, grimacing. "I'm not sleeping with him."

"Then explain these!" He waved my notes in the air, desperately. "Please."

"Tutoring!" I sputtered. "He's my tutor." I took a deep breath. "Statistics."

Like the word was all the explanation Henry needed, relief seeped into every single one of his features. His shoulders sagged, he took a deep breath, and Henry closed his eyes in what seemed to be a silent prayer to a God he didn't believe in.

"Tutoring," he affirmed to himself in a half-whisper, then took another bite of the banana, as if the fit he'd just thrown never happened. Swallowing, he nodded in another self-assuring gesture. "He's your tutor."

"Yes."

His voice was calm when he said, "So get another one."

"I can't simply *get another one*," I huffed, sitting back on the bar stool.

"Why not?"

"Because," I groaned. Henry's brows rose in anticipation. "Because Shaw said *this* is my only shot at passing his class. McCarthy as my tutor. Once a week."

Henry shook his head as if he'd been there for the conversation and that wasn't what Shaw had said at all. "I'll be your tutor instead."

Hello, offer number two.

"Are you Shaw's TA?"

"No," he said. "But I'm better at statistics than McCarthy."

"You think you're better than him at everything," I pointed out, and buried my face in my hands.

"Because I am."

"Sure."

"Athalia—"

"*What?*" I didn't mean to shout the word at him. His demeanor had been entirely too calm for that, and yet my head jerked up forcefully.

A short silence hung between us before Henry gave me an apologetic smile, rounding the kitchen island. Propping himself against it by my side, his hand ruffled my hair in that way he knew I hated, but I knew he loved. Even if it felt like one every time, it wasn't a malicious gesture. Actually, it was probably the way Henry said, *You know I love you, right?* because he never said the words. I couldn't even remember the last time he had.

"I'll talk to Shaw," he suggested, voice low. As if he knew even the smallest thing could set me off now.

"That's probably the worst idea you've ever had, Henry," I said calmly, mostly to compensate for my outburst seconds ago. "Shaw hates your guts almost as much as mine."

"So what?" he asked. "He should know better than to put you and McCarthy in the same room. I'll talk to him."

I didn't mention that Shaw probably had other things to worry about than a stupid rivalry between his top students.

"There's no point." Shaw wasn't going to budge; McCarthy wasn't going to quit. That was all that mattered.

Henry rose back to his impressive six foot one, and circled the kitchen island again to throw the banana peel into the trash under the sink. "I'll talk to him," was all he said.

"No you won't," I retorted, suddenly fierce in my stance.

"*Athalia*," he groaned.

"Henry."

Exasperated, his hands flew up. Henry was so easy to aggravate, I almost saw the appeal in McCarthy's actions. At least that way he was paying attention to me. "I just don't want that asshat—"

"Asshat?" My smile did slip out now. "*Very* original."

Henry waved me away half-heartedly. "Whatever," he huffed. "I just don't want that guy anywhere near my little sister, that's all."

"I'm twelve minutes younger than you." I shook my head slightly. "Which is why I don't need you to baby me. In fact, I don't need anyone to baby me. I'll handle the situation with McCarthy like any adult would—by myself."

He pointedly ignored the last statement. "And yet, you're born a day after me. Twelve minutes or not, Athalia, you're my baby sister. Period."

"Henry—"

"Either way—" He shrugged like he hadn't interrupted me, heading for the door. "Don't worry. I'll handle it, *little sister*."

"Don't you dare—" I was by his side again before I could even finish my sentence. "*I* will handle it."

Unfazed, Henry opened the door, only hovering in the doorway long enough to give me an unbothered smile as a parting gift.

Little shit.

I took a deep breath, leveling my voice. "Dylan McCarthy will not get anywhere close to your *little sister—*" I mocked. "At least not closer than the desk separating us at all times. Now, let me just deal with this by myself. Okay?"

"Sure," Henry said as he left, but he didn't mean it.

Chapter 3

"You're sure this isn't a costume party?" Wren's voice traveled through the barely lit street, music blaring through the walls of the colonial-style home we stood in front of.

Shifting my attention from the Greek letters above the entrance, I grinned at her. "Positive. But if it was, you might still qualify." The military boots, dark tights with a run in them that disappeared under a skirt, everything in her favorite color: black. It was giving witch—if witches went to frat parties.

"Fuck off." Wren rolled her eyes, probably rethinking the entirety of our three-year-long friendship. I gave her one last look, and when her smile matched my own, I pushed the door open.

A few cheers erupted from the crowd inside, not because they necessarily knew who we were (or cared), but simply because, to them, more people equaled more fun. More singing, more dancing, more possible hookups.

"Athalia!" Two arms pulled me into a bear-like hug, and I only knew who it was when a big hand ruffled my hair in that way I hated.

Henry.

"Didn't know you'd be here." My voice was muffled against his chest, and I was already too tipsy from pregaming to care about the fact he'd just ruined an hour of hairstyling in five seconds. Probably too taken aback by the fact that I was in Henry's arms. That he was *hugging* me.

Before I could fully understand what was happening—*why* it was—Henry let go, then surprised me a second (or third?) time when he embraced Wren just as enthusiastically. It gave me time to consider my twin. His brown hair was styled just enough to seem casual, when I knew it took him almost as long as it took me to get ready. He wore a black polo tucked into tailored pants, somehow pulling off that golf-course vibe casually.

While Wren patted his back—waiting with an upturned nose until he was ready to let her out of his hug—I considered another fact. Henry was drunk, and Henry did not usually drink.

Help me, my best friend mouthed.

"All right!" I announced, wrestling Wren out of Henry's grip. I barely managed a "See you around!" shouted in Henry's general direction before my best friend dragged me through the crowded living room of the frat house. The last thing I saw was Henry giving a friendly salute.

Wren dusted off her black top in a way that was just so her, it had my heart swell with affection. At the wide, distracted grin on my face, she did a double take. "Athalia—" she warned, taking a tentative step back. "I know that look. Don't—"

But my arms were slung around her before she could finish the sentence. Her five foot two came up to my shoulder, on which she slumped her head in resignation. "This is my least favorite thing about you," she muttered into my hair.

"My great hugs?"

She barked a laugh before correcting my assumption. "That

you get so touchy when you're drunk," she tsked. "Apparently, you and Henry have that in common."

"Speaking of drunk . . ." I wiggled my brows, and Wren sighed.

"Right. The drinks are over there." She laughed, gently turning me toward the kitchen counter. "I'm gonna find the bathroom, then meet you there." She turned back toward me only when the crowd had almost swallowed her whole, then pierced me with a look I knew all too well. "Take. It. Easy!" she shouted over the music, her voice taking on that motherly tone as she enunciated every word. What she meant by that was, *don't be black-out drunk by the time I get back.*

Naturally, I honored her words with a shot.

If there was one thing about Wren Inkwood that was almost as certain as death and taxes, it was the fact that she'd be looking for a bathroom within the first ten minutes of arriving at any party.

She didn't drink alcohol—never had—but while I'd been pre-gaming to our 'getting-ready' playlist at home, she couldn't *not* drink something. *It's the principle of it, Athalia,* she'd always say. So, she opted for water.

Gallons and gallons of water. I suspected that's why her skin was porcelain-like. Inevitably, it also sent her looking for the nearest bathroom by the time we got to our destination. Like clockwork. She went to pee; I waited wherever she'd park me that night.

Tonight, it was the makeshift bar on the granite counter of the kitchen.

I shook as the alcohol burned down my throat, wiping the residue off my lips. Turning back toward the counter, I knew before I even touched anything, that the drink I was about to mix myself would end up way too strong.

"Well, this has never ended well before." It took me a second to realize the words were directed at me, but I twirled toward them, startled by the proximity of the body now in front of me.

My eyes wandered up the white dress shirt—the top two buttons open—before my eyes found his piercing blue ones in panic-riddled recognition. A playful smirk hung in the corners of his mouth.

When most people thought of the devil, they imagine horns and hooves, red skin, and even redder eyes. When *I* thought of the devil, however, he was all blond hair, blue eyes, and cute curls. Coincidentally, as 'Highway to Hell' played in the background and drunk college students blurted it louder than it was playing, he stood right in front of me.

"Let me take care of that." He grabbed the red cup right out of my hand, fingers brushing mine in a gesture I knew was deliberate. I found out a little too late that, with Jason Montgomery, everything was *always* deliberate. A little wistfully, he added, "Your mixers were always way too strong."

I had that same thought around a minute ago.

The realization freaked me out enough to keep my mouth shut and accept my full cup when he turned back around. Maybe the alcohol already in my system had something to do with that? Maybe the unwanted insecurities still riddling my thoughts around him did, too.

Taking a sip, I had to admit that my ex-boyfriend was as good at mixing his drinks as he was at cheating on me.

"You used to talk more."

Great observation, I wanted to say. The possibility that I still talked just as much to the people I actually wanted to talk to hadn't even crossed his mind. I knew him well enough to know that it wouldn't either.

Stunned by his audacity—and my audacity to still let myself be stunned by him—I simply nodded, lips pressed together in a thin line. Jason leaned against the bar behind us while I desperately searched for a familiar face in the crowd. Unsuccessfully.

"Used that mouth of yours quite often, Pressley," he continued.

I groaned loudly, but I doubted he even heard me over the noise around us. (I wasn't sure if I could still consider it music. I probably would after a few more drinks.)

"Pretty skillfully, too."

Fuck. Me.

In a mix of annoyance and rage and *I can't believe he said that!*, I turned toward him, so quick, I lost balance for a dreadful second. With my hand holding onto the bar he still leaned against, the full weight of the alcohol I'd consumed until now kicked me. Hard.

"Jesus fucking Christ," I finally snapped. "You've got some nerve."

"Oh," Jason hummed, nodding to himself. "She speaks."

Honestly, the J-name should've been my first blindingly red flag. Yet, despite all odds and previous beliefs, I fell head over heels for Jason Montgomery just three weeks into my freshman year. Probably more so because my parents would've loved him, because my brother had loved him, and because everyone (excluding Wren) had told me we were practically perfect for each other. The thought was repulsive now.

But back then, knowing nothing of Jason—apart from the

fact that he was the Montgomerys' golden boy, with a bright future ahead, and the charm of someone who had been raised to be nothing but charming—he was perfect. Handsome, too.

"This." I gestured between the two of us, finding an amused gleam in his eyes. "Is not happening."

"What's not happening?" Jason's hands flew up in mock surrender. "I'm not trying to make anything happen, Athalia." The only thing giving him away was his smug, subtle smirk. I hated the way my name sounded on his lips. "But honestly, after you egged my car and slashed a tire, I thought we were even."

The tire was an accident. Sort of.

He leaned closer, his voice low. "I'm just trying to catch up with an old friend here." As he straightened back up, I hoped it was the alcohol that sent a light shiver down my spine. Taking a step forward to stand opposite me, he added, "We *are* friends, right?"

And I was trying to come up with the best way of telling him that I would rather eat my own foot—

"I think I'd know about that."

For a moment, I wondered whether it was my own voice that had become deep and sulky, carrying a cool kind of indifference. Perplexed, my hand reached for my mouth. I was pretty sure I hadn't said a damn thing. If I did, though, it would've been just a little meaner than that.

Then, my head snapped to the arm that carefully placed itself around me, a beer in hand, just by my shoulder. I jerked at the touch, taking a step away, only to bump into a body that hadn't previously been there. My hazy mind couldn't put two and two together. The blasting music—it could be classified as that again—had sucked the last bit of coherency from my brain.

What I did notice, though, was that Jason took a step back because of whoever that arm belonged to. And that was all it took for drunk, simple-minded me to relax into the stranger. I even managed to whip up a smile, fueled with a confidence that usually went out the window when Jason was around. Meanwhile, he wasn't even looking at me.

"McCarthy," he said by way of greeting.

The name alone was enough to startle me. Jason still focused on him, and my own eyes skirted up the black T-shirt, noticed the silver necklace disappearing underneath its collar, and registered an annoyingly familiar jawline, before taking him in as a whole.

McCarthy had an arm around me, but he hadn't acknowledged my presence much more than that. His attention was entirely on Jason.

In any other situation, I would've shoved McCarthy off me before I could even be sure it was him. But now, with the way Jason responded to him, McCarthy was useful enough for me to stick by his side.

"What a sight to behold," Jason said, snapping out of it. His eyes flicked back and forth between us in record time. I swallowed deeply. The room started spinning. "Never thought Brother Dearest would approve." His eyes slid back to me. "Where is Henry, by the way?"

Henry wouldn't approve. He'd kill both of us if he saw McCarthy's arm around me. I had to keep myself from looking around frantically just at the mention of my brother.

McCarthy did what Jason hated most: he ignored him. Instead of answering, he turned to me, raised his brows, an edge of—surely faked— concern in his features. "Care to join me outside?" he asked coolly, nodding to the backyard.

And I wasn't even lying when I said, "Yes, please."

Chapter 4

"I'd thank you—" The crisp autumn breeze swallowed my words. I was lulling, probably. Swaying and hiccuping as we made our way to the garden bench. "But being here with you is probably just as bad."

To be honest, nothing was worse than spending another minute in the suffocating presence of Jason Montgomery, but McCarthy didn't need to know I was lying. So, I doubled down. "*Worse*, maybe."

"You could just say thank you, you know." I felt the bench shift underneath his weight when he sat beside me, and without looking at him, I knew a self-satisfied smirk played on his lips. The same one that he couldn't seem to suppress whenever he realized just how lost I was during our tutoring.

"I didn't need your help," I clarified, only because the sheer thought of that cocky smile irritated me.

"Of course not." Still that same undertone in his voice.

"I had it under control."

"Of course you did."

I expected a mocking grin, could practically see it before I even looked at him. But when I did, his eyes were on the night sky above, not even glancing in my direction, and not a smirk in sight.

There were too many lights surrounding us to see anything

significant up there, and the few stars you would usually see were covered by clouds. Still, his attention didn't waver.

"I'm being serious," I pressed once more. The silence probably wasn't longer than a few seconds, but to me, intoxicated and annoyed, it felt like minutes passed by before I went on. "For all you know, you could've been cockblocking me." When the accusation finally made him look at me, I gasped. "Oh my God." The words were slurred more than usual, spoken as I pointed an accusatory finger at him. "That *is* what you were trying to do, isn't it?"

He shook his head and I think for the first time, I saw what could've been classified as a genuine smile on his lips.

"Got me." His hands raised playfully before he gave me a look. "I think I'd definitely end up aiding and abetting something if I saw any girl in Montgomery's vicinity without heroically rescuing her." His nose crinkled at his own joke.

"We used to date." I didn't know why I felt the need to clarify that. In the five seconds of silence that followed, I felt stupid for doing so.

"I know."

I jerked back to look at him, surprised above all else. McCarthy keeping up with my dating history was . . . unexpected.

The only light came in waves and flickers from inside, and yet, it was fairly easy to make out his jawline, the tip of his nose and chin. I imagined his cheeks tinted a light pink from the chilly air around us. Every now and then, he would blow one of those floppy brown hairs out of his face after the wind had knocked them into it.

And as my head began to clear just slightly, I wondered

how I had ended up here: drunk and alone with Dylan McCarthy—who hadn't said anything in a few minutes—his eyes still set skyward, looking somewhat... content.

I cut those thoughts short, attention lazily drawn to the opening door as someone stepped through. Scanning the backyard, they hesitated, then walked toward us, somewhat determined.

"Athalia?" My name rang out in the dark, and I only recognized her—and her voice—when she stood right in front of me. I stumbled when I jumped up. I blamed the alcohol for both.

"What are you doing?" Wren didn't bother lowering her voice. "Here. With him," she specified, eyes flicking toward him.

I snickered. "I was just asking myself the same thing."

McCarthy decided to perk up from behind me at that. "Hello to you too, Inkwood," he said in that sarcastic tone of his I was getting to know quite well. He took a sip of his beer and stood—all while Wren glared at him.

Instead of answering, she looked back at me, and I only vaguely registered McCarthy heading in the direction of the door.

"What did I say about taking it easy?" she muttered, though her features relaxed now that McCarthy was gone.

"Sorry, Mom!" I let my head fall onto her shoulder with a laugh, and it's like that one gesture brought back the events she'd missed. Dragging my best friend back inside, I filled her in on my encounter with the blue-eyed devil; so busy with that, I didn't notice he was talking to my brother at the other end of the room.

Chapter 5

I couldn't quite remember how I got home. But when I woke up in my comfortable bed the next morning, my body ached and my head thudded.

For five terribly short minutes, I contemplated my plans for the day. With the study session written in my calendar in bold, capital letters (underlined twice with a red pen), I tried not to hear an "I told you so" in Wren's voice. Obviously, she had. And I barely remembered my own excuse when she'd explained, in great detail, how I was going to regret going out just ten hours ago.

There were too many things I needed to get done to simply skip. Again. It's what I'd done last week. And the week before that. It's how I had ended up here, with reading due Monday, an essay worth twenty percent of my international management grade, and Statistics II homework. The latter obviously the worst of them all.

I could type a few thousand words. I could read a few pages. I couldn't, however, wrap my head around correlation coefficients and whatever else McCarthy had in store for me. Technically, figuring all that out was *his* job, but I didn't like his smug expressions and amused hums when I didn't know what he was talking about.

If I showed Shaw I could do this by myself, got an acceptable grade in the next test, perhaps I wouldn't need McCarthy at all. I'd be rid of those ridiculous looks and condescending sounds before I'd gotten used to them, and that was motivation enough to finally swing myself out of bed.

Just that instead of swinging, I slowly, deliberately, carefully slid from underneath my covers—ignoring my spinning surroundings—and groaned as I clutched my throbbing head. I thought I might throw up, but I managed to drag myself to the kitchen instead.

The sun peeked through the windows—a rarity in HBU fall, when it mostly blessed us with grey, rainy days. It was a perfect day for a stroll to the library, studying at one of the tables by its large windows. Unfortunately, it was an awful day for a hangover. Too bright.

"Fuck." I flinched, hands falling from my face, previously shielding my eyes from the brightness. "Sorry." I tried to give Wren my best hungover smile after almost bulldozing into her by the coffee machine. Though, all I got back was a single nod before she turned to grab the steaming cup under the machine. My brow furrowed.

"When did we get home last night?"

A few seconds ticked by. "Around two."

I blinked at her, hesitating at the awkward tension. "Oh, okay." My eyes narrowed as she went to leave. "Thanks."

She faltered in her steps, turned around to look me over once, clutching her mug shaped like Lin Manuel Miranda's Hamilton's head tightly between her hands. "For?"

"Getting me home."

"Sure." Wren nodded, turned to leave again. She stopped right before disappearing into her room, as if she'd *just* reconsidered her stance on talking to me. "I could hardly leave you by yourself with the company you would've kept." The attitude in her voice was undeniable now, and at least I knew I wasn't imagining it anymore. "Who knows, though, you seemed to be enjoying yourself."

"What's that supposed to mean?" I didn't mean to snap my words; I was genuinely curious. And confused. But my hangover seemed to be shortening my temper even further and now I had an attitude, too.

Wren snorted drily, though she was clearly not as amused as she wanted to portray. "Nothing," she managed. Before shutting her door, she added: "Forget I said anything."

Great.

Today was not the day for arguments. I had things to do and papers to write, and I wasn't in the mood to fight or even speak to anyone with an attitude. I wanted a calm day. One in which I'd spend most of my time in the library, reading, writing, and studying. Ideally, I wouldn't have to talk to anyone at all.

So, after taking painkillers, a hot shower, and an espresso shot (in that order), I strolled to the library, ready to conquer my demons between books and burned-out college students.

And it was going great. By four o'clock I'd finished that godawful essay and was through the reading materials for the past two weeks. If you ignored the coffee I'd spilled across the wooden table, the chair I'd rammed into the knee of a student passing behind me, and the loud snore I accidentally let out during a particularly boring chapter, I was thriving. *Really*.

Productivity over humility. Wasn't that what they said?

"Athalia"

My head jolted at my whispered name, messy curls inches from my face when I looked up. Heather leaned across the table toward me, a wide grin on her heart-shaped lips.

Heather, Henry, and Reuben lived in the mirror apartment across the street from us. Once I'd moved up on the waitlist and managed a last-minute spot at Hall Beck U., it had been too late to rent off campus, so I'd ended up in the dorms. The second Henry had heard about someone moving out across the street from him, he'd reserved the apartment, and Wren and I moved in at the beginning of sophomore year.

My brother and I didn't speak often—we weren't even particularly close. But when we did, it was always because he'd managed to fix something in my life that I wasn't able to. A problem solver, through and through.

Hey, you, I mouthed at Heather. After the librarian issued me a warning for that snore earlier, I assumed with two noise violations I'd be out of here. My brother's roommate cared half as much, though. Fishing a stack of notes out of her bag, and lining them up with the book she'd taken off the shelves, Heather cheerily chatted away.

Although I relocated to one of the long, dark wooden tables—shielded from Ms. Jones' direct line of sight, courtesy of the high bookshelves on either side—I threw a nervous glance, wanting to make sure the librarian wasn't lingering around a corner, just waiting to kick me out. Fortunately, all I saw were the bent necks and bad postures of students hung over their pages, lots of books (of course), and the changing colors of leaves through the massive window-front on the other side of the aisle. No grey, pinned-up hair, thin brows, and tiny glasses on a sharp nose in sight.

"I'm not going to lie," Heather quipped, English accent muddied after the three years she'd spent at HBU. "You look godawful." A sympathetic smile followed her words, and I couldn't help but huff. Her eyes ran across the statistic notes neatly lined up in front of me. The sympathy on her face turned into pity when she looked back at me.

"At least you'll be rid of him now." She nodded to my notes with a knowing look. "But yeah, I guess that means having to do it yourself again. Pick your poison kind of thing, isn't it?" Her eyes had already drifted to the book in front of her, scanning the table of contents.

That's why she didn't notice my confusion until I said, "What?"

"What?"

"I'm going to assume you're about to explain what you're talking about?" I asked hesitantly. Heather's eyes flicked across my face, her brow furrowed before she waved me away with a "come on now . . ." look.

"You know," she insisted, amusement still lingering in her voice. She nodded to my statistic notes again. "You'll have to work on passing statistics yourself now." She laughed.

I was not, because I still wasn't catching on.

"You must have known that once you were rid of McCarthy, you'd have to learn all that by yourself." She gestured to my papers once more. "Which is why you're here . . . studying statistics . . . by yourself." Her eyes met mine again. "Right?"

A few seconds of silence ticked by.

"Please don't tell me—" she began.

"*Rid of McCarthy?*" I said at the same time. "What's that

supposed to mean?"

Her head fell into her hands and the subsequent groan was way too loud for a library. "No way," she mumbled into her hands, voice lowered again. "*NowayNowayNoway.*" Her eyes snapped back to mine. "Henry didn't tell you?"

"Tell me what?" My patience was beginning to wear thin. With her. With this subject. With my thudding head at the prospect of what she was saying.

"I'm so sorry—" she began, immediately cutting herself off again. "I thought, you know—" Her head shook again. "I thought if he was going to talk to Professor Shaw, he'd do it because *you* asked him to. Or suggested it. At least that you knew about it. *Bloody hell.* Why—"

"Heather." I reached for her arm and she finally refocused.

"Oh, right." She cleared her throat. "Henry talked to Professor Shaw about your tutoring setup." She said the words as if she couldn't get them out fast enough. Then, to my dismay, added, "Well, not talked, really. Emailed him."

I blinked at her.

"He emailed him." If I sounded the words out, maybe they'd make more sense. "After I specifically told him to stay out of it. After I specifically told him to let me handle this by myself." Heather's expression grew more horrified with every word. "After all that. He emailed him?"

"Oh God." Somewhere in the distance, the librarian shushed us. I barely noticed, perceived it somewhere in a distant corner of my mind, maybe, because I was still trying to wrap my head around other things. How much of an asshole my brother was, for one.

A few things were going through my mind.

1. Where did men get the audacity?
2. How could I be sharing the same genes with that particular man?
3. What . . . the fuck?

I could pinpoint the exact moment confusion turned into anger. It was right after I'd excused myself from Heather. Right when the chilly air hit me, and a gust of wind whipped hair into my face with full force. It was the wrong day for that, and I wasn't just angry anymore. I was furious. And a little embarrassed.

Embarrassed by the fact my professor would now think I was sending my star-athlete brother to handle my business. Furious, because my star-athlete brother couldn't comprehend that I was old enough to live my own life, competent enough to deal with problems myself.

And, quite frankly, livid, because the only time I warranted my brother's attention seemed to be when there was a problem he didn't think I could fix. I was 99% sure the reason I got into HBU—one of the best schools on the East Coast—was Henry's pointed remark (threat) that the only way he'd be attending was if his sister would. That, if they wanted the star athlete, they'd have to take the under-qualified twin, too. I'm sure our last name on the gym in big gold letters helped his persuasion.

Thanks, Pressley Center for Recreation.

Apparently, I was only worth Henry's time if I was the problem. When I might not get into college, when I couldn't find an apartment, and, apparently, when Dylan McCarthy Williams was involved.

"Pressley!" My voice echoed across the soccer field before I even reached it. In the distance, behind the waist-high handrail and between the trees circling it, I could see a few heads whip in my direction, confused and annoyed at whoever dared to interfere with their sacred training, and so close to the NCAA championship at that.

I found him quickly. Number eight casually jogged toward me, casting a pleading look in his coach's direction. An edge of concern riddled my brother's expression when he came to a standstill on the other side of the railing.

"Look, Lia, can this wait—?"

"No," I seethed.

"I'm in the middle of practice—"

"*I don't care*, Henry."

He didn't like the way I raised my voice at him. In front of the team, in front of his coach. It bruised his incredibly fragile ego; I could tell. "You know what I *do* care about?" I mused, trying my best to hide just how angry I was.

Restless in front of me, he dared a few glances across his shoulder, trying his best to will his team to continue what they were doing, instead of eavesdropping on a clearly uncomfortable conversation.

"I care about you not butting into my life every chance you get."

His face fell at my tone, though not in recognition or understanding or guilt. Blinking down at me, brow furrowed, there wasn't a single thought behind those beautiful green eyes. He had no clue what I was talking about. And that made it worse.

"Oh my God." *I can't believe this.* "You don't even think you did anything wrong."

His silence confirmed that.

"You know," I began. "You do not have to play concerned

brother every time you spot a chance to flaunt your wealth and influence in order to stroke your ego." His expression remained clueless. "I don't need your help with this. I can go to some stupid tutoring once a week, even if I don't like the guy, and *yes*—even if *you* don't."

And there it was. A spark of understanding. Before he could answer—

"Pressley!" The shout came from behind him. "Get your ass back on the field!" My gaze shifted to spot the source of those words, but I could've probably identified the lackluster shout, the annoyed tone, even without looking. "You're holding up the entire game!"

From the way he stopped short to the look he sent me, it was obvious McCarthy could sense the tension from where he stood, and he didn't feel the need to move closer toward it.

I looked back at my brother. "Nothing to say?"

"I've got a lot to say," he suddenly snapped, eyes back on me. "But this argument is not worth skipping practice over. It's not even worth *having*. I'm dealing with shit you don't know anything about, and I did you a favor, despite that. You can thank me when you realize it."

Something snapped. In me. Between us. My next words were more unhinged, though hushed, because as much as I wanted to embarrass him, I did not need personal issues aired out in front of the HBU soccer team.

"You have no right to just reach into my life and change what you don't like," I hissed. "We talk once a month and *this* is when you decide to butt in?" I tried to make the accusation sound snippy—to make him feel guilty about shutting me out, about the fact we'd become part of each other's lives merely out of some kind of genetic obligation.

"Clearly I have to. Because you would've continued going to those stupid lessons, with your stupid thin walls and McCarthy's stupid face." The mere mention of McCarthy's name made a vein pop on Henry's forehead. At least he felt the argument was *worth having* now. At least he was talking to me.

I almost laughed. "You're acting like a ten-year-old, Henry—"

"I just don't want you to spend time with him, for fucks sake!"

"And I don't want you to control my life. *Look!*" I cheered, sarcastically. "Seems like we're both not getting what we want."

At that, he ducked under the white handrail we argued across, grabbing my arm to drag me out of the team's sight. If this were a cartoon, there'd be steam coming out of his ears.

"You can't tell me what to do—"

"I can try!" he shot back, finally coming to a halt behind the changing rooms.

"You can't!" Pretty sure I shouted that. "If I want to, I'll continue going to McCarthy's stupid lessons. If I want to, I'll see him outside of them, too. If I want to—" It was out before I could stop myself. "If I want to, I'll go out with him. Get a drink. Go back to his place. I'll do whatever the hell I want, Henry. You're not the boss of me, and I'm not twelve anymore."

And that's what seemed to do it. What sent him over the edge. I almost smiled at the way his head turned a deep shade of red with fury.

"That's what you want?"

No.

"Maybe I do."

Henry's eyes closed in an unsuccessful attempt to calm himself. But he sensed my bluff, I could feel it. "No, you don't."

There it was.

So really, I had no other choice but to double down. I had to. My hands were basically tied.

"Maybe I already am."

"You're not." A beat, and his eyes narrowed, as if he just remembered a vital piece of information. "So Jason was telling the truth, then?"

It was all I could do not to flinch at the name, not to yell and scream at the mere fact my brother had talked to my ex-boyfriend behind my back. About me. Saying I didn't care about what would be a lie. But it seemed to make Henry believe the lies I was telling him.

So, with the tiniest smirk, I shrugged.

I had the upper hand now, and that's all it took for me to relax into the feeling of it— forget that he'd betrayed me not once, but twice now. Not just with the Shaw thing, but by talking to the guy who had fucking ruined me a year ago.

"God," he groaned. "You're fucking infuriating, Athalia—"

A whistle sounded, another voice called for Henry (in that no-bullshit way only a coach could muster), and it must've reminded him of where he was supposed to be. On the field. With his team.

Not behind the locker rooms, arguing with his sister—speaking more than a few words to her for the first time in months, even if they were unpleasant.

So just like that, red-steam-engine Henry fled the scene.

Chapter 6

I didn't like being angry at my brother.

We'd grown up fighting more often than we got along. And I wasn't sure if he'd just gotten older, or if he really did seem more unhinged today than I remembered him ever being. Even when we were shouting and screaming through our entire summer house so loudly the walls shook—he'd never seemed quite so on edge.

I'm dealing with shit you don't know anything about, and I did you a favor despite that.

We argued, we fought. Then, our parents died, and all of a sudden our fifteen-year-old lives were thrown into a whirlwind of lawyers, press, and therapists. To me, it felt like Henry was all that was really left of them.

After the accident, it was hard to plan for the future. Mom and Dad had planned theirs perfectly, and it didn't matter at all when air turbulence had catapulted them into the Atlantic. What the fuck was the point when life was so, *so* fickle? When somebody could be a constant in your life at one moment and wiped out of it the next through no fault of their own?

The realization had made me want to cling to my brother like a lifeline. I never wanted to let him out of my sight, never mind accept what had become apparent quite quickly: he did not feel the same way.

At fifteen, Henry bought his first planner and became the crisis-averting top student and athlete he was today—with a mind for nothing but his meticulously planned, picture-perfect future.

Even though that meant we weren't fighting anymore, it kind of felt like I'd lost my brother that day as well. When we'd been hurling petty insults at each other, pulling hair and scratching skin, at least we'd still been talking.

It's all I could think about now. We were fighting, yes, but at least we were *talking*. At least he'd been looking at me, speaking to me, probably thinking about me. In a way that I should probably unpack with my therapist, I felt . . . cared for. Loved. I hadn't felt that from Henry in so long, just the very hint of it made me itch for more.

That care had never extended past grades and career prospects—had never reached into my personal life. Until now.

I tried to suppress the memories of better times, with parents who were alive and loving, when my greatest worry had been if Henry had snatched the last chocolate bar out of the fridge or how he'd messed up my hair on picture day. All of it was coming back to me now.

The way they'd tear us away from each other, take us into our respective rooms—Dad with Henry, Mom with me. I didn't know what my brother had been told all those years, but Mom's words lingered in my head even now.

"*Listen here,*" she'd say, softly. If I cried she'd wipe my tears. "*Henry has a hard time coping with his feelings the right way. But your brother loves you very much, Athalia. He admires your strength, your kindness, your humor. A little piece of him wants to be just like you.*" She'd say, "*And you love him, too, don't you? His bravery, his confidence?"* Depending on how bad the particular fight had been, I would argue with her on that point. But in the end, she'd always won. *"See?"* she'd say. *"You'll always have each other. Your brother will take care of you, and you'll take care of him long after either of you need it. And you'll find it so annoying—"* She'd continue in a whisper. *"He's a little annoying, isn't he?"* she'd joke. And I'd laugh every time. *"But you'll be with him much longer than you'll be with us, Lia."*

A few things about Henry Mom didn't mention . . . He wasn't just brave and confident, although he was. He was also stubborn, arrogant and could never, ever be wrong. And all of that got worse when he felt like he wasn't in control. Of a situation, of his life—apparently *my* life too.

Sitting on a wooden bench perched up behind the main building of HBU, I noted that Henry Parker Pressley was an asshole. Then, despite my brother's selfishness and ignorance, I scolded myself for wanting his attention like a child, regardless.

If I'd been more like him—driven, determined, destined to play pro sports or academically ahead of the rest of our classmates—maybe we'd be closer now. Maybe I wouldn't need a fight to feel close to him, at all.

Unfortunately, I was none of those things, and a part of me was still that fifteen-year-old girl clinging to her twin brother.

"Please don't tell me you come here often."

Startling, my spine straightened, and I squinted against the setting sun. McCarthy was still in his crimson shorts, a hoodie thrown over the jersey, and his hair still damp from the shower he must've taken after practice.

Could this get any worse?

"You're really the last person I want to see right now,"

I admitted, eyes shifting from his towering frame to the townhouses—mostly occupied by fraternities and sororities—across the field separating the main campus and frat row.

"Is that so?" As if to prove a point, he planted himself on the bench beside me.

"Today is not the day, McCarthy," I warned.

If a looping track of my fight with Henry playing over and over wasn't enough, fate wanted me to stare the reason for it straight into his big brown eyes. I closed mine.

The reason for it.

A wave of awareness flashed through me like lightning.

McCarthy was the reason for it.

Not my need for independence or that I'd yelled at Henry. Not that I'd interrupted practice and caused a scene.

It was McCarthy. The mention of him, the thought of me spending time with *the enemy*.

I just don't want that guy anywhere close to my little sister. Wasn't that what he'd said?

I sorted through the information behind closed eyes, neurons firing, before I opened them wide.

If McCarthy hadn't already taken a seat, I would've offered it now.

In a magical turn of events, he wasn't the last person I wanted to see. He was exactly who I *needed*, sent not out of spite, but as my one-way ticket to Revenge-ville. And if it meant I had my brother's attention for a little while longer, who'd complain? Certainly not me.

"That seems dangerous." His words drew my gaze back to him, only noticing the sly smile on my lips when McCarthy pointed it out. Literally. His finger circled my grin a safe distance away when he added, "I've never seen you smile like that, Pressley. It's terrifying."

"Good." I turned my body toward him, considering all my options carefully. The entire plan was still forming in my head, and once the words were out, I couldn't take them back. "I have a proposition."

"I'm listening." McCarthy's brow rose with interest. "What has that *marvelous* brain of yours produced this time?"

My body deflated with a groan, gleaming eyes narrowing into a glare. "If that's a reference to my statistic skills—"

He cut me off with a snort, his head tilting slightly. "Skills?"

It was easy to forget how infuriating the guy opposite me was. With his thick, dark hair and the hint of a dimple working its way into his cheek, it was almost like that was the point.

"You know what—" I was close to dropping the whole thing, but his hands shot up in mocked defeat.

"All right, all right." Amusement still played in his features. "I'll admit it, I'm interested to know what's going on in that little—" He cut himself off at my reinforced glare, clearing his throat. "In that *very big* brain of yours. Spill."

Despite the urge to abandon my plan, I saw it through.

"I know you deeply despise my brother," I began, still not quite sure how to go about my proposal.

No way back now.

McCarthy huffed. "Masterful deduction."

"Well, I present you: the one thing that'll show him just how much you really do."

Chapter 7

I regretted asking as soon as his lips had split into a wide, victorious grin.

"If you wanted to take me out this badly, you could've just asked, Pressley."

"Can you . . . *not*?" I muttered, suppressing a groan. "If I wanted to go out with you, I'd be going out with you."

A challenging smile deepened the dimple in his cheek. Despite the self-assured grin, his mouth remained closed. Just how I liked it. Though, in this situation, some feedback would've been appreciated.

"So." Still awaiting an answer, I brought us back on track. "What do you—?"

"Yes." It was almost like he couldn't get the words out fast enough now. The amusement on his face disappeared, leaving the hint of a grin behind.

"Yes?" My brow creased, anxious at the gunshot of an answer.

He simply repeated himself. "Yes."

I'd expected to do some groveling to strike a deal with him. A *You'll-do-this-for-me-and-I'll-do-that-for-you* kind of thing. What I didn't expect was a "yes." Quick and precise, no bullshit. I wasn't used to it from McCarthy.

I studied him. With his head turned to me, arms propped

on the backrest of the bench and both brows raised as he waited for my next words, it was hard to believe I'd just asked him to be my boyfriend.

A fake one, yes. But a boyfriend nonetheless.

The breeze had his brown hair in constant motion and indifference laced every part of him. A *yawn* escaped his lips.

This was too easy.

"What?" His head tilted slightly, and now he was fighting hard to suppress another smile. "I said yes."

"I heard that." I snickered halfheartedly. I was focused on finding something in his demeanor that revealed the lie. Or stalling for time until he'd break into a fit of laughter because I'd actually believed him. Neither happened. "Why?"

"*Why?*" he repeated. My uneasiness only seemed to make his amusement grow. "Why not?"

"Oh, I don't know," I cooed. "Maybe because it means you'll have to actually spend time with me. And you don't particularly like me."

Poor Princess Pressley. Can't believe someone wouldn't be thrilled to spend time with her.

McCarthy shrugged, eyes shifting. "I don't *particularly like* your brother any more." He mocked my choice of words.

"And you want nothing in return?" I asked, still wary. "God knows you wouldn't do me a favor if your life depended on it, McCarthy. So, what's the catch?"

He stretched beside me. With his arms in the air and long legs extended, he was the picture of tranquility. Our eyes connected when he opened them again. "I'm getting everything I want, Pressley."

And for some unknown reason, he looked genuine. It still

wasn't enough.

"And what would that be?"

There *had* to be a catch here somewhere, right?

McCarthy sighed. "Let's see—" He pretended to think over his answer for a moment. "A beautiful girlfriend on my arm when I walk around campus—" He immediately cut himself off as amusement glimmered on his face. "I'm sure people won't mind the horrible attitude, unfunny jokes. Right?"

"Because you're such a comedian," I spat back, ignoring the *beautiful* and latching onto what I knew him for: the insult. "Just say no, and I can find someone else." I was bluffing. There wasn't anyone on this planet my brother would like to see me with less. But McCarthy didn't need to know that.

"I said yes," he reminded. "I'm sure you remember?"

"You're not acting like that's your final answer," I said. I shook my head quickly. "So, I'd rather skip the back and forth and move on to you saying no, like you will anyway."

"So little faith," he mused. "I'm saying yes, *let me be your fake boyfriend*, Pressley." His voice took on a fake pleading tone when he intertwined his hands in front of his chest. "Do you want me to beg? Is that what you want?" He pretended to get on his knees. Of course, he never would.

"So you're serious?" I deadpanned. Not a hint of humor on display.

"Dead."

"And you want nothing in return?"

McCarthy thought for a moment. "*Fine*," he conceded. "Even if seeing your brother lose his mind is enough for me, if you want me to want something in return . . ." He eyed me just to make sure I realized how ridiculous it sounded. "Let's just say you'll owe me. A favor for a favor."

Can't complain now.

"All right." But something about the calm demeanor, the lightning answer felt . . . *off*. I couldn't shake the feeling. "And you're sure you know what you're—?"

"—Getting into?" he cut me off, and I nodded. "Yes, I'm sure. I'm sure I want to see you be my girlfriend, and I'm sure I definitely want to see your brother when he realizes. Is that enough of an honest answer?" His brows rose to make a point. "This seems like an incredibly easy way to do so. So yes, I'm in. It was your idea. What are you so hesitant about?"

"Your ability to be a convincing boyfriend." It slipped out. And I didn't regret it.

"I can be a very convincing boyfriend," he rebutted.

I snorted humorously. "You don't even date."

"I go on plenty of dates."

"Yeah, but you don't *date*, do you?" *Please don't ask me how I knew that.* "Like, the same person, multiple times. After she slept with you?"

I didn't really mean to be as caught up on the subject of his dating history as I was. Girls just talked: when they were in the library, when they were getting ready to go out, when they were drunk in bathrooms. And if you stayed to listen, you could hear their conversations through the closed doors quite easily.

Why couldn't he just agree with me so that I wouldn't have to drive this point home *so hard?* He knew I was right.

McCarthy's lips broke into a smirk, and I wished the ground opened up beneath me, before he had even opened his mouth. "Is this a frequent topic in the Pressley household?" he asked curiously, smiling. "My relationships? Dates? Say, do you have a file of every girl I've been with?"

"Can't really blame Henry after Paula." I shrugged quickly, shifting my eyes to study the brick wall behind us. "Besides," I added in an amused drawl. "That file would be *thin*, only proving my point." I dared a glance toward him.

"Paula?" McCarthy tilted his head, a little hesitant as he ignored the rest of my words. "Castillo?" I nodded. "What does Paula Castillo have to do with anything?"

"Oh, you know, just the fact she basically cheated on him. With you." The thought was enough for the semi-permanent scowl on my face to make an appearance again., but McCarthy's unapologetically loud laugh pulled me back to reality. "*What?*" I snapped.

"Oh, you know." He mirrored my words. Something must've still seemed incredibly funny to him. He was still laughing. "Just the fact that Paula is my friend—my *neighbor*—and I never touched her beyond a hug when *Henry* fucked up."

"He didn't—" I cut myself off. I wasn't here to defend my brother's actions, much less understand whatever relationship he did or didn't have. "Whatever," I huffed instead.

McCarthy snickered. "Whatever indeed," he said. "Which means I'm perfectly qualified to be your fake boyfriend, Pressley. Are you happy now?"

And honestly, the reality of my proposition only dawned on me now. I scrambled. "This has to be convincing, you know? It's important that it's convincing—"

"It will be."

"You can pretend to be a good boyfriend?" The longer I thought about it, the more this felt like a huge mistake. Maybe I shouldn't have asked in the first place. "Have you even been in a relationship before?"

His eyes narrowed. "Yes, I can pretend to be a good boyfriend. Thank you very much."

The fact he pointedly ignored the other question was answer enough.

"You can pretend that you think about me nonstop, that you're totally and endlessly enthralled by me?"

"Yes." At least he seemed convinced.

"You're gonna have to be *so* in love with me, McCarthy. And if this doesn't work, I swear to God—"

"Don't worry," he said, and a faked smile graced his lips. "I'm a great actor."

And that was that.

"A few ground rules—" I wanted to continue, but he rummaged through his bag, and for some reason, that required my full attention. *Was that . . . ?*

I stifled a laugh when he pulled a little notebook out. "You're taking notes?"

"Don't laugh," he scolded, trying to keep his own amusement in check. "Every agreement should be put in writing. No?"

"Spoken like a true business student," I agreed. "We'll do date night every Friday. I'll pick you up from practice. Make sure Henry sees."

His protest came quickly, eyes glued to his book. "Can't do Friday; every Thursday?"

"What if I'm busy Thursdays?"

"Are you?"

"Maybe I am." *I wasn't.* "But I'll make it work."

McCarthy snorted. "Thank you *so* much. I'll be forever in your debt—" He stopped himself. "Oh, wait." Smiled. "That's you." He added a wink.

"You're hilarious," I deadpanned. "Thursday it is."

Clearing my throat—to suppress my annoyance and to distract from the smirk on his lips—I went on. "We could soft launch on Monday." Two days from now. "Talk after class, smile at each other. Go all in a few days later. Keep it up for a month or two? Until the new year, maybe?"

McCarthy scribbled furiously, nodding along to let me know he agreed. When his pen stilled, he looked up at me through thick lashes any girl would be envious of.

"*All in*. What does that entail?"

If I was being honest, I hadn't decided yet. Up until now, I'd managed to make it seem as though I had thought about this thoroughly before bringing the idea to him. In reality, I was making everything up as I went along, not sure what would come out of my mouth when I opened it.

"Public display of affection is a must. You know, holding hands and all that." An amused expression on his face, he willed me to go on. "So, light PDA. Nothing above that, of course. And only when Henry is around, obviously."

"Still not quite catching on." Casually, he twirled his pen between his fingers. Something about his eyes batting to mine, innocence in them he couldn't have faked better, told me he wasn't as clueless as he was pretending.

"You know." I trailed off, brows rising.

"Let's assume I don't. Gotta make sure I get this as accurate as possible, right?" He pointed to the makeshift contract in his lap.

"Why don't you just put 'No sex' down, then?" I shot back, already growing irritated. Maybe this really wasn't the best idea.

"Put it in capital letters, too."

"Oh no," McCarthy sighed dramatically. "However will I cope? After all, that was the only reason I agreed in the first place." He pinned me with a look that said the opposite. "Now, are there any non-obvious rules to this masterplan of yours?" He leaned back. "Or do you just like to think of a world where I can't keep my hands off of you, Pressley?"

At the end, our Fake Dating Contract consisted of exactly seven ground rules. Beneath them, both of our signatures beamed brightly.

#1 Fake-Date-Thursdays.
#2 Delivery Period: November 1st–January 1st.
#3 No Sex.
#4 Exclusiveness is guaranteed. (Single activities to be postponed until after the duration of this agreement)
#5 Athalia Payton Pressley is obligated to support her fake boyfriend Dylan McCarthy Williams at his soccer games.
#6 Both parties involved can't, under any circumstance, break character.
#7 Don't fall in love with Dylan McCarthy Williams (or Athalia Payton Pressley).

Number seven was McCarthy's addition, and after I had added my own name (and then he added parentheses around it), I was okay with it. He'd made sure to underline the *Don't* and wrote it in bold, capital letters, like I needed the reminder.

"Pleasure doing business with you." I held out my hand for

him to shake.

"The pleasure's all mine, trust me."

Chapter 8

I tried to self-care my way into thinking this was a good idea. When Wren came home that night, my wet hair was in a towel and my face covered in a blue mask. I sprawled across the brown couch in the living room, watching *Gilmore Girls* with a glass of wine in hand. Wren's rattling key gave me a five second heads-up before she stood in the door. My eyes narrowed, assessing posture, stance, expression.

Her weird tantrum this morning had been the start of what turned out to be an awful day. But in the grand scheme of things, Wren didn't fuck up nearly as badly as Henry had.

Leftover tension hung in the air. She took me in cautiously, only shifting her gaze to take off her shoes and jacket. Leaving them by the door, Wren cleared her throat and I braced myself for whatever continuation of our argument we were about to have. It seemed inevitable.

"You look absolutely ridiculous," she deadpanned instead, dissecting every minuscule reaction of mine to calculate her next words carefully. I assumed she caught the amused twitch of my lip before I could make sure they'd stayed put.

That earlier tension visibly fell off her. She carelessly let the paper bag slip out of her hand, and a loud, theatrical sigh left her lips.

"Ugh!" she humphed, heading for the couch I was sitting

on. "I am *so* sorry, I don't know what came over me this morning. I probably just slept horrible, you know? Parties are not my thing, and staying up late isn't either. And while you were playing *some* variation of beer pong, Henry would not stop chewing my ear off."

My body reacted to the mention of my brother's name. There was nothing I could do about it. "Since when does he drink, by the way—?" It took Wren a second to catch it, then she faltered in her wordy apology. I hadn't heard her talk this much in one sitting since we went to see *Hamilton* last year. It was my first time. Her fourth. Or was it fifth? "What was that?" she asked.

"Nothing." I wasn't a terrible liar, but Wren knew me like the palm of her hand. Seeing as she knew how to read them, that said a lot.

She looked at me curiously, leaning in as she blew strands of black and blond hair out of her face. Then, she said "*Henry*," as if to test the waters. Slowly. Cautiously. And, of course, I flinched again. "*Aha!*" she exclaimed, finger in my face, before she jumped back victoriously. She only realized what being right meant when she quickly settled. "Sorry."

I accepted her apology by letting my head fall onto her shoulder. If she cared about the blue goo currently seeping from my face onto her hoodie, she didn't act like it. Instead, her hand cupped my shoulder in a makeshift hug before resting her own head on top of mine. We remained quiet for a while. Our attention was on the screen, and I think we were both grateful for the silence it filled.

"Before you tell me everything—" The groan I let out was meant to show how little I wanted to talk about it, but the way she squirmed out from underneath me to get up did intensify the sound. Wren knew I'd tell her, whether I wanted to or not. She was right.

"Before you tell me everything," she repeated, sterner, a hint of humor in her voice, "I got takeout from Prem's."

Prem owned the Indian place down the street, which, coincidentally, had the best takeout in the entire state. And even more importantly: the best *Bhatura* in the United States of America. A weakness of mine. A comfort not many things could bring me. Now that Wren mentioned it, I could smell it from here. My eyes probably lit up and my mouth watered as I shot upright, full attention on the brown bag Wren was currently retrieving from where she'd dropped it earlier.

"Apology accepted," I said as soon as the container saying '#12 no onions' appeared on the coffee table, followed by the Bhatura wrapped in foil. My heart jumped at the sight.

"I'd hope so," she muttered with a laugh, leaving her food on the table to get cutlery from the kitchen. "Also: got some of that left?" She pointed at her own face, finger circling it.

I snorted. "You called my face mask ridiculous five minutes ago."

Wren simply shrugged. "Bathroom?"

When she came back, her short, colored hair was tied up as best as she could manage, traces of blue catching on the edges of it here and there. The mask covered her already clear skin messily, but entirely.

Wren was aware of my weird brother issues, so when I told her about our fight, and then my inevitable I-wish-I-were-more-than-an-inconvenience-in-his-life epiphany, she wasn't surprised. She ate and listened, every now and then throwing in an outraged "*Motherfucker,*" or "*What?*" Usually, when she'd just taken a bite.

At the end of my monologue, Wren considered me. "So . . . ?" she asked. Our food was done and Netflix asked whether we were still watching.

"So what?"

"What's the plan?"

Ah. The plan. Of course Wren knew I'd want to get back at him. Shame she won't like it. At all.

It seemed McCarthy had made quite a few enemies in his three years at HBU. Coincidentally, on the top of that list were the two people closest to me. Henry at number one, of course, closely followed by Wren Inkwood—for some reason not quite clear to me.

Before today, I'd never really questioned why either of them disliked him so much, never cared enough to ask.

Hell, I wasn't even sure what *my* problem with him was. Take Henry out of the equation, and I was left with pretty much nothing. Except the way his lips curled knowingly when I gave a wrong answer.

"Funny story," I muttered, faking a single laugh as my eyes roamed the living room, like I'd never seen Wren's bookshelf against the wall behind the couch filled exclusively with historical texts and fantasies. Never sat on the smooth brown leather of our couch, facing the TV on the opposite wall. Like the loft's open floorplan and the green-white checkered carpet under the coffee table were new. And like Wren's polaroids decorating the short hallway to the front door had only been hung this morning. I scrambled for the remote between us, telling the screen that, *yes, we are still watching; please fill the lingering silence now!*

"Is it?" she asked. "Funny?"

"Well," I began, eyes flicking to Wren long enough to see her eagerly awaiting my response. "Let me preface this by saying my methods may be flawed, but they are always effective." I was stalling. Clearly. "So, while the means of achieving my revenge might not be ideal, the outcome will be worth—"

"Just spit it out, Athalia."

Fuck it.

"I'm going to pretend to date McCarthy for the next two months." The speed in which the words flew out of me could win a Guinness World Record. "Exclusively," I added reluctantly.

It took her a good thirty seconds to comprehend the jumbled mess I'd just thrown at her. When she got it, her brow stretched high, and she leaned back, in some kind of shock. For a moment, I think she froze.

I didn't know whether it was five seconds or minutes or hours. I didn't realize I was holding my breath until she said, "Okay."

"Okay?"

"It's gonna piss Henry off." She mulled it over once more, expression twisting into a grimace. "It's definitely going to piss him off. Bonus points for getting the attention you so clearly crave. A quick fix for something that, at some point, you *will* have to talk to Stephanie about." The fact Wren knew my therapist's name was evidence enough that she'd gotten to know me way too well in our three years of college together.

"I mean, it's a solid plan. Except for the *one* unpredictable, right? If McCarthy is one thing, it's probably unpredictable. See how I said probably? That's because he's so unpredictable,

I don't even know—" It felt like Henry had rubbed off on her. Wren didn't usually ramble, but she was definitely doing so now. Rambling on and on and on and—

"—Okay," I cut her off, hands lifted in surrender. "I get it. It's an idiotic plan, but if it works the way I want it to work, it'll be the best thing I can do. If McCarthy doesn't act like a jerk—which is unlikely—and if spending time with him isn't insufferable—also unlikely—I might not even regret this." I was also rambling now. "But it *is* a good plan," I insisted.

Wren sighed. "It's an okay plan," she said, but smiled.

Going to bed that night, I checked my emails, in the hope that any of next week's lectures had been canceled. Instead of the sweet relief of one of those messages, there was one thing waiting in my inbox:

<D.M.WILLIAMS@HALLBU.COM> 6:33 PM

Pressley,

Find attached a copy of our written contractual agreement.

Unkind regards,
D. M. W.

Chapter 9

During the *soft launch* stage, I could count the number of times my and Henry's eyes met on one hand. He was stubborn enough to barely look at me, and I barely wanted to look at him.

And now, with two hours until my first lecture, here I was. Being stood up by my fake boyfriend, on our first fake date. Wasn't life just marvelous?

Wren had said this was a bad idea. And I didn't want to admit it, but I'd had some serious doubts of my own. McCarthy was unreliable, selfish, arrogant. Those weren't great qualities to have in a business partner. Worse in a boyfriend.

"Fancy seeing you here."

The sinking feeling of my own humiliation got replaced quickly. Now that McCarthy's voice drawled through the air, all I could bring myself to feel was annoyance. As carefree as ever, he took a seat on the other side of the small table, right by the window. My gaze moved toward him slowly.

"You're late." I dropped the spoon that had just been stirring my coffee back into the cup. His brown hair was still damp. He shrugged his jacket off, revealing the compression shirt that clung to his outline. My eyes flicked back up, ignoring the tight fit around his arms before I could accidentally linger.

"You're early," he corrected quickly, eyeing my cup. "We agreed on 9:30."

"9:15." I was sure I'd said 9:15, and I was sure he'd agreed to 9:15. Why else would I be sitting in Daisy's Coffee at 9:15—

"You said 9:15," he confirmed. Unfortunately, he went on, "I said I won't make it for 9:15, suggested 9:30, and you shrugged. Which, in my world, means you agreed." His smirk was unbearable, even before he added, "To 9:30."

I sighed more in annoyance than defeat. In my defense, that conversation had taken place in the same Statistics lecture *he* had told me to pay more attention to. And I had felt Shaw's eyes on us the entire time we were having it. I'd been prone to agree to anything he'd said, just so he would shut up.

"Ah, she remembers." He smiled when my gaze met his again.

"You're insufferable, McCarthy."

He reached across the small table for my drink, took a long sip and placed it right in front of me again. "Just think about what you might've done to deserve a boyfriend as insufferable as me."

I grimaced. "Charming," I muttered as he wiped the whipped-cream moustache off his face. To make sure no one saw the unfiltered urge to murder him dash across my features, my eyes shifted.

Daisy's was the only coffee shop perfectly located between my apartment and the business buildings we had most of our classes in. Relatively modern—painted white with accents of pink here and there, tiles ran along the front of the counter to the pastry display behind a glass front. To the right, the counter's modern white tiles morphed into dark wooden planks. The light, clean floor was replaced by ancient-looking wood, and flowers and plants spread out across the entirety of the other side of the building. The walls were red brick, instead of white paint. Daisy's Coffee and Daisy's Daisies shared the space—a coffee and flower shop in one.

It's what was charming about the place. Two entirely different concepts—clashing, yet somehow working together so incredibly well.

And on sunny days like this one, Henry preferred to walk to class, get a coffee from Daisy's on the way instead of a cup from his machine at home, before heading into the nightmare we called Accounting. That little habit of his was the only reason I was still sitting here, surrounded by flowers, fresh pastries, and a guy I wasn't sure would come out of this alive, if I had it my way.

"So, you've been studying?"

Right away, I knew this wasn't about Statistics. "Of course."

To his initial email, I'd replied with a similar one.

<A.P.PRESSLEY@HALLBU.COM> 9:20 AM

McCarthy,

Find attached a document of all the things my boyfriend should know about me. Should you not memorize each of these points, I, your future fake girlfriend, will be thoroughly disappointed, as well as forced to fake break up with you.

Insincerely,
A. P. P.

To which he'd replied:

> <D.M.WILLIAMS@HALLBU.COM> 10:35 AM
>
> Pressley,
>
> Find attached my own list of fun facts. I'll be expecting just as much commitment from you as you are from me.
>
> PS: Did you know your favorite animal tortures other sea creatures for fun? Thinking about it, I can see why you like them.
>
> Worst,
> D. M. W.

It's how we'd ended up here: full-blown quizzing each other on the content of our respective document.

"Best friend?" I asked.

"Wren Inkwood, history major. Dislikes me strongly. Mine?"

I tried to hide the disappointment at his correct answer, instead focused on the response he expected from me. "Blake Zachary, computer science."

So far, we'd gone through full name (McCarthy Williams, Dylan), age (twenty-three), favorite color (green) and parents' names (Natalie McCarthy and Lincoln Williams). We were moving quicker now, the next question already on his lips before his last had even been answered. He was enjoying this, hoping to make me slip up, just as much as I wanted him to.

"Hometown?" he asked, and the answer flew out of my mouth effortlessly.

"D. C. Mine?" Determined to see him fail, I leaned closer, elbows on the table despite my many etiquette classes.

Unfortunately, his answer was just as confident and correct. "London, Chelsea. Moved to New York when you were five, grew up there."

I groaned at the victorious smile on his lips, watching the dimples in his cheek deepening with the sound.

"Seems much easier for you to study me than correlations and regressions," he pointed out. By now, the lack of distance between us was apparent. The more challenging the question, the closer we'd drawn to one another. So far, no one had been intimidated, and no one had gotten an answer wrong. We were just competitively staring at each other in the middle of a café, not enough space between us for comfort.

"Well." I cleared my throat, leaning back into my chair to break the tension. "There are few things duller than correlations and regressions."

"Aw," he said with a cruel smile. "Did you just admit I'm interesting, Pressley?"

My eyes rolled with an equal mix of amusement and disbelief. "Being more interesting than statistics is *not* a compliment."

He shrugged. "I'd say that's subjective. Don't you think?" He waited for my response somewhat eagerly, as if my words were next week's lottery numbers.

"Have I mentioned that you're insufferable?"

"And yet you begged to fake-date me."

My head shot back in his direction, and he looked at me like it was the exact reaction he'd aimed for. *Fuck.*

"I did not beg," I clarified. "And at this point, I regret even politely asking."

"No you don't."

And I would have one-hundred percent disagreed with him, if Henry hadn't just walked through the door. Instead, my body stiffened, and my brother noticed me immediately.

Henry's gaze lingered on me for a fraction of a second before shifting unnaturally quickly to explore the familiar shop.

He looked at the handwritten chalkboard menu as if he wasn't going to order what he got every single morning. His attention shifted onto the various bouquets of flowers on the other side of the room, even though he'd bought at least half of them for Paula at some point. And then, as if he couldn't help himself, his gaze flicked toward me again.

If an expression could be made of steel, his was stainless. Not a twitch in the mask he was wearing for ego-preserving purposes. It was infuriating.

God, I really needed this McCarthy thing to work out.

"He's behind me?"

I startled. At McCarthy's voice, the reminder that he was actually here, and we were really doing this. Fortunately, it was the nudge I needed to get it together and put my—no doubt risky—plan in motion.

Nodding, I smiled as if he'd just promised me the world. A quick glance behind him told me Henry had a hard time not showing interest in the guy his *little sister* was sitting across from. But his relatively calm expression told me he hadn't yet recognized the back of his enemy's head. "How good is your fake laugh?"

McCarthy didn't reply. Instead, his lips parted in a grin, his nose crinkled, and he squinted slightly as a perfectly natural laugh filled the store.

I didn't think anything could've prepared me for the sight. Or the sound. Or the way I could grow accustomed to hearing it more often. The slight rasp, the hint of a giggle bubbling in the back of his throat when he threw his head back.

Damn it.

I only vaguely noticed the recognition on Henry's face when I sneaked a peek behind the heavenly smile in front of me. Clearly, I wasn't the only one surprised to hear that laugh.

"You do that often?" I wondered, eyes shifting back to McCarthy.

He winked, and it was a shame Henry stood behind him. "Only with you."

"You should know your girlfriend is *incredibly* funny. There's no need for fake laughs." My eyes narrowed and I leaned across the small table to emphasize my point. To make sure Henry couldn't interpret this any other way.

McCarthy gasped in surprise, laughed, and then shook his head. All in all, he was playing the part as if his life depended on it. And I was unironically thankful for it.

"How come my fake laugh is so well-practiced, then?" The accusatory tone in his voice made me crack a smile as he leaned on the table as well.

"Your other girlfriends must've been tools." I shrugged, making sure to break eye contact only for a second, and only because I knew the ringing of the bell above the door had announced Henry's departure, even before I saw him walk off through the window. No coffee cup in hand, aggravation lacing his steps.

My gaze fell back to McCarthy, a sense of accomplishment radiating through me. His brown eyes were close enough for me to make out their different shades. His face, close enough to notice the minty scent of his gum lingering in the little air left between us.

He was *close*. And he must've realized at the same time.

"What are your favorite flowers?" As he asked the question, he sat back. The unbothered, well-rehearsed look on his face was back on full display and I was sure he knew Henry had left without so much as a glance over his shoulder.

"Why?"

"As your boyfriend, I feel I should know."

"What makes you think I have favorite flowers?" I asked, relaxing into my chair.

"Come on," he teased, as if it was obvious. He gestured me up and down once. "You're a *billionaire's daughter*. You simply must have favorite flowers." The concept seemed amusing to him.

"And you're a millionaire's son," I challenged. "What are *your* favorite flowers?"

McCarthy shrugged. "My mother's are lilies." I took that to mean his were too.

I looked at Daisy's bouquets across my shoulder for inspiration. Roses, sunflowers, peonies, daisies, orchids. Eventually, I sighed as I turned back. "Tulips, I guess."

He pondered my answer. One look, and he probably spotted the bouquet of pale pink tulips, just like I had. "Least favorite?" His gaze shifted to me again. "Which should've been my first question, actually."

"Now *that's* an answer I can give you." Because picking

favorites was . . . hard. Figuring out the pros and cons of so many good things, only to find the *best*. Knowing what you disliked, however, was as easy as falling asleep after pulling an all-nighter. It came naturally. Quick, like an instinct you followed. "Red roses."

Chapter 10

Henry skipped our Accounting lecture, which I thought was childish. Then again, it meant the plan was working. In return, I had a bounce in my step and a smile on my face for most of the day.

Even if I wasn't speaking to my brother, at least I knew he was thinking about me. I hadn't been this certain about that since our parents died.

I could tell by the look that washed over him when he spotted me in the hall. The way his head whipped in the opposite direction before I even really looked at him. He was on his way home, I was on my way to McCarthy's tutorial, and that fact probably wasn't lost on him.

Divine intervention or a simple coincidence? When McCarthy's head popped out of his TA office before I even reached it, I said a silent *thank you.*

The hallway was long, though the door to McCarthy's office was barely ten feet from where my and Henry's paths would cross. The light beige walls were peppered with doors to my left and windows to my right. Between every window, the bust of some historically important person was placed on a slim, wooden podium and I thought Henry might walk into President Abraham Lincoln himself, with the way he eagerly avoided my gaze.

"Pressley!"

I wasn't used to my arrangement with McCarthy just yet, and the friendliness of his tone caught me off guard. As Henry's gaze shot toward him, it seemed he wasn't familiar with the sound either. Though, when someone called your name, it was second nature; you'd check, right?

The look that passed between the two could've frozen lava.

McCarthy raised his hand and gave me a lazy smile. One that hopefully said: *Oh, my girlfriend, I'm so glad to see you.*

"Would you look at that," I muttered, as I sidled past him into the tiny office. "You can actually sound like a decent human being when you try." He shut the door behind me with a thud, gesturing to the uncomfortable chair.

"You'd be surprised how kind and generous I can be when you're not around."

"I'd guess about just as much as Shaw on a bad day." My brows rose. "Right?"

Unfortunately, McCarthy's attention was already on the source of my demise for the next sixty minutes: *Statistical Interference I.*

"Have you read this before?" He held the book out to me, a brow raised critically as he sat.

"Sure." I leaned back, and the gesture made him drop his hand with a theatrical sigh. He knew that the honest answer was a big fat *nope*.

"It was required reading last year." He made a point of opening, turning, and placing the book in front of me. Then went on without checking to see if I was even looking.

Then again, if I weren't looking, I wouldn't know he wasn't checking.

"It's got a chapter on everything you're failing to understand." His finger slowly ran across the table of contents, giving every relevant chapter a purposeful tap. The null-hypothesis: *tap*. Calculating probabilities: *tap*. Confidence intervals: *tap*.

I didn't know why my eyes were practically glued to the book. *The book*—not the ringed finger running across it.

McCarthy turned the page slowly, continuing to run his finger across every chapter of the table delicately. A-B tests: *tap*. Correlation coefficients: *tap*. I noticed a vein that ran from his knuckle upward, and my eyes followed it mindlessly. Regressions: *tap*. They were nice hands. Firm, tough-looking, veins running across the back. He wore rings, too. Three silver ones.

My eyes jumped up to his quickly. I wasn't quite sure how long he hadn't said anything, and I was even less sure of how long his hand had remained on the page. When our eyes connected, his brow rose in amusement, waiting for any kind of reaction. I huffed as I stalled for time.

"The thing is also, like, a hundred pounds, McCarthy," I finally retorted. "There's no way—"

The book snapped shut, and I was sure the only reason he closed it was to keep me from talking. His patience was already wearing thin, five minutes into the whole ordeal, and I wasn't sure whether to feel proud or a little guilty. Being Shaw's TA must be hard enough without the burden of having to teach statistics to a hopeless case like me.

"What is your problem with this?" he asked, with an equal mix of aggravation and confusion in his voice. "You're not dumb, Pressley, but somehow you don't want to understand."

"That's probably the nicest thing you've ever said to me," I quipped, and McCarthy's eyes rolled in annoyance.

"I'm being serious."

"And that might be the problem." As the silence that followed my statement lingered, I dared a glance at the man opposite me. A hand ran through his dark brown hair, eyes on the wooden table. In a wave of unprecedented guilt, I sighed. "I don't know," I admitted.

"You're not even trying," he pointed out.

Rightfully so. I wasn't trying. And I didn't know why I wasn't trying. At the very least, I always tried.

Perhaps it was the fact that, no matter how hard I'd try with this, I'd never be my mom. I'd never be Naomi Yung, the woman who had changed the way we applied statistics in business today. Way past her death, her success was a lingering presence. Last semester, I'd stumbled over her name three times trying to study for this damn class.

I'd never be her.

The thought made me sick.

Henry was basically Dad, living up to his name and the reputation of a Pressley in soccer. He'd go pro after college, just the way he was supposed to. The draft was but a month away, and I wasn't even worried. Everyone knew he'd make it.

Why couldn't I be just a little more like either of our parents, too?

Could I be—if I just tried a little harder?

I wasn't quite sure what trying in statistics looked like, but the following tutoring session with McCarthy was not it. The bounce in my step and the smile on my face were wiped away by the end of it.

I watched as his nose scrunched, trying to decipher the notes in front of him. His brown hair fell into his face as he read through the words, as unsure about them as I had been. His tongue poked the inside of his cheek, he squinted, then flicked his eyes toward me.

You're totally staring at him, the voice inside my head blurted out as soon as our gazes connected. It was right. I was staring. *Why was I staring?*

He held our eye contact steadily, though. So technically, was he staring at me too?

The smile he gave me was all dumb and teasing and uncontrolled, and the dimples in his cheek were a brief reminder. He was irritatingly attractive. It was a fact. Probably one that contributed to why I disliked him so strongly. Probably one that contributed to why Henry did, too.

I shook my head to snap out of it. "So—" I began. I didn't get very far.

"You were totally staring at me." McCarthy bit his bottom lip to keep from breaking into a toothy grin. Apparently, he'd picked up on it, too. "Don't shake your head like that." He went on. "Athalia Payton Pressley, you were *totally* staring at me," he said again, dropping the sing-song voice.

I mulled over his accusation for a moment. "Stop being a five-year-old, McCarthy."

He was grinning now. *You. Were. Totally. Staring*, he mouthed back, then redirected his attention to the notes in front of him. Before I could retort, a knock on the door cut me off.

He took a double-take at the clock on the wall—3 PM, on the dot—and then sighed. "I'll email you the details for tomorrow," he said, handing me my notes back, before raising his voice for a louder *"Come in."*

And he did. Over the tip of his long nose, Professor Simon Shaw studied us somewhat curiously. His black hair hung into his features messily, and I almost couldn't see the way his brows rose when I stood up.

"Where do you think you're going?" he asked, head slowly turning in my direction. Standing still, I was glad he didn't expect—or at the very least didn't want to wait for—a response. "If you could fit five minutes with me into your, no doubt, busy schedule, Miss Pressley." Shaw's hand extended toward his office, inviting me inside with a snarl.

He didn't ask me to join him; he expected me to. Even if I'd had the most important appointment of my life in those five minutes, I still would've followed him in without a second thought.

A single glance across my shoulder showed McCarthy mouthing a sarcastic *Good luck* my way before he closed the door between us.

Professor Shaw's office was brighter than McCarthy's. Bigger, too. And tidier. Though, with the number of times I'd been in here, I wasn't surprised by that. The chair on the opposite side of his desk looked more comfortable, too, but I didn't get the chance to sit in it.

"There's no need," Shaw said when I was about to. "This will be quick."

So I stood.

"How are you finding your tutoring? Making any progress?"

The urge to throw McCarthy under the bus was huge. This was a once-in-a-lifetime opportunity to destroy the flawless reputation he'd built with staff at this school. *Even the janitors love him*, was what Henry had said once, clearly annoyed by the fact.

Still, despite the golden opportunity, I nodded. McCarthy was doing me a solid, so this was hardly the time to stab him in the back.

"Yes, sir," I muttered. "It's only been two hours so far, but I feel like I'm getting the hang of it."

"Great." His mouth dropped into a straight line. "So why did I need to get an email from your brother expecting me to drop these sessions?" My cheeks flushed bright pink before I could stop them. "*Expecting* me to grant you a free pass?" he snarled with clearly faked curiosity in his voice.

"Professor—" My mouth was dry when I spoke, and I cleared my throat before I could go on. Shaw stood behind his chair, squinting at me and making the most uncomfortable eye contact in the history of eye contact.

"Just because your parents have earned *their* reputation at this school doesn't mean either of you have, Pressley," Shaw hissed, his voice still dangerously low. "Just because you're their daughter and he's their son, doesn't mean you get to waltz around this school—*my* class—and tell me what *you* might prefer I do."

He was right, of course. Henry had overstepped massively, overestimated the influence he might have around athletes and coaches as Felix Pressley's son. He did not have it here, and he should've known that before he sent the goddamn email. I could kill him.

For some reason, I still didn't rat him out. I really wanted to, more than I wanted to throw McCarthy under the bus. But instead of telling him that Henry should be the one in trouble—that it was his idea entirely and he hadn't even consulted me beforehand—all I said was "I know," followed by, "It won't happen again."

Shaw nodded, his mouth twisting in discontent, despite my words. "It is a shame," he drawled, studying me. "With all that your mother accomplished in the field, I was excited to hear you'd joined my class last year." He shook his head in disappointment, sighed. "It's a shame you're not living up to her reputation, Miss Pressley."

Chapter 11

When I got home that afternoon, the details McCarthy had wanted to email me were waiting in my inbox.

<D.M.WILLIAMS@HALLBU.COM> 03:12 PM

Pressley,

If you survived Shaw, I'll meet you in front of the Alexandrian Library tomorrow. Three PM sharp.

Happy Fake Date Thursday Eve! You better get your hopes up.

Disrespectfully,
D. M. W.

"*This?*" was the first thing I wondered when McCarthy walked up to me that Thursday. "This is what you had in mind? What I was supposed to *get my hopes up* for?" My tone was disbelieving as I watched him, a copy of *Statistical Interference I* in hand.

"Well, did you?" The corner of his lip quirked at the prospect. As he took a seat beside me, leaving the bench on the opposite side of the picnic table empty, I rolled my eyes.

"Of course not." I might not know McCarthy well, but I knew him enough to lower my expectations when he suggested I raise them. I shook my head again. "Normally, dates involve a movie, dinner, drinks. Flowers. Not—" I pointed at the 100-pound book now resting on the table between us. "—that."

"And usually, dates aren't at three o'clock in a college courtyard, to make sure a certain someone would see you."

Touché.

"Besides," he added. "This is perfect. It makes sense. I'm your tutor. This—" He gestured back and forth between us. "—is a cute, unsuspecting study date. Taking in the last of this year's sun in front of the library your brother happens to be in for . . . how much longer, again?"

I shrugged. "Like half an hour."

"Half an hour," he echoed, checking his phone for the time and nodding in confirmation. "See? Perfect."

If there was one thing about Henry, it was that he always followed a schedule. He had since he was fifteen years old, and he stuck to it religiously. It's what kept him grounded, productive, and on top of his game. *In control.* And as someone who'd been with him since before his first to-do list, I knew his routine better than my own.

Mostly because the only routine *I* followed was Indian takeout on Saturday nights, and even that lacked consistency most weeks.

We lived very different lives, my brother and I. Every second that wasn't planned out was a wasted one for him. Life was sacred and having one he could be proud of in ten years' time seemed to be the most important thing.

I . . . didn't quite operate that way. What happened, happened.

Life went on regardless of the mistakes you made, regardless of who lived or died. So why invest so much energy into living a perfectly planned-out life when we all ended up in a casket? He'd tried often enough to fix my attitude. Every year, I'd get some kind of planner for my birthday. Once, he'd stolen my iPad password to download one of those calendar apps. The only reason I hadn't used it was to annoy him.

"You know," I huffed, attention back on McCarthy and the devil's testament in his hand. "The only reason I had any motivation to study statistics by myself was to avoid seeing you every Wednesday. Now that I'll have to see you regardless, what motivation is there?"

I was back to not wanting to even try. *What. Was. The. Point?*

"Proving me wrong?"

His head tilted slightly as he waited for me to grasp the concept. My eyes narrowed. I continued evaluating the stakes.

"Prove you wrong how?" Suspicion laced my voice.

"I told Shaw you're a hopeless case. He asked after your... *conversation* yesterday."

Oh.

I knew I was a hopeless case. McCarthy knew I was a hopeless case, and Shaw probably thought I was a hopeless case, too. But there was a significant difference between *thinking* and *hearing it confirmed by your TA.*

"You can't just—" I wanted to argue, my raised voice faltering at his next words.

"—He agreed with me. But that provides you with an amazing opportunity." I didn't have to ask what he meant, and he didn't have to say it out loud again either. A short silence lingered before he did, anyway. "Prove us wrong, Pressley."

I didn't want to give him the satisfaction of agreeing with him, but he was onto something.

I hated being underestimated as much as the next person—it's what growing up with an overachieving brother did, I assumed—and so the opportunity to prove McCarthy wrong, to prove Professor Shaw wrong . . . it was inviting.

So inviting that I actually tried to listen the next time my tutor explained the basics of statistics and what we could do with them. Sure, trying wasn't doing.

That blue Frisbee being thrown into the blonde girl's face, who had been exceptionally talkative on the other end of the grass even before it had hit her in the head, was still more interesting than why we needed a null-hypothesis. And the look on my brother's face when he spotted us half an hour later was still more satisfying than finally understanding what a null-hypothesis was supposed to do.

At one point, even as I tried to listen to what McCarthy was saying, I'd caught myself analyzing the curve in his dimple, the rasp in his voice after he cleared his throat, and how voluminous his hair was. I briefly wondered if he used 3-in-1 shampoo, though hoped to God he didn't.

I'd love to say this sudden detail-awareness was nothing to worry about: everything—*everyone*—was more interesting than statistics. But there was something in the glances he threw me that made them exhilarating enough to still think about back in the comfort of my own home. And there, he was competing with *Gilmore Girls* and Wren and good snacks . . . not the definition of a null hypothesis.

He shouldn't have still been on my mind, but there he was.

Accompanied by the memory of his hopeful look when he asked if I understood something, and the faked pout when I deadpanned *no*.

Chapter 12

"No," Wren insisted. I could tell how hard it was for her. "Athalia Payton Pressley, I'm not going." My full name was added for dramatic effect. So was the grim look on her face, the crossed arms, and the threatening tone in her voice.

I pointed out the window. "We're already in the car." My voice was calm, but stern.

"Because you didn't tell me where we were going!"

"Because you love going to games!"

Hence why it was so hard for her to say no. She wanted to see HBU kick some ass. She wanted to be in the stands, cheering and booing and trying to explain what was happening to me, who'd been trying her hardest to avoid anything soccer-related since the ripe age of six. Apparently, I'd run out of the room screaming until I was out of earshot whenever Dad and Henry had started talking about it—which had been always.

So, yes, Wren loved to drag me to the games. She loved being there. She just didn't want to be there for *my* reason.

"This is kidnapping," she protested loudly, moving to open the passenger door. Panicked, I enabled the child lock. "The only reason you want to go is your fake boyfriend, who I don't want to see, by the way!"

Her eyes darted around, looking for another exit. Though, unless she wanted to smash the window, she had no way out.

"So, let me out of this car before I smash the windows."

I took one deep breath before fastening my seatbelt, and turning the key until the engine roared below us.

"*Athalia*—" A warning note played in Wren's voice, and I tried my best to ignore it. Instead, I threw her a winning smile and pulled out of the parking lot. "I'm going to kill you one day." I'd been waiting for the defeated sigh that followed her words. Dramatically, she put on her seatbelt and officially gave up.

I could tell her that I didn't *want* to go to any game. That it was in the contract and there was no way around *fake* supporting my *fake* boyfriend. But she wouldn't care either way, and I decided to avoid the topic of McCarthy as best as I could.

"I love you, too," I retorted carefully. "Now, just trust me when I say we'll have an incredible time, eat lots of junk . . . and the next time we're in New York, I'll sit through another *Hamilton* show with you. Deal?"

Her posture relaxed beside me, and out of the corner of my eye, I could see a smile threatening to spill across her face. She hesitated before she nodded. "Deal."

In my opinion, soccer games had always been too long. Whenever I watched my brother's high school games, or we'd flown out to watch Dad play; my short attention span was simply not made for ninety minutes of . . . anything. Add a fifteen-minute break to that and it was almost unbearable.

Sure, the rush of a win and even the lows of a loss were exhilarating. The energy shift when the right team scored. The yelling, the screaming: it was fun. Especially when a player was family. But that was just it. There were other things to do that were more fun than even the best soccer games.

I skipped most of the games I was invited to.

Due to my contractual obligation, that wasn't an option anymore. As if that wasn't bad enough, I was just as contractually obligated to cheer for the one guy I used to root against. Yes, that meant I could gloat a little whenever Henry would leave a hole in their defense, but it hardly mattered. My brother was on fire today.

Everything that had been bubbling up within Henry over the past week only seemed to make him a better player. It's like he channeled his annoyance, irritation, and anger into kicking that ball as hard, as fast, and as aggressively as he could. Somehow, it worked . . . so long as we ignored the yellow card he'd earned himself within the first twenty minutes of the match.

Now, ninety minutes in and with two minutes of overtime left, the game was pretty much settled. Our stands were roaring with chants and whistles and screams, and I was sure I heard someone uncontrollably sobbing from the other end of the bleachers.

Wren had her arm wrapped around me, pulling me into her rhythmic jumping, as if I didn't have to kidnap her to be here in the first place. A wide grin played on her face and her eyes followed the ball with a speed that was inexplicable to me.

When the sound of the final whistle finally rang across the field, Wren's hands flew in the air, and our popcorn bucket right with them. No one around us winced—even seemed to notice—as she showered the rows in front of us with popcorn. 2–0.

She hugged me, the stranger beside me hugged me. And I let myself get swept up in the excitement of an amazing win.

An honest mistake. It wouldn't happen again.

"That was in-cred-i-ble," Wren said, excitement still vibrating in her voice when we pushed out of the tightly filled rows stands, her arm interlocked with mine. "Henry was amazing today," she added apprehensively, side-eying my reaction.

I couldn't do anything but agree. She was right. Although I didn't watch him play often, today was one of his best performances by far.

"Maybe the key to him going pro is us fighting." By the pitying look on her face, my attempted joke didn't land the way I'd hoped.

And just to add salt to the wound, arriving by the sideline to congratulate my boyfriend very publicly, the first person I noticed was my brother. The proud grin on his face, how good it felt to see him happy and accomplished. I wished I could be rooting for this version of him. Maybe, in some sisterly way, I still was. But that wasn't what revenge looked or felt like.

"You were late."

My attention was forced onto the striker I was here to see. And he lacked a shirt. A self-righteous smile graced his full lips, but I'd be lying if I said it was the first thing I noticed. Or the second.

The smooth abs and the sheen of sweat covering his entire upper body definitely came first. The bright lights illuminating the field now that the sun was setting only underlined the predicament I found myself in.

Don't stare, Athalia.

My eyes shifted as soon as I could force them to, but the little glimpse of his bare chest I'd caught was enough to last a lifetime. I tried my best to remember what he'd said when he so rudely took over my entire field of vision with his perfect upper body.

I cleared my throat. "And you should've been busy playing, instead of checking whether I was or wasn't on time."

The dimple in his cheek almost distracted me from the damp, sweaty hair hanging over his face. Instead of retorting, he glanced Wren's way.

The high of the win must have worn off as soon as McCarthy had made his presence known. And it seemed his exposed chest probably didn't have the effect on her that it had on . . . me?

Wait, no. There was no effect.

"Inkwood," he greeted with a nod.

Wren didn't say anything. Instead, she faked a wide, exaggerated smile and leaned against the bleachers with her arms crossed. I decided not to push her any further. Being here was enough for me, and more than enough for her.

"So . . ." he hummed, leisurely propping himself against the handrail separating stands and field. Right behind him, Henry beamed brightly as he spoke to Coach Hepburn. "We're going out to celebrate after this," McCarthy said. "Care to join me?"

Surprisingly enough, his eyes flicked back and forth between Wren and me, inaudibly extending the invitation to both of us. We replied simultaneously.

"Yes."

"No."

"A few of the guys are bringing their girlfriends; I'd hate to rob them of the pleasure of meeting mine." Though his voice sounded genuine, and was picked up by Henry exactly that way, the grimace on his face couldn't have been more ironic.

"*We—*" I gave Wren a warning look. "Would love to."

Before she could protest—and she was well on her way to doing so—I mouthed the word *Hamilton* in her direction. Her lips shut tightly, as if they were about to disobey her if she didn't keep them glued in place. When I looked back at McCarthy, I smiled as if I hadn't just blackmailed my best friend for the second time today.

"Great," he said.

Great.

Although it was early Sunday evening, the streets were bustling with all sorts of people. Drunk college students, workers just getting off their eight-hour shifts, and homebodies picking up takeout at the Chinese place we'd just passed.

"I'm staying an hour. Tops," Wren warned as we neared the address McCarthy had given us.

"And I love you for it." I came to an abrupt halt, my gaze lifting from my phone to scan our surroundings for some sort of sign. The blue location dot hovered right by the destination pinpoint, though the name of the bar, or any sign of it, was nowhere to be found.

"Awesome." Wren sighed in an *I-told-you-so* manner, leaning on a low fence behind her. "This is a joke, right?"

I turned with an apologetic expression. "There's pizza—" She waved toward the small shop on the other side of the street. "Chinese—" Her head gestured in the direction of that, too. "But I don't see—"

Before she could finish her sentence, a broken neon sign right above her head flickered slightly. The light was so dim, it was barely noticeable. But I could make out a huge arrow pointing down and a cocktail beside it.

Thank God.

"I do!" I grabbed Wren by the wrist, then steered us toward the stairs leading into the apparent underground bar.

"You're so quick to expect the worst, Inkwood," I teased as I pushed open the door. The light scent of beer, peanuts, and sweet cocktails indicated we were in the right place. It screamed college sports.

I spotted the HBU soccer team right away. It was hard to miss thirteen loud men and their plus-ones celebrating a win. I was surprised they even had a table for a group that big in a place so small.

As we walked toward the team, confidence edged into my stride, and even Wren had picked up her slouch into a begrudging walk. Before we reached the group, an unfamiliar voice hollered and another joined in with a, "There she is!"

"The woman of the hour," another cheered as he pretended to bow in the chair in front of us. Beside him: McCarthy, who was busy smacking the guy upside the head, before turning our way with a tight smile.

"Ignore them," he pleaded. The image of carefree, fun McCarthy shocked me right away. No scowl in sight.

I waved at the entire group with a quick *Hi*, eyes flicking across them. On the opposite side of the table, Henry tried his best to ignore the playful commotion around him. Pretending to be immersed in his phone, but probably typing a bunch of nothing into his notes app just to look busy.

If I hadn't been so focused on the lack of Henry's attention, maybe I would've realized the seat beside McCarthy was the only one free *before* Wren threw herself into it. I guess she deserved it for having to go through this in the first place.

"I'll just grab an extra chair." I gestured to the neighboring, much smaller table.

McCarthy already nodded in agreement when the boy beside him perked up once more, laughing. "Nonsense!"

"*Caden*," McCarthy warned. To no effect.

Caden's box-dyed blond buzzcut contrasted his dark brows, but complemented his blue eyes, which gleamed in amusement as his hand landed on McCarthy's thigh with a dull thud. "There's a perfectly good seat right here!" he exclaimed, patting the leg beside him.

McCarthy threw a deathly glare at his friend, but it turned into an unreadable expression when his gaze drew to mine.

I blinked at him.

Was he actually considering this? Me? On his lap?

Nothing but clothes separating us, no room to mess up our relationship facade? After all, Henry was right across from us. Any argument, any looks that didn't say *We're-in-a-happy-healthy-relationship*, and he'd know how fake it all was.

How embarrassing would that be?

McCarthy shrugged, brow furrowed as he tried to read my expression. Then, as if giving up, he pushed his chair back with a scraping sound that was almost entirely drowned out by the surrounding conversations and the low music in the background. His arms opened, and a prompting look washed over him.

And one glance at my brother's face ushered me right into McCarthy's lap.

Chapter 13

McCarthy was comfortable. His lap didn't feel like one at all—or maybe I was just glad to spare my ass from sitting on chairs that looked as comfortable as blunt boulders. Even if that meant McCarthy's legs cushioning it.

I tried not to think about that at all. About the muscles rippling his thighs, or that I was sitting on them.

Despite my greatest efforts, I was still aware of the arm slung around my waist and the murmur of his and Caden's conversation, though. And I startled when McCarthy shifted underneath me.

"Sorry," he muttered, drawing my attention from my conversation with Wren and Laila, the girl beside her. She'd turned out to be someone's sister. I wish I remembered whose.

McCarthy's grip around me tightened when I turned his way. Which was a bad idea, by the way. His brown eyes were mere inches from mine, so close I could feel his breath catching against my nose.

It made ignoring him underneath me *that* much harder. His fingers curling around my hip didn't help.

I tried to adjust my new position. My arms ended up around his neck, and I honestly didn't mean for them to. Because it meant his undivided attention on me, and my undivided attention on him.

He tensed below me, and I paused my wiggling abruptly, like I'd suddenly realized what sitting—*wiggling*—in his lap really meant. "Sorry." I cringed, honestly. "Just trying to get—"

"Comfortable," he whispered, voice strained. An odd choice, I thought, to whisper in a loud, dingy sports bar. I didn't like how intimate it felt.

McCarthy swallowed hard, eyes never leaving mine. Undivided attention.

"Are you?" he asked, voice still low. "Comfortable? Because I distinctly remember you saying light PDA, and the way you're nestling into my crotch is anything but—"

"I'm not!" I hissed, but the second I lifted some of my weight off him, I couldn't deny it. Horrified wouldn't begin to describe how I felt, and I was glad for the low lighting when heat crept up my neck.

He huffed. The way I felt it on my skin only exaggerated the color in my cheeks. "All I ask is that you have some mercy on me, Pressley." Something low in my belly coiled at the rasp in his voice, and I was so focused on suppressing the feeling, I forgot to . . . say something. *Speechless*. I'd never been speechless.

"Great." McCarthy nodded, the corner of his lip twitching. "So you're comfortable?"

"Yes." Even if I weren't, I wouldn't dare move. I was scared, not of the consequences, but by how much I wanted to know what they'd be. How much I wanted to shift in his lap just for the sake of it—

"Dude!" The word broke the spell between us, and judging by my train of thought, I should've been glad for the interruption. I turned to follow the voice, wincing when it meant I was wiggling again. Getting away from McCarthy's intense look felt like sweet relief in itself, but the low chuckle right by my ear would follow me into my dreams that night.

Sitting next to Henry, Dude Guy hit Henry's chest hard enough to get his attention, then nodded in my general direction.

"Isn't it weird?" He sounded amused, but Henry's smile fell as soon as he followed his teammate's gaze. I looked anywhere but at my brother.

Right then, I was painfully aware of McCarthy. The fact I was still sitting on top of him, close enough for his breath to tickle my neck when he picked up his conversation with Caden again. It took all my willpower to focus on the voices on the other end of the table, instead of the sensations all over my body.

Dude Guy elaborated. "That McCarthy is dating your sister, I mean." *Thanks for the clarification.* "I'd kill anyone at this table who tried—" He cut himself off, and my eyes flicked in their direction to see the guy throwing a threatening glare at no one in particular. "But my sister's also sixteen, so . . ."

Henry's eyes closed for a moment to gather his composure. He looked like he was about ready to commit murder himself. Then, his eyes slid in our direction once more, a deadly glare in them. I shifted uncomfortably in my seat—*wait, no.* McCarthy's lap. Goddamn it.

McCarthy drew in a sharp breath, head turning toward me. I wasn't sure if he meant for his hold around my waist to tighten. But it did.

"Pressley," he hissed, voice low and deep. "I'm really trying here." But I didn't want to focus on that, or him, or how tense he was all of a sudden. How he held me closer to keep me in place.

My eyes and ears were already on my brother again. The latter sighed, seemingly letting out all built-up frustration, then took a long sip from his glass.

As if to emphasize his point—as if he knew I was listening and as if he knew how desperately I wanted to hear his answer—he didn't look away when he said, "Couldn't care less, Michael." Then, he smiled. Right to my face.

Which made an awful thought pop into my head.

Was the reason Henry supposedly didn't care that he knew? Knew me well enough to know I wouldn't intentionally spend more time with McCarthy than seriously needed? Knew me well enough to anticipate the surefire revenge coming his way? Knew me well enough to figure out that *this* was it?

With how much distance he'd put between us, I didn't think he'd know me at all, but . . .

My head spun. I panicked. I stood. Short-circuited. A few heads turned my way curiously, quickly turning away again when they realized nothing was going on. Only Wren and McCarthy were both looking at me with equal interest in figuring out what I was planning.

Funny you should ask. I didn't know, either.

"Getting food," I lied quickly. I nodded to the bar and hoped to God they served nachos or fries in this place.

And thank God they did.

I took my sweet time reading each and every food item on the menu.

Cheesy nachos. Onion rings. Peanuts.

I was in no rush to be sitting opposite my brother. Or on top of McCarthy, for that matter. What was the point if Henry was already fully aware of everything? Any previous confidence in my plan had vanished.

Who would've guessed it'd be me begging Wren to leave well before she had the chance to ask me? Apparently, her conversation with Laila was delightful. One glance told me as much.

With my eyes back on the menu, I sighed.

Mozzarella sticks. Wings. French fries.

"Athalia."

My head shot back up at the sound of my name. The dim light revealed a vaguely familiar smile.

"Blake?" If I sounded surprised, it's because I was.

Blake Zachary, all charm and big smiles. Remembering McCarthy's list, Blake was his best friend. Tall, dark, and handsome; he was the very definition. We'd been on the same beer pong team once, but that was as far as our acquaintance went.

"You enjoying yourself?" His dark eyes trailed back to me while he gave the bartender his order. Compared to McCarthy's honey brown, his were an almost abyss-like-black, deeper and darker, and I definitely needed to stop thinking about eyes that weren't in front of me right now.

"Uh-huh," I muttered. Nodded. "You?"

"Celebrating a win's always nice," he agreed. "Better than a loss, anyway. Thanks, man." He gave a grateful nod to the bartender when he returned with drinks.

"I feel we should get to know each other better," he continued, his voice smooth and silky. "Now that you're *dating* my best friend and all. I hardly know anything about you. Nothing, apart from the fact that you're awful at beer pong and supposed to hate Dylan as much as your brother does." There was something challenging in his eyes, yet his calm demeanor didn't crack.

"Are you trying to do a background check on me, Zachary?" I teased, and it brought a slight smile to his face.

"Not at all." Blake raised the glass to his lips, taking a sip before he shook his head. "Sorry," he said. "Trying this new approach called Intimidating Best Friend. Wren's got it perfected." His eyes flashed behind me. "How did I do?"

"Awful. Really quite awful." I laughed then, and was relieved when he offered me a single one as well.

"Good." His eyes wandered down my sweater, halfheartedly tucked into the pleated skirt, its grey almost as dark as the tights underneath. When his eyes came back up to meet mine, it was too dark to read his expression. "Let's try that again, then."

And he was actually quite pleasant to talk to once he dropped the act of concerned, intimidating best friend. We chatted for a solid ten minutes, before he turned to order another non-alcoholic drink for Mike. Whoever that was.

As if I'd just remembered, my attention darted to the laminated menu still sitting underneath my fingertips.

"That must be one hell of a snack." I startled at the familiar voice coming from behind me. My head whipped up in recognition, and I eyed the bottles of liquor behind the bar. "Whatever you ordered, better be worth the twenty minutes it took you to get it."

McCarthy knew nothing had been ordered. He just wanted to see me squirm, and I wouldn't give him the satisfaction. Not after he'd left me speechless once already tonight.

"I'll probably go with the nachos. What do you think?" I pretended to read that damned menu yet again. In the corner of my eye, I could see Blake's attention shift from the much busier bartender to his best friend.

McCarthy's arms wrapped around my waist from behind, head resting on my shoulder and his body flush with mine. To keep up our facade—obviously. Despite having sat on his lap for the past hour, this felt different enough for my breath to hitch. Hopefully so lightly it went unnoticed.

When he spoke, his voice was barely a whisper. "I think," he began, his lips hovering right by my ear. "I think you might've forgotten you're supposed to be my girlfriend. Not his." The little nod in Blake's direction had his lips graze my skin. A subtle touch. Nothing major. I ignored the goose bumps running down my neck when his hot breath tickled it. And I ignored the urge to lean into his tall frame behind me.

One of his fingers absentmindedly trailed along the dip of my waist, though the fabric dampened most of the impact it would've made.

Listen. It's been a while. This was not about who did it, and more the fact it was being done in the first place.

The light scent of beer mixed with his cologne, and I wanted to shove him off me just to feel like I could breathe in something other than his intoxicating scent. Instead, my eyes closed for a brief second so I could get it together; then I turned around.

I didn't realize how close that would leave us standing. A few inches, not more. His face, his eyes, his lips, all right there. Trying to get just a bit of distance between us, I hit the bar half an inch behind me, my head still angled up to catch his eyes.

They were rapidly taking in every part of my face. Drinking in every faint freckle along and around my nose, the green eyes I'd inherited from Dad, and the flushed cheeks I blamed on the stuffy air in here.

Remembering his words, I scrambled for a reply before the

silence became deafening. "I'm bonding with your best friend," I gasped in irony, my voice low. "You should be thrilled. At least we get along." My eyes moved to Wren, still immersed in her conversation with Laila, and he caught my drift without having to follow my gaze.

A smirk formed on his lips, and his head tilted slightly. With a raised brown and a know-it-all tone, he said, "My best friend, who's had a thing for you since you picked your brother up from practice the first time?" His lips were by my ear again to make sure no one would hear his next words. "And proceeded to chew off the entire team's ear about it? I'm just telling you what it looks like to them." He shrugged when he brought much-needed distance between us.

"All right, all right, cool it." I rolled my eyes, hands flying up in playful defeat. The urge to rest them on his chest came up. Briefly. Kind of. I mean, it was right there. Instead, I lowered them. Before he could say anything else, I made sure I had the next word. "So." I trailed off, finger tapping the menu. "Nachos?" I looked up at him through mascara-covered lashes.

McCarthy tried his best to suppress a smile. He searched for the bartender—Gene—behind me, then let his hand slip from my hip to my hand, tugging it lightly to get me in front of Gene and my nachos ordered.

By the time I turned around, Blake was long gone, sitting in his previous spot at the table behind us. Five minutes after that, I was back on McCarthy's lap, both of us unbothered by the other's presence, maybe for the first time.

Chapter 14

I stood in front of our lecture hall, in the middle of a busy corridor. Glued into place. "You've got to be fucking kidding me," slipped past my lips, and I refused to take another step. No matter how hard I tried, I couldn't shift my gaze. Couldn't do anything beyond staring.

Like he was a car crash you desperately wanted to look away from, but couldn't.

In all his glory, there he stood. Wearing sweats and a white compression shirt, every muscle in his upper body outlined. Shamelessly put on display. Leaning against the wall opposite of our lecture hall, McCarthy's arms were crossed lazily. The red rose between his fingers stuck out like a sore thumb.

Various insults crossed my mind when I closed the few feet between us.

McCarthy smiled brightly, tongue between his teeth and the dimples in his cheek prominent.

He knew exactly what he was doing.

"You are unbelievable." My voice was hushed, laced in annoyance.

"I got this for you." Extending the single red rose toward me, he decided to play dumb. "I remember you told me they were your favorite." The cruel smile on his lips made this worse. "Or was it your least favorite? Ah, damn. I can't remember now."

I tried not to follow the bobbing of his Adam's apple when he swallowed heavily, stalling for time. His teeth latched onto his bottom lip as he looked back at me, trying his best to hide the insufferable grin threatening to spill across his features.

He was failing. Miserably. "Doesn't matter now, does it?"

Groaning, I finally plucked the rose out of his hand, managing to dig my thumb into not one, but two thorns on first contact. Two seconds, and I wanted to throw the thing back in his face.

"God," I pretended to swoon instead. "What did I do to deserve such an attentive boyfriend?" My voice was laced with loving kindness. My face basically told him to go fuck himself.

"All the right things," he said with a wink. His shoulder gently bumped mine when he brushed past me toward the lecture hall, which was beginning to fill up. He lingered in front of it until I decided to follow his lead, and I managed to catch a last glimpse of the back of Henry's head as he rushed into the room.

"You know why I don't like them?" I asked rhetorically, attention on the rose as I twirled it between my fingers. He shuffled into the same row as if it was second nature—normal, even, for us to sit next to each other.

"*Oh-oh*, let me guess!" Mocking excitement played in his voice. Letting himself fall into the seat beside me, he went on. "They're basic, boring, cheap?" He quickly shook his head. "*No!* I've got it. That one time in your least favorite summer house in the south of France, your brother picked one of the roses off the bushes and blamed it on you. Your allowance was cut in half as a punishment, and how would you be able to survive off a thousand dollars a week, right?" His tone had become even more mocking, trying his best to mimic my voice.

"I sound nothing like that."

"I mean, *the audacity*," McCarthy went on, still grinning widely. "I totally understand why that would put you off them forever."

My eyes rolled so forcefully I feared they might get stuck. I didn't know why I still struggled to keep a smile off my lips.

"No," I sighed theatrically, attention shifting from his dimples when Professor Carter walked into the hall. She closed the doors behind her with a forceful thud, and I shook my head. "But he did push me into a bush when we were summering in The Hamptons. Consider me traumatized for life."

I wasn't sure how hard he'd tried to hold it back, but from the way that laugh spluttered out of him—rang through the entire hall, and earned us both a cruel glance from Carter—it hadn't been hard enough.

And the real thing was miles . . . no, lightyears ahead of the fake laugh he'd showed off oh so many times during the course of our fake relationship. I had considered it nice, but this one—the real one—made it feel halfhearted and weak by comparison. Giggly, somewhat boyish, and definitely . . . cute. Unexpected.

McCarthy's eyes were already wide when they met mine. His hand covered his mouth, eyes jumping back and forth between the professor and me, seemingly just as confused. His cheeks flushed at the unwanted attention.

"Something funny, McCarthy?" Carter's voice rang through the room, and even from up here, I could see her her eyes darting between us.

The earlier display of amusement washed off his face, and

his answer came out as quick as lightning. "No. Sorry."

"Never took Pressley for quite the comedian," she said, earning herself a few snickers from the room. After throwing a final glance our way, she focused on her laptop once again.

"You'd be surprised," McCarthy muttered under his breath. I was sure the words weren't meant for my ears. It was almost a compliment, after all.

The red rose between my fingers found its way into my bag, and I made sure it didn't get crushed when I took out my laptop to take notes.

Unfortunately, that wasn't the end of it. Not by a long shot.

By the end of the week, I had four identical, disgustingly perfect and thorny roses sitting in a vase on my windowsill. One for each day of the week. I pushed the fifth one into the vase, throwing my bag to the floor and myself onto my bed afterward.

My emotional support blanket covered the floor, along with . . . half of the contents of my closet, probably. It was time for a serious deep clean, but between classes, fake dates and the extra statistics work McCarthy had sentenced me to, there hadn't been enough time to consider one, never mind actually doing it.

My eyes trailed back to the only thing that seemed orderly in here.

McCarthy was having a field day with these roses. Every time I saw him, he had one in his hand, looking as proud as ever. As if it was the first time he'd given me one and he just couldn't wait to see my face when he held it out to me. It didn't matter that it had become predictable by Wednesday. His nose still scrunched up in the same way when he spotted me.

Anticipation still lingered in his every expression, and a wide grin still snuck onto his lips when I rolled my eyes. Every. Time.

Turning my attention from a vase filled with my least favorite flowers, I tried to concentrate on the task at hand: mustering up the motivation to get ready for the party Henry would be at tonight.

Inevitably, that meant his favorite power couple would be there, too.

Chapter 15

It was 11PM when McCarthy showed up at my door, ensuring he was ready to live it up. He did not look the part. As if on cue, a yawn rattled through his chest.

"We don't have to go," was the first thing that slipped past my lips. I thought it was . . .

"*Wow*," he gasped. "So thoughtful of you."

Yeah, it was exactly that.

"I know." I continued, my tone exaggerated. "I just care about you so much. You should know that by now."

I rushed back into the kitchen, knowing McCarthy had let himself in when I heard the door shut. "It's also the fact that I would like people to know I'm amazing company to keep, and my boyfriend falling asleep on me would say quite the opposite." It definitely had nothing to do with the fact I was nervous. "Beer?"

The question hung in the air as I opened the fridge, rising to my toes to reach the top shelf. When he didn't answer, I looked over my shoulder.

McCarthy was shrugging out of his dark Carhartt jacket and hanging it over one of the stools. When he walked over, I took that as a yes, quickly grabbed a can out of the fridge before he could, and turned back around with a victorious smile.

Being faster than him felt like a small win in itself. I might've gloated more if I wasn't immediately faced with his chest. It took him less time to get to me than I'd anticipated, and as the smirk slipped from my lips, it appeared on his. Without breaking eye contact, his hand curled around the can, finger grazing mine before I could let go.

I did not want to interpret the way his touch scorched my skin. The way color rose to my neck.

"No, thank you," he said, voice lower as he placed the beer back on the top shelf. Cool air hit my back, and a shiver ran down my spine. McCarthy was close enough for me to feel the suppressed chuckle in his chest. His head basically hovered above my own, and I thanked God for the height difference that put some distance between us.

He took in the contents of my fridge, ignoring my body pressed between him and the cold air coming from behind me. "We're not supposed to drink. *Captain's order.* But it's his birthday, so I'm sure he'll make an exception and just torture us for our decisions in the morning. Got something stronger? Sweeter?" he asked, hand curling around the corner of the fridge. "Please?"

He seemed different tonight—more unpredictable.

Fuck, something was definitely wrong with the guy, when *please* and *thank you* out of his mouth made you feel on edge.

I took the opportunity to duck under his arm, escaping to clear my thoughts of . . . him. I didn't want to notice the outline of his toned arms, the short sleeves showing them off. My eyes really just *grazed* them. Anyone's would have.

"Oh, McCarthy." I hummed playfully, overcoming the single flutter in my belly. Because I was nervous. About the party. "I'm flattered. But you can't have me. Remember that contract?"

He tilted his head, huffed in amusement. "And what a shame that is, right?"

What a shame. I ignored his words. *Nothing to read into here.* Leaning against the counter beside him, I looked anywhere but his way. To distract from everything about McCarthy that clouded my judgement. For starters, his presence. Followed by the scent of his earthy aftershave, the sound of his snicker and the way I could feel his eyes boring into the side of my face.

"This isn't really a soda household. Sorry. Didn't take you for a sweet tooth," I admitted.

"That's fine. Many things you wouldn't take me for," he retorted, then pushed off the counter to stand in front of me. "Ready?" His eyes flew down my frame when he asked, as if to approve the way I looked before he turned up on frat row with me on his arm.

"Don't know," I admitted. My honesty kind of surprised me.

It seemed he mirrored the sentiment. Gave me a tentative look before another once-over. "Seriously?" he asked.

In answer, I pushed myself off the counter and headed for the full-length mirror in my room. Since Wren was busy, I'd gotten ready by myself for the first time in a long time, and I wondered whether the lack of a second opinion had affected my outfit decisions. You could never go wrong with a black dress, but . . .

"It's a bit basic," I concluded loud enough for him to hear my words in the kitchen, a single wall between us. Or maybe it was too much? I thought back to my last frat party, trying to remember whether people wore dresses to them. Distractedly, I twisted and turned in front of the mirror beside my bed to see all angles.

It was decided. I hated it.

In defeat, I dropped my hands with a groan. McCarthy showed up in my door the next second, and our eyes locked in the mirror. He leaned against the doorframe, filling it.

"You're not seriously thinking about changing, are you?" His eyes fell down my body again. Maybe even lingered on my backside. *Who knows?* I certainly wasn't keeping track.

"I am." I puffed out a breath. "It's too much. Or too little. Maybe too—" Annoyed, I tried to fix what, in my head, had become the unfixable.

Riding the hem of the dress further up my thigh, I turned from side to side. I cupped my boobs, pushing them up, wondering if maybe I should've gone with the push-up bra instead of the no-bra option that left me looking relatively flat. In a matter of seconds, this had become a fashion emergency, and I'd forgotten all about McCarthy's presence in order to fix it.

Until a strangled groan that wasn't mine reminded me. Two large hands turned me, and I stared right at McCarthy. Startled, I looked up, green eyes big with surprise and my hands awkwardly falling from my breasts. He held onto my shoulders as he took a deep breath, trying to lessen his clear annoyance at how long I was taking.

At least that's what I thought it was, until his gaze dropped lower for a fraction of a second.

"It's perfect," McCarthy snapped, dark eyes back on mine. "Heads will turn, Pressley. No doubt about it." The sarcastic undertone I was used to made an appearance again, and somehow it calmed my suspiciously fast beating heart. "But if I still want to get the chance to show you off, we'll have to leave this apartment eventually."

I still ended up changing. Just my choice of shoes, though. And I regretted the knee-high boots for one reason only: their plateau heel. Neither of us wanted to be designated driver, but walking over to frat row had been one of his worst ideas.

Not even halfway through the twenty-minute walk, I forced him into an Uber. Necessary, if I wanted to survive the night. And five minutes later, we thanked the driver and jumped out of the car. Our destination was as obvious as the nose on my face.

Loud music, neon lights, laughing people. You could smell a frat party from a mile away, especially if it was a birthday bash for the captain of the soccer team. Which was how McCarthy knew Henry would be here, and which was why, inevitably, I was here too.

Not daring a glance in McCarthy's direction, I slipped my hand into his. Big, and warm and solid, closing around mine without a second of hesitation.

This was our first official outing as a couple. This was *different*. It had to look real to everyone, from every angle, all the time. Not just to Henry. Not just when he was around or looking.

Always.

For the next few hours, I had to make sure every fleeting glance, every look, every touch would make our relationship look real. Somehow, that didn't seem quite as challenging as it would've been a few weeks ago.

Chapter 16

We made a beeline for the drinks. We knew we needed alcohol's help if we wanted to pull this off and look casual while doing so.

Leftover pieces of pizza were scattered across the kitchen counter, some still in the box, some . . . not. It was crowded back there—*everywhere.*

The couches that had been pushed to the walls of the living room were at full capacity, and so was the makeshift dance floor they made room for. Sweaty, drunk, happy bodies that were no more than a blur moved across it, hands either in the air or on someone else.

Smaller groups were sitting and standing on the stairs. Someone had just fallen down the stairs, so technically, they were lying on them too. To say this was the most crowded party I'd been to would be an understatement.

My eyes returned to my company for the night. Apparently no longer interested in something sweet, McCarthy opted for a beer. Canned and probably warm. Taking a sip, he squinted in displeasure—to the surprise of no one. The cheap wine in my plastic cup didn't taste much better, though.

"D!" The friendly shout caught my attention.

"Kenny." He sounded just as pleased to see the vaguely familiar guy approaching us. They did that man-hug-that's-not-really-hug thing, before McCarthy forced another sip of piss beer down his throat, this time without a reaction. "You seen the birthday boy?"

Kenny shook his head, and dark blond hair flopped into his face. "Not yet—just arrived." His eyes slid to me. "But I *do* see you brought a date." I gave a polite smile, not thinking a handshake was cool enough for the occasion. "And a nice one at that." His attention was back on my fake boyfriend.

Dude, I'm right here—

McCarthy's brow furrowed. "She's right there." He lifted our intertwined hands for emphasis. For a second I'd wondered whether I'd thought out loud. "You can give *her* the compliment, not me."

Kenny's eyes widened, though he made a point out of not looking at either of us. His uneasiness made me smile, and he let out another nervous laugh.

McCarthy put him out of his misery a few seconds later by announcing we were going to look for the birthday boy. A pat on the back later, and we were gone, swallowed by the crowd.

"Don't take it personal," he said, leaning closer to make sure his voice carried over the music. "Kenny's got a real problem with talking to women. Especially pretty ones. We've tried to teach him, but he just goes into full panic mode. I'm talking sweaty palms, red cheeks, stuttering."

"Just like you, then." I shrugged, knowing I was as wrong as the sun rising in the west. He knew it, too.

"Yeah." He dragged the word out. "*Exactly* like me."

We found the reason for this party by the fireplace in the back, surrounded by people. Big Mike, the birthday boy, wasn't big at all. Big Mike was also Dude Guy, aka Michael from the bar. And so when McCarthy casually propped his arm around my shoulders, pulling me closer in the middle of our conversation, Mike's brows rose in sync with the smile on his lips.

He seemed to have a particular interest in our fake relationship, because he interrupted McCarthy in the middle of his sentence to say "What in God's name is this?" eyes jumping between me and him. McCarthy gave me a quick glance that said *I'll handle this*. Fine by me.

"I know you don't have much experience with the opposite sex, but I assumed you'd know a woman when you saw one—"

"—It's my birthday, asshole. You're supposed to be nice to me! And I wouldn't worry about *my* experience when *you're* going to experience Pressley shitting himself when he sees you're here together." He paused, and gave me an apologetic smile. "The other one," he clarified unnecessarily.

That took me by surprise.

No one had ever referred to Henry as *the other one*. That had always been me.

"Let him." McCarthy shrugged.

"Well, was only a matter of time, anyway. Wasn't it?" Mike's tone was easy. But my body basically pressed against McCarthy's made it impossible not to notice he'd tensed up.

"And besides." Mike went on. "It's definitely making him a better player, isn't it? So, we all win here."

McCarthy relaxed at the mention of soccer. God, reading him was so much easier when I was close enough to feel every single one of his muscles move.

"He's never played better," he admitted. "He runs, like, twice as fast, is twice as confident—our defense is up tenfold thanks to him. Brown won't stand a chance next week. Won't even get the ball past Pressley with me around." His eyes slid to me.

"Or her."

That was my cue to leave. Soccer talk had always been my cue to leave.

"Well, you're welcome, guys." I laughed as I gently wiggled free of McCarthy's grip. "I'll be right back, just gonna find the bathroom."

"Upstairs," Big Mike instructed, and I thanked him with a thumbs-up, already too far to want to yell over the music.

I squeezed past the pairs and trios sitting and standing (but no longer lying) on the stairs and wound up in a much quieter, but not entirely empty corridor, and then slipped into a bathroom.

I spotted McCarthy the second I returned to the hallway, and my body's reaction surprised me more than the sight of him. When he pushed himself off the wall to walk toward me, I actually smiled. *At* him.

I didn't have time to form a single thought before he was standing in front of me, and I was swept up by the whirlwind that was Dylan McCarthy Williams.

In the blink of an eye, he moved. *Us.* His hands on my waist gently nudged me left, into a room I hadn't previously known to be there. His touch only lifted to open the door before turning me in his grip and using my poor, helpless body to close it from inside. I was stuck.

Between him, and an unmovable object.

I looked up at him, wide-eyed and confused.

"Sorry." And he sounded sincere. His hand stayed curled around my waist, and I didn't make any indication of wanting him to remove it. My skin burned under his touch, despite the layer of fabric between us.

"Pressley." His words did absolutely nothing to explain. Not even when he nodded at the closed door I was still pressed against.

"Yes?"

"No." McCarthy shook his head quickly. "The other one."

There it was again.

I swear my eyes lit up, and I didn't know why or how or what. I just knew not being *the other one* felt great. And, secretly, I think that's why he had said it. Not that he'd ever admit it. "Behind you," he added.

It clicked when someone hammered against the door. McCarthy locked it in one swift motion, leaving the part of me he'd previously touched cold and empty.

"Athalia!" Henry sounded angry, and I flinched at the hiss in his voice, pressing myself against the door harder just to make sure he couldn't get in. My eyes were still fixed on McCarthy's, now merely inches from mine, and I blinked slowly, unsure what to do.

"Quick thinking," I admitted, voice thin, trying to relax into the situation. Unfortunately, my body wasn't ready to calm down—he was too close. Looking down at me, his hot breath tickling my nose.

"And the rest is up to his imagination, I guess," McCarthy said.

I'd rather not have my brother imagining any of that, but that was the point, right? Henry didn't know we were just standing still, locked in place. Or that this was the closest we'd ever been to each other.

"Can you believe this shit?" His voice came from outside, the complaint challenged by someone whose calmer response wasn't as easy to hear. Henry scoffed. "No, Reuben, I can't just—" He cut himself off with an exaggerated groan.

Couldn't care less my ass.

"Athalia!" It echoed again. When I looked up, the lack of distance between McCarthy and me forced a sharp intake of breath.

Had he always been this close or was I just losing my mind?

The smirk on his lips. The knowing snicker he let out . . . I sighed. "Shut up."

"What?" He laughed lowly, defensively. His hands shot up to display his innocence, and it brought a bit of distance between us. "That's all you, princess. It's not my fault you get nervous—"

"—I'm not." My answer came too quickly, though. Felt too forced. "I don't. You don't affect me at all, McCarthy." But I was laying it on way too thick. *Great.*

I wish I could blame it on the alcohol, but a cup of cheap wine didn't make me blush and stutter, and it certainly didn't make me look so stupid.

"I don't?" he pouted, and I jerked slightly when his finger trailed up my arm playfully, proving the opposite of everything I'd just said to him. "What's all this, then?" Goose bumps trailed his touch. God, someone take me out of my misery. *Please.*

Just that I wasn't quite sure I'd want to be anywhere else.

"You have to get used to being this close to me, Pressley." His gaze shifted to follow the trace of his finger, all the way to my collarbones. Heat climbed into my cheeks.

I swear I didn't want my head to turn. Granting him more access wasn't a conscious decision. When he spoke, a shiver ran up my spine. "You can't get nervous with every little touch."

Again, I meant to deny the accusation. "I don't—" But I cut

myself off when he gently hooked his finger under my chin, tilting it upward to connect our eyes. Our lips almost did, too. I couldn't ignore how close they were.

"Relax," he said, his voice dark and rough like I'd never heard it before. He sounded... strangled, focused, intent on catching every reaction on my face. So there was absolutely no way he hadn't seen me look at his lips. "I'm your *boyfriend*, remember? If you want this to be convincing, you have to seem used to this." His mouth moved right to my ear before he whispered, "To my hands all over you. My lips on your skin."

It sounded like a promise. One he seemed desperate to keep when his breath stuttered and his mouth moved—

"Athalia!"

Fuck.

Henry's shouting brought me back to this reality. Pretty sure I'd temporarily entered one where I wouldn't have minded McCarthy to go on with whatever he'd been about to do. I almost wanted to curse Henry more than I wanted to get back there. *Almost.*

My head fell against the wooden door in defeat.

"I know what you're doing, Athalia!"

That caught my attention. My eyes widened—no, I'm pretty sure they doubled in size. McCarthy, of course, seemed as cool, calm, and collected as always. He moved his finger beneath my chin to my lips, silently shushing me. Unsurprisingly, it did.

And he was right. Right? Henry couldn't possibly know. If he did, he wouldn't be furiously hammering against the door.

He wasn't good enough at reading people—not good enough at reading *me*. Right?

"You're fucking pathetic for this, Athalia. Seriously—" came from the other side of the door. "My expectations for you were low, but holy fuck, *McCarthy?*"

Oh.

My hand flew to the handle. Well before I had even made the conscious decision to open the door and physically fight my brother, my temper had decided for me. And I really thought I'd have to fight McCarthy too, when his hand prevented mine from unlocking the door.

He lifted it quickly at my glare, only ruffling my hair with a devious smile on his face. At my questioning look, he shrugged. "Just gotta make you look right. Ready?"

I took a deep breath, determined to sell this thing. "Whatever it takes."

McCarthy opened the door so forcefully that Henry almost fell through it.

My brother startled at the sight of us, probably half assuming I wouldn't cave, half certain his words were exactly what would make me. We'd grown up learning exactly what buttons to push to get the reaction we wanted, after all.

"I know what you're doing," Henry repeated.

"I heard you the first time." My voice sounded cold, unbothered. I thought I was doing a good job of hiding my panic-ridden thoughts.

"Good." His eyes slid to McCarthy, gaze so threatening, I wouldn't want to be in his shoes. "So you can stop whatever this is now, because I know—"

Which was when I cut him off before he could confirm my earlier fear.

"I don't know what you know, Henry." I could probably guess, but I ignored that pointed voice in my head. "I don't care what you think you know. All I know is that you don't know shit."

Did that even make sense? I was too angry to reason.

Oh please his face said. "You know exactly what I'm talking about. Why you're parading him around like a new purse. Why you only do so when I'm around. None of the people I've talked to have even seen you hold hands, never mind kiss—"

"You've been going around asking about me?" That was the first time McCarthy said anything. His brows drew together, tongue poking the inside of his cheek in irritation. Yet, he sounded almost monotone.

"If you're supposed to be messing around with my sister; hell yes I am!" Henry didn't hide the anger surging behind his green eyes as well as McCarthy.

It had always been their dynamic. Henry blew up quickly, got angry fast. But I hadn't seen McCarthy truly angry once. Just annoyed, bothered, irritated . . . the list went on.

It's probably one of the reasons they didn't get along. McCarthy seeming unbothered only served to piss Henry off more, and Henry blowing up so quickly probably amused McCarthy. It was a vicious cycle.

While one look told me McCarthy hadn't been happy about the revelation, I couldn't help feel somewhat . . . victorious. When had Henry last cared enough to ask me a question? Never mind asking *other* people.

"What?" Henry spat during the short silence. "You think I'm just going to let you—"

"We kiss," I blurted. His very accurate observation that we didn't seemed most threatening to the plan, and my brain must've latched onto that fact, scrambling to fix the hole in our story. Both their heads flew in my direction. "So much. *All* the time."

Was I laying it on too thick? Judging by McCarthy's warning nudge, he seemed to think so.

"No you don't." Henry didn't miss a beat. Probably because he didn't want to think about the possibility. "You're full of shit and you know it. Just. Give. It. Up."

But he must've known that wasn't an option. We'd both been born with the same ego, inherited from father dearest. There wasn't a way in hell I was going to admit this was fake.

"We just were." I gestured into the room behind us. We might as well have been, with how close we'd been standing. Henry followed my gaze, but his response was as immediate and confident as the last one.

"No you weren't." I hated the little curl of his lip when he knew he was right. And I hated the way my nose twitched when I knew I wasn't.

There was a single beat of silence between this moment—where I was just as convinced as Henry that I wouldn't be kissing McCarthy—and the next, when I was an inch away from doing so.

If I had to explain how and when McCarthy had managed to turn me on my heels, or when and how I had managed to wrap my arms behind his neck, I wouldn't be of much help.

We acted in perfect sync without having to say a word, exchange a glance. The whole thing was a blur, right up until my lips were nearly touching his and I felt myself hesitate when my back hit the wall behind me.

This was McCarthy. My tutor. Fake boyfriend. Guy I couldn't help being somewhat attracted to, no matter how hard I tried not to be. Kissing him wasn't a great idea, but I could feel the heat of his breath and his hands on my hips and—

Whatever it takes, I'd said. *This* was what it would take.

His breath hitched against me, his hand gently curled around my face. I saw Henry storming off out of the corner of my eye, but that didn't keep me from seeing this through.

Whatever it takes.

His lips finally on mine. My hands in his hair.

Yep, definitely not 3-in-1 shampoo.

It was probably ten seconds before I came up for air—not enough time to warrant how I felt. Flustered, turned on. A little needy. The low, muffled sound of disapproval McCarthy let out almost made me go in for round two. He cleared his throat, probably hoping it would cover the noise, but I was hyper aware of every single sound and motion coming from him. The unevenness of his breathing. The look in his eyes that made an unwelcomed rush of *more* surge through my body.

Nope. Nopenopenopenope.

"That wasn't a good idea." His voice was barely a whisper. Because we'd just crossed a boundary that was hard to put back in place, I assumed.

I felt glued in place. Maybe a part of me didn't want to move away from him at all, which was absurd. *This is McCarthy*, I reminded myself. *You don't like him—shouldn't want him anywhere near you.* And yet.

I finally looked down the corridor. Henry was gone, but I hardly cared. I'd known, and done it anyway.

Not a good idea.

For many reasons, it was probably the worst idea I'd ever had.

1. He's Dylan McCarthy Williams.
2. I just *kissed* him.
3. And it kind of felt too good to just . . . forget.

So why wasn't I regretting it? I swallowed when I looked at him again, correct in suspecting that his eyes had never left my face.

Chapter 17

We walked home in silence.

Henry probably took off while McCarthy still had his tongue down my throat, and I was too sober to pretend whatever had happened didn't . . . happen. So I'd left McCarthy standing in the hallway, ready to march home by myself.

It hadn't even been a full minute before he caught up with me on the sidewalk. He probably shouldn't have left without saying goodbye to his friends, but I wasn't mad about the company.

Yes, that surprised me, too.

McCarthy broke the comfortable silence between us five minutes and six blocks later.

"Was it that bad?" His shoulder bumped mine jokingly, and the gentle motion almost threw me off my heels. If it weren't for his hand immediately reaching for my waist to steady me, I would've probably face planted the sidewalk.

There was a sly expression on the pink lips that had been so soft and welcoming—

"Awful," I confirmed before my cheeks could heat up enough to reveal I was lying. "Absolutely terrible."

We continued down the road.

"Agreed." He nodded thoughtfully. I only glanced his way because I knew I'd spot the smile he was trying to hide, and

I kind of wanted to see it. "Very poor effort from your side."

"From my side?" I rested my hands on my hips, coming to a halt to scowl at him. Half because I wanted to sell my fake outrage, half because my feet were killing me and I didn't think I could walk a single step further in those boots.

"*Yep.*" He popped that "p" so self-assuredly, my eyes practically rolled out of my head.

"Right." In response, I rolled my "r" as condescendingly as I could. He laughed, then kept moving. And though I was in so much pain the second my feet moved off solid ground, I followed him like a lost puppy.

"I *am* right."

"Sure," I snickered. Giving up the shoe battle, I looped my arm through his—putting all my weight on him—before letting out a loud, satisfied sigh.

He didn't bat an eye at it. Or me. Just laughed softly and asked, "You good?"

My first response was another groan. "My shoes," I complained, "are killing me." To emphasize, I dragged him to a stop and wiggled my heeled boot in front of him.

"If you keep this up, I swear we'll arrive *after* my alarm goes off. Which is at five in the morning." Without a word of warning, he dragged me across the sidewalk, coaxing loud insults and complaints out of me, then pushed me to sit on a hard wooden bench. Another sigh of relief fluttered through the air.

"What are you doing?" I asked as he started fumbling with his shoes beside me, and the sound of my voice guided his eyes to mine. Almost like he couldn't help it.

Something about him looking up at me through those dark lashes, his brows raised . . . it did something to me.

Something I couldn't think about further.

"I'm giving you my shoes," he said matter-of-factly. Just like that. No laugh, no explanation. Just McCarthy taking off his shoes and *giving them to me.*

"What?" Perplexed would be an understatement. "You really don't need to—"

"Shut up." He said it without even looking at me—right as he slipped out of his sneakers.

I think I preferred that side of him. The side that told me to shut up and didn't catch me off guard with random acts of kindness. At least I knew what to do with that version of him.

Kiss it, apparently.

"You keep on wobbling in those shoes and we'll never make it home." He placed his pair in front of me.

"I can walk barefoot."

"I'm not letting you walk home barefoot." He acted like it was the most absurd suggestion. Like he wasn't about to do so himself.

"Why not? It's a good idea, actually." I leaned forward to take my own shoes off. His offer was simply too nice, and I didn't know how to deal with that.

But his hand grabbed my wrist, and I hesitated. My grasp lingered on the heel of my shoe, ready to slip it off, and I made sure to keep my eyes on the pavement. Because I knew he was right beside me, the scent of his cologne prominent in the air. Everything around me screamed *McCarthy*, and I didn't think I could take seeing him, too.

"Pressley," he said, a note in his tone that was unfamiliar. "Put on the damn shoes so we can get home."

So I did.

My heeled boots dangled from McCarthy's hand and his white socks turned darker with every step we took. Beside him, I was still wobbling, but only because his shoes felt at least twice my size.

As we walked, I wondered if he accidentally ended up on my left side or if he somehow knew about the sidewalk rule.

The comfortable silence that followed was one of my favorite things about being around McCarthy. We didn't have to keep forcing conversation; we could just shut up around each other without a lingering awkwardness.

"Why do you hate me?" I asked without any of the accusatory tone you'd expect in a loaded question like that. I actually wanted to know. Who wouldn't be a little curious?

McCarthy scoffed. I could feel his head turning in my direction, though my eyes stayed on the road in front of us. In the distance, some cars rushed past our small college town as we approached my apartment building. I'd gotten used to the size of McCarthy's shoes, and only limped half as badly as I had in the beginning, when he'd made fun of me for it.

In return I'd called him Bigfoot.

"I don't hate you. If anything, I hate your brother. And I pity you for how long you've been having to deal with him."

"Well." I shrugged, kicking a pebble into the strip of grass to my right and almost losing his shoe in the process. A glance at him confirmed he'd seen the entire thing. His smile was wide, but at least he had the decency to look down while he tried to get it under control. "Same difference. Why do you hate him?"

"Have you . . . met your brother?"

I snorted. Loudly. And I immediately regretted it as the sound traveled further through the empty streets than I'd expected. When I looked at him, he was no longer apologetic about the grin on his face.

Before I could saying anything, McCarthy came to a halt. He held out my shoes, and I only recognized the redbrick building beside us as my own when he nodded toward it. "You're welcome," he teased as I took them from him, stepping out of his sneakers.

Despite the sarcasm he probably expected, I meant it when I said, "Thank you."

He probably didn't know how to deal with that any better than I had with his shoe trade, and I told myself that maybe we were even now.

But a thanks didn't match up to walking barefoot so I wouldn't have to wear uncomfortable boots. Not by a long shot.

"Seriously," I tried again. "Thank you."

Nope. Still miles behind him. He remained silent. "All right, then." I nodded toward the door of my building as if he didn't know we had arrived. "I'll see you Monday?"

He nodded. His hands disappeared in the pockets of his jacket. "Just get in and I'll be on my way."

Ugh. Stop. Being. So. Nice.

"Thanks." At that point I felt stupid. I hurried to find my keys in the small bag I'd brought with me, to get out of his sight before another useless *thank you* came out.

Scrambling inside, I turned back only when I'd made it into the elevator. My gaze met McCarthy's, just as he was about to leave. Unsure what to do, I gave him a smile. One I meant, too.

To my surprise, he returned it without missing a beat.

Thanks, I mouthed one last time.

For good measure.

Chapter 18

Our morning coffee at Daisy's became somewhat routine. Only that this week, McCarthy had canceled. The email hadn't given away much. *Something came up. Wouldn't make it in time.* I hadn't replied, and my fingers definitely hadn't been itching to type a passive-aggressive response.

Not that I was curious to know what had come up.

Not. At. All.

We hadn't been alone since The Incident five days ago, which was what I'd decided to call it in my head. Mostly to keep from thinking about what it had actually been: a kiss. A good, damn near perfect kiss.

When I knocked on his office door the following Wednesday, the eighth rose he'd slipped into my bag in our lecture earlier peeked out of it. Apparently, he still found that to be as hilarious as ever.

I'd gotten used to the sarcastic "I'd rather not" that he'd shout through the closed door whenever I knocked, but I didn't wait for it this time. Itching to get back into that room, I pushed open the door. That was my first bad decision of the day.

Because that's when Shaw looked down at me—in the literal sense. I stuttered to a halt. Maybe if I didn't move at all, I'd blend into my surroundings enough to be spared his wrath. Despite the muted colors I wore and despite my utter stillness, he still stared condescendingly over the bridge of his crooked nose. Shaw's stoic expression didn't waver, his blue eyes boring into my own.

"Oh my God," I exhaled loudly, noticing the amused twitch of McCarthy's lip at my flustered state. "I'm so sorry, I didn't expect anyone to be here at this time—" Redundantly, my eyes jumped to the clock on the wall above the offices' connecting door, where it read 2:00 on the dot. I knew it would.

"So why'd you knock, Miss Pressley?"

"I—"

"If you think Mr. McCarthy Williams has no other obligations as my TA, other than tutoring you, there's no reason to knock, is there?" Shaw's brow rose. "Especially if you don't have the decency to wait for an answer."

"Sorry," I croaked. It was all I could say without adding a "cranky bitch" at the end of my sentence, and I was lucky I had that much restraint in the first place.

Shaw turned away from me to face McCarthy standing behind his desk. Immediately, my tutor, fake boyfriend, the guy whose lips I was still thinking about wiped the smug expression off his face. I raised my middle finger behind Shaw's back.

"In any case." The professor cleared his throat. "We're done here, aren't we?"

McCarthy nodded. "Yes, sir. I'll get right on this." He lifted a stack of papers in emphasis. Shaw gave me one last, lingering look of pure evil before disappearing into his office.

"You asshole!" The words flew out of my mouth as soon as Shaw was gone, head turning in McCarthy's direction with lightning speed.

"What was I supposed to do?" he asked, as if phones, and

calls, and texts didn't exist.

"Oh, I don't know. Give me a heads-up, maybe?" I sat in my chair, bag slipping to the floor. "Text me, call me. Fucking email me, if you have to." Annoyed, I added, "You knew just fine how to do that a few days ago."

"Oh." His head tilted as he took me in. "You're talking about Daisy's." As he leaned back in his chair, a satisfied sigh left his lips. "Have you been wracking your little brain about me? Why I wouldn't make it? What must've come up?"

"You think entirely too highly of yourself."

"Did you—" He gasped. "Did you *miss* me, Pressley?"

"Oh my God," I groaned, head falling back. "I did not miss you," I clarified. To myself and to him. "I have not been wracking my brain about you and I do not care why you canceled or what came up."

McCarthy snorted, went on without a care in the world. "Don't worry, Princess. I wouldn't dare cancel on you if it weren't of the utmost importance." His gaze leveled with mine, the nickname rolling off his tongue in a snicker. "Coach wanted to speak with us before class. About the upcoming Brown game."

"*I don't care.*"

"Right." He underlined the cockiness in his voice with a wink. "By the way," he added. "If you want me to spontaneously notify you about who might be in my office at which time and for what reason—" I went to interrupt him again, but McCarthy raised his voice playfully. "I should probably have your number."

I gave in, stretching my arm across the desk for his phone. It only took a second until I held it in my hands, unlocked.

"Don't sign me up for any weird spam with this," I said, typing in my number begrudgingly.

"Or what?" Judging by the smug expression on his face when I handed him the phone back, he was enjoying this a little too much.

"Or I'll have you killed." My sweet smile didn't match the icy, serious tone. McCarthy chuckled, actually chuckled, and it was kind of cute.

"I'd like to see you try, Pressley."

"Pearson product-moment correlation?"

I wasn't exaggerating when I said this was probably the hundredth time that phrase had come out of his mouth in one tutoring session. Thinking positively, which I'd been told to start doing often enough, I was pretty sure an hour ago I'd never heard of the term before. Progress, right?

Still, that didn't help much when I was supposed to define it. With so many new words in my vocabulary, they were all scrambled and mixed together, forming one giant statistical mess in my head. The odds of getting the definition of a Pearson product-moment correlation right were pretty slim.

I groaned. McCarthy had given up his seat on the opposite side of the desk, saying he needed to walk off his frustration. Fine by me. Until he'd decided to lean against my side of it for a more . . . intimidating approach.

His words, not mine.

Convincing him (and myself) that I had no problem being close to him, I positioned my chair right in front of him. It didn't leave much space between my angled knees and his extended legs. I could catch a glimpse of his hopeful expression as I looked at the ceiling.

How he still had any hope left after this, I didn't understand. I had given up a long time ago. Still, I tried my best. I owed it to Mom, at the very least.

Pearson product-moment correlation.

It's kind of like high school English class—memorizing terms and definitions. I'd been great at that. It had been the only subject where I hadn't been standing in my parents' shadow. Something I'd been better at.

Better than Mom and her algorithm-equation-brain, and perhaps even better than Henry with his lack of creativity, which did not benefit him when it came to building mnemonic forms. Another thing I'd been great at. Only now, instead of defining cinquain poems and sonnets, McCarthy was asking about a certain type of correlation. Which meant some kind association between . . .

"Measures strength." I began, wary. He nodded. "And direction of association between two variables?" I half-guessed, half . . . didn't?

To my surprise, McCarthy's face didn't fall in disappointment this time. He didn't roll his eyes, or opt for a teasing comment, before asking the same question again.

"That's it!" He smiled. Widely. "Well done."

In some distant corner of my mind, I noted how good his praise felt. Like I'd accomplished something by making him proud. I couldn't help the smile that took over my entire face until I noticed it was there, and until I grasped that the reason for it was *his* smile. It dropped as soon as the realization did, and McCarthy mirrored me.

"We should probably end this on the only positive note we're gonna get out of you today," he suggested. The shift in attitude made me squirm in my seat, nose flaring at his sarcasm.

"*Ha-ha.*" I didn't want to admit he was probably right. "Have a little more faith in me, McCarthy."

Perhaps the way to master (or at the very least, not fail) this class was to stop thinking about how great a statistician Mom had been, and consequently, how awful I was in comparison. Instead, focusing on what I'd been better at (e.g. memorizing) seemed like a step in the direction.

McCarthy hummed lowly. "The problem isn't *my* faith, princess."

There was that nickname again. The one that wasn't supposed to make my stomach flip and my lips twitch. It was an insult, after all. A dig at everything that screamed privilege about me. So I glared at him.

"You still think this is going to end well?" We'd been doing this for a while, and I was nowhere near a passable grade. Exams were fast approaching, too.

McCarthy just shrugged. "Of course." He said it so convincingly, he almost had me. "If you fail, it means I've failed," he reminded me. "And I don't do that."

He was right, of course. If there was one thing bigger than my ego—which was clearly failing me at the moment—it was his. And when McCarthy said he wouldn't fail, he wouldn't.

My eyes lingered on him for a little while longer. His lips were parted slightly, a pretty pink and a little puffy, probably from gnawing on them whenever he'd waited for me to answer a question. His brown eyes roamed the room as if he didn't spend hours in here every week. He made a point out of not looking at me, and I kind of enjoyed just watching him.

That snapped me out of it fast.

I wasn't successful when I cleared my throat to banish the thoughts of his pretty face and prettier lips. Instead, I was reminded that they'd been on mine just a few days ago.

Enough.

I shot up so quickly, my body needed a second to catch up. My chair scraping against the wooden floor filled the room.

And there he was again. Turning toward me, unintentionally all up in my face. Every effort to keep my mind from going *there* went out the window.

"Hey, listen—"

"Look—"

We started simultaneously. A nervous laugh cut through the silence. Mine apparently. I wondered what the fuck was going on with me and since when I nervously giggled. Because of a man, of all things.

"That . . . *thing* on Friday," he started again, a little hesitant. I wanted to laugh because he called it a thing and I called it an incident and I was just about to bring up the same topic.

His brow furrowed, trying to gauage a reaction, but I stayed quiet, just nodded.

"Big mistake, right?" His tone took on a casual note. He even tried to force a laugh I could see right through. And it hit me like lightning. Dylan McCarthy Williams, the picture of irritating nonchalance, was nervous. I never thought I'd see the day.

That alone was enough to keep my spirits lifted despite the nature of this conversation.

"A huge one," I assured him. Because apparently it made me nervously laugh and care when he canceled. I couldn't have that.

"And it can't happen again," he continued, brown eyes finally on me again. They traveled up and down my body once, making him swallow thickly. "Right?"

I shook my head. "Never."

My chest rose and fell heavily underneath my top, and there was a twitch in his stoic expression.

He didn't say a thing. Just looked at me.

And then, it happened again.

One hand curled around my waist while the other cupped my cheek so lightly, hesitantly, you wouldn't think his lips were exploring mine the way they were. A rough groan slipped past his lips as mine parted, and that sound alone was enough to make it worth it.

In one swift motion, McCarthy turned our intertwined bodies, my legs pressing into the desk he'd been leaning against. When I scrambled on top of the table, our lips barely disconnected. A second later, he was standing between my thighs, pulling me closer.

Things were happening fast.

My hands found his hair and he stifled a groan when I pulled it.

Really fast.

His touch was scorching. Every trace of his finger, every sound he groaned into my mouth made me burn. For him. With him.

And every time he pressed his lips against mine when I was about to pull away showed me how much he wanted this, and how little truth there'd been to his earlier suggestion.

It can't happen again. What a liar.

"I signed a contract," he panted, like he was trying to remind himself of the fact. Of every reason why we'd put NO SEX on the damn thing. "So have you." His hands cupped the back of my head, thumbs still on my cheeks. He swallowed hard, like it took everything in him not to kiss me again.

He should. *I* should.

But McCarthy held me in place so I couldn't move toward him, either. "Do you tend not to honor what you sign, Pressley?"

I can't find it in me to care when you're standing between my legs like this.

If he wanted to play it this way, though, we could. If he *really* intended to honor that part of our agreement, the least I could do was make it as hard as possible. "Are you sure this is a game you want to start, McCarthy?"

Somehow, he knew exactly what I meant. "Playing it with you would be an honor."

Chapter 19

> [Unknown number], Wednesday, 8:55 PM
> > Congratulations! You've won a $ 1,000 gift card of your choice. Click here to claim now.

I was well on my way to blocking the spam number, when a second text followed.

> [Unknown number], Wednesday, 8:55 PM
> > And take your boyfriend out for a nice dinner with it after his game on Sunday.

I rolled my eyes, and snapped that smile off my face.

> ME, Wednesday, 8:56 PM
> > fuck you
> > I'll be there

> ME, Wednesday, 9:22 PM
> > for contractual reasons, of course

> MCCARTHY, Wednesday, 9:22 PM
> > Of course.

Wren was only half annoyed when I'd asked her to join me. Of her own free will, she was cheering in the stands, hands thrown in the air when McCarthy scored the 1–0 against Brown.

My own holler that followed the goal was more surprising.

I watched the HBU boys tackle the striker with a group hug. I couldn't hear their cheers and yells over the boos of the crowd that was eighty percent Brown students. It made sense—being a good two-and-a-half-hour drive from campus made sure there were hardly any of your own students there.

It didn't matter, though. We were still winning. Home or not.

By halftime, we were still up. I let myself fall back into the seat, my heart beating too fast for comfort and exhaustion catching up with me as soon as the adrenalin of our performance stopped pumping through my veins.

"Look what I brought!" Wren's spirits were still unusually high. Winning must've had that effect on her.

Her shoulder-length, split-dyed hair was messy when I turned, cheeks red from the cold *and* the yelling to overpower the negative Brown energy she'd told me she *sensed*. In her hand was the Polaroid camera I got for her birthday last year. The black color matched half of her hair, as well as the HBU hoodie she was proudly wearing.

"I want to remember *beating Brown's ass* in their home stadium for the rest of my life," she said, making sure her voice was loud enough to be picked up by the crowd around us.

I rolled my eyes, but I couldn't suppress the smile on my face. I loved seeing her so carefree and happy. Even if it required someone else's misery—in this case, *Brown's*—I didn't care. I never had. I never would.

Maybe I should've gone to more of these games with her.

A tsunami-sized wave of guilt rolled through me at the thought. It came out of nowhere, and was so unexpected I almost took a sharp breath in surprise.

Wren shook the camera in her hand once more, snapping me out of my 'I'm-a-horrible-friend' realization. Impatiently she requested, "Would you?"

I nodded when I took it from her, lining up the shot before Wren poked her tongue out, smiling so wide her eyes squeezed shut.

"So you're keeping a record of rooting for McCarthy?" I teased, slipping the camera into my bag and shoving that guilty feeling down with it. I replaced it with the only coping mechanism I knew: sarcasm.

"Don't even start!" Snatching the photo from my hand, she grimaced. "He's always been on the team. I've always cheered for the team. That doesn't mean I wouldn't laugh if he fell on his face." Which must've reminded her: "Remember when he got that fistful from the random goalie one time? In the middle of the game?"

Obviously, I hadn't been there, so I shook my head.

"God," she sighed. "What I'd do to be able to relive that moment." I could *hear* the smile on her face.

"What happened?" I wondered, suddenly *oh-so-interested* and, again, wondering why I didn't go to these games more often.

Wren shrugged as she fell into the seat next to mine. "God knows. I wasn't focused on the specifics of it." It looked like she was watching the scene play out in front of her mind's eye right then, and the pleased smile on her face was concerning.

But she was happy, and even if it was my fake boyfriend's

misery she was happy about, so be it. I didn't care about him. Or why he'd gotten punched in the face.

HBU won 1–0. As per McCarthy's prediction, Henry didn't let a single shot get through their defense. Most of the time, he was acting like a goalkeeper himself, minus the hands.

A few roars of victory rattled through the stands. Though mostly, the sound of defeated sighs, curses and boos surrounded us. My attention was entirely on McCarthy.

Despite the low temperature and freezing rain, the entire team's shirts came off the second the whistle announced their victory. McCarthy jogged from his position in front of Brown's goal all the way to our own, glee filling every single one of his bouncy steps.

I only realized I was staring at him when his head turned in my direction, and our eyes met instantly. He didn't even have to search the stands. He'd spotted me as soon as the teams had gotten onto the field. Then again, I'd made it easy for him by lifting my middle finger high in the air as he scanned the stands. He'd blown me a kiss in return.

A winning smile graced his lips now. Widening when he realized I'd been watching him, putting his dimple on full display, even from a distance.

I rolled my eyes. Tried to force my mouth to act accordingly. Failed at that. Miserably. My smile stayed put as I continued clapping, gaze following him to the other side of the field.

"How are we getting home?" Wren asked. My lips finally straightened.

Neither of us felt up for a two-hour drive at nine in the

morning, so we'd carpooled with Laila (who I finally figured out was Michael's cousin, not sister) and her friends. Knowing there wouldn't be space for both of us to get back, because she'd told us said cousin would ride home with them. She'd told us again, and again, and again. All we'd said was: *future-us will figure it out*. And I despised past-us for it.

I sighed. "How *are* we getting home?"

Wren shrugged.

Great.

"You could've clapped harder."

"You could've played better."

"I didn't hear you cheer *once*, Pressley."

"You never will."

I ended up in McCarthy's car, if you couldn't tell. The run-down black Jeep wasn't what I'd expected him to be driving, though I liked its charm. Compared to my G-Wagon, it had character.

It took almost thirty minutes to convince Wren to take the only seat left in Laila's car. Once I'd succeeded, I turned in McCarthy's direction, ready to humiliate myself. Of course, he'd watched the entire thing unfold in amusement.

He'd leaned against his car, unbothered by the pouring rain, and his brows raised expectantly. I knew he wouldn't let me off the hook without the words coming out of my mouth. He wanted to hear them. From me.

So, I asked him to give me a ride. And he opened the door for me without another word.

"Admit it, that was one hell of a goal." One hand held onto

the steering wheel, the other fell around the stick.

It *had* been one hell of a goal. I could admit that . . . just not to him.

"It definitely . . . went in," I agreed, nodding thoughtfully.

He was biting his bottom lip to try and keep his smile from showing. Unsuccessfully.

If only to distract from every inappropriate thought in my head, I rummaged through the bag I brought. I inspected my keychain as if I hadn't been carrying it with me since I was nine years old. I felt the soft material of the scarf I'd decided to take off when McCarthy started blasting the heating. And I dug deeper, simply to keep myself busy.

Busy, busy, busy. *Don't look at him*, I warned myself. It'll only remind you of . . . The Incident.

But there it was. What I'd been trying to forget ever happened. *Very successfully*, might I add. The thought of his lips on mine, the scent of his cologne lingering in the air, the feel of his thumb drawing distracted circles on my cheek as his hand gripped my waist. All things I barely even thought about anymore. Couldn't you tell?

I wasn't oblivious to the burning of my cheeks, and I could imagine the color of them just as well. *Distraction*. I grabbed the next thing I caught between my fingers. And I whipped out Wren's Polaroid camera before knowing what it was.

"Smile!" My voice was eerily high as I held the camera up, pointing the lens at me and the man to my left. I didn't wait for him to comment.

So much for distraction. Looking at the fully developed picture several minutes later, I wasn't sure how well that had worked out for me.

With McCarthy's wet hair all messy, and his damp shirt stretched across his biceps, I felt distracted *by* him, not distracted *from* him. The way he looked at me instead of the lens didn't make it better. I clipped the Polaroid onto his rearview mirror and carefully watched his reaction.

"That kind of defeats the purpose of it," he commented matter-of-factly, eyes continuing to flicker to the photo.

I shrugged. "Don't be so boring," I teased. "You're going to die one day, McCarthy. If it's gonna happen this way, crashing at sixty miles an hour because of *one* polaroid in your mirror, we deserve it."

The thought of him dying was less pleasant now than it would've been six months ago. It made my insides clench and tugged at my heartstrings in a way I didn't want to interpret. Fighting the feeling, I added, "Nothing really matters."

A laugh slipped past McCarthy's lips, teasing and ironic and beautiful.

"Except money, right?" I assumed this was another one of those instances where he forgot *he'd* grown up with just as much money as *I* had.

I shrugged, not giving him the satisfaction of successfully winding me up. "Money matters less when you've always had it," I said. "You of all people should know that."

He gasped, pretended to be shocked.

"Don't get me wrong," I quickly added, rolling my eyes before I turned in his direction, catching his gaze. "It's great. Probably the best thing that's happened to me. But I didn't work for it, it's always been there. You know?"

"How very self-aware of you," he snickered, then shifted into a higher gear, gaining speed. "It's heartwarming to hear you're aware of your privilege. I didn't know you had it in you."

"Well, you didn't work for it either, did you? We're in the same boat, whether you like it or not."

"*Right.*" He dragged the word out. "Only that I worked three summers in a row to buy this car, and the sole reason my dad is paying my tuition is so I wouldn't take a scholarship spot away from someone who actually needs it."

"So that makes you a better privileged rich kid than me?" I didn't mean to sound irritated, though my ability to package my delivery into the appropriate amount of sarcasm suffered when I got annoyed.

"Arguably, yes." He looked pleased with himself, probably noticing he'd succeeded in getting under my skin. Again. "Anyway," he pressed on. "Speaking of the best thing that's ever happened to you, money can't really be on top of that list. Can it?" I was a little amazed by how swiftly he dropped the sarcasm in favor of genuine curiosity. It gave me whiplash.

"What?" I snorted. "Are you expecting to hear your name?"

"Will I?" His grin was goofy, unguarded, when he dared a glance my way.

"In your dreams, maybe."

"Yeah, most definitely in those." My eyes snapped back onto him. Like he didn't just say what he'd said, he continued. "What about family, friends? Aren't they up there?"

He'd have to have lived under a rock for the past seven years to be unaware of my family's . . . fate. About the fact I didn't really have one. Sure, Henry was still there. But barely.

"Are you . . . trying to get to know me, McCarthy?"

"And what if I am?"

It was a good question. What if he was trying to get to know me? I didn't have an answer to that one just yet. So I shrugged, and thought about his initial question.

"Family?" I clarified. "The one that died when I was fifteen or the one that I'm currently conspiring against?" It's not like he didn't know. If you followed soccer the way McCarthy did, you probably mourned Dad's death when it had happened. He might still remember where he'd been when he found out. Felix Pressley was enough of a legend in his field.

But there was a gravity to the words. Something McCarthy couldn't have begun to comprehend. I only did when they'd slipped out of my mouth ten seconds ago.

I'd been so busy plotting the perfect revenge, I'd completely lost sight of the bigger picture: my brother was the only family I had left. And we were not on good terms.

I wasn't even sure if I wanted to be on better terms, especially if he kept walking through life like an only child, remembering he wasn't only when I inevitably became an inconvenience. Henry only cared when he saw something in my life he deemed worth fixing, and then he crossed all boundaries in order to do so.

My eyes closed, and I feared if I said another word, looked at the wrong person at the wrong time, it might all come crashing down. The dark reality that I couldn't say family mattered most, when it never had to them.

If it had, maybe my parents wouldn't have decided to spend Thanksgiving in the Bahamas without us. Maybe they wouldn't have gotten on that plane, wouldn't have flown straight into the turbulence that made sure they never got to step off it again. Maybe I wouldn't be dreading the day others gave their thanks.

And then, maybe Henry wouldn't have grown up trying to

compensate for the lack of control he'd felt that day by focusing on nothing *but* control. Maybe that way, he wouldn't just think about himself, and his career, and his future, but actually stop to consider the people he'd lost on the way. The fact that he'd probably lost a little bit of himself on that way, too.

"What about Wren? She's family, isn't she?" he asked.

During our first year of college, when my mood had gotten gloomier as Thanksgiving approached, Wren put the pieces together relatively quickly. Like most people, she'd known who my parents were and what had happened to them. And even if she hadn't been familiar with the exact holiday they'd died on, one quick Google search would've told her.

So it hadn't been rocket science to figure out why I was closing off to people. Why I'd spent my days under the blanket, reading or texting or crying. Very quietly. Apparently just not quietly enough, because the next thing I knew, she'd thrown half of my closet into a bag and announced she'd be waiting for me in the car. No room for ifs, buts or whys.

We'd only know each other for three months when she took me to spend Thanksgiving with her family. For the past three years, she'd insisted on doing so for every other holiday, too.

Christmas? I was there.

Easter? You guessed it.

Fourth of July? Yup.

From the moment we'd arrived that first Thanksgiving, Delphia and James had welcomed me with open arms. Nobody asked about my bad mood or got upset when I locked myself in their guest room for twenty-four hours. Instead, if I didn't show up for dinner, there was a plate waiting outside my door. Most of the time, I did eat with them, but when I didn't, there was compassion.

They understood me. Valued me. Maybe even . . . loved me, a little bit.

In three years, they had shown me what family meant more so than people who'd been in my life forever.

"Doesn't have to be blood for it to be real." McCarthy must have been aware of where my thoughts were leading me. His voice was calm and kind, when he interrupted them. "You can choose. You always have a choice."

Understanding, I thought. That's what he was giving me.

Chapter 20

When I came home from class on Monday, the kitchen was littered with dough-covered bowls and the whole loft smelled like heaven. The last time I'd seen Wren bake like this, she had gotten a C on her final and caught Jason cheating on me the same afternoon.

She was a stress baker if I'd ever seen one. So the tray of chocolate chip cookies and the dozen red velvet cupcakes were enticing... and concerning.

Sliding a third batch of something into the oven, she paused when I walked in. Calculating each and every word, movement—even the way I breathed, because this was a delicate situation, and even asking what was going on might have been enough to set her off. But I did. Ask, that is.

She unfroze, the tray rattled as she slid it all the way in, and the oven door thudded before Wren emerged from behind the island, back to me.

"Do you like him?" She sounded eerily calm. Casually, she dusted off her white apron and placed it on the counter like she was a contender on MasterChef and had just been eliminated.

"Who?"

Wren turned on the spot to lean against the counter. Her hair laid perfectly, even after a serious case of stress baking. There was flour on the tip of her nose, and if I hadn't been so confused, I might have thought it was cute.

"You're not dumb, Athalia." In other words, *take a wild fucking guess*.

I almost snorted at the suggestion. "McCarthy?" I asked. The only thing keeping me from laughing was Wren's blank expression.

"*Dingdingding*," she muttered sarcastically. "The one and only."

"What about him?" My words were still as calculated as before, and I was on high alert as soon as his name had slipped out of my mouth.

"Let me paraphrase. Are you two fucking?"

I shook my head so quickly I felt dizzy.

"What the fuck?" Okay, so my words were no longer calculated.

Wren shrugged, her narrowed eyes were the only crack in the unruffled facade she tried to put on. "Why would you say that?" I added.

"Heather and I had lunch today," she said casually. Heather, my brother's best friend with a big mouth that usually worked in my favor.

"She's one hell of a talker, isn't she?" Wren was playing with me at this point. "Just talks, and talks, and talks. And she says just... the funniest things." Wren arched a brow. "Doesn't she?"

"Like what?"

She ignored my question and asked her own. "Are you?"

I shook my head again. "Obviously not."

"So, you just kissed him?" She began collecting those batter-stained bowls. When her back was facing me again, somehow thinking became easier.

"How do you know about that?"

The water stopped for a second, the first bowl clinking when she maneuvered it into the dishwasher. "Heather talks," she repeated, as if it was obvious.

And Henry talked to Heather. So for Heather to be talking to Wren, it meant—

"Don't be so smug about it," she muttered. I *was* looking smug, because it meant despite my doubts, the plan was working. Another bowl made its way into the dishwasher, louder than the last.

"The point of this is for them to think we're—" For some reason, it felt wrong to say the word.

"—Fucking?" she offered. "Screwing? Fooling around? There are *so* many words for what you two are supposed to be doing." The third bowl made it into the dishwasher, clinking, rattling, cutting her off. "You've only ever been prude about these things with Jas—" She seemed to change her mind, grimacing. "He who shall not be named."

I snorted at the unexpected choice of words. Then, I fully understood the meaning behind them and immediately fell quiet. Wren, of course, knew exactly what was happening in my mind, so I pushed it to the furthest corner of it. "No. I don't like McCarthy. We haven't *fucked*." My nose crinkled with the word, but Wren's observation rang through my mind and I quickly went on. "Why do you care so much?"

The last bowl was dropped into the dishwasher and when she looked up at me, there was a whirlwind of emotions on her face. I flinched at the sight.

"Oh, I don't know. Maybe it's because I care about you, Athalia. Have you ever thought of that?" She shook her head.

"I don't want to see you hurt. Again. I don't want to pick up those pieces. Again. I just don't want to see you like that."

"You're overreacting," I spat, and I didn't even feel sorry. "For any of that to happen, I'd have to care about him in the first place." *Which wasn't what was happening.*

"You do, don't you?"

"No."

Wren wasn't the type to get all up in your face when she was angry. Instead, her hand curled around the edge of the kitchen counter so hard her knuckles turned white. Her nostrils flared.

"I know you. I know when you care, I know when you don't. I know when you lie, and I know when you tell the truth. I know—"

I cut her off. "You don't know everything, Wren." *Because you didn't tell her everything,* echoed in my mind. "And it seems you hardly know me at all, if you think that's what's happening." I didn't know if I was angry with her or myself. Either way, my voice became louder, more fierce with every word.

I honestly wasn't sure why I hadn't told her about the kiss. At least the first one would've been safe territory, part of a plan that seemed to be working perfectly. A little too well, if my best friend was starting to doubt how fake this arrangement between McCarthy and me was.

But if I wasn't talking about it, I could pretend it hadn't happened. I could probably pretend it hadn't been *that* good a kiss, too.

Wren sighed. Something sad, almost pitying played across her face.

"You have awful taste in men, Athalia Payton Pressley." I blinked at her. "I'm your friend. You talk to me about every peck at every party, but you obviously chose not to disclose this one, for some—well, the obvious reason. That's all I'm saying: I thought I was your friend." She headed for her room.

If there was one thing worse than a fight, it was running away from it. I'd always been the type to face conflict head on. Jason, my ex, had been the opposite. I think that might've been the hardest part of our relationship. *Before* the cheating happened.

Someone walking away made me panic, think that if we didn't solve it now, I'd feel this shitty for the rest of my life. I always worried we might not get the opportunity to fix it later.

So the next words I spoke were unhinged, uncalculated, raw, panicked. Anything to continue this... fight? Right here, right now.

"I thought we were friends," I sneered. "But clearly, you're more interested in acting like a jealous girlfriend."

Wren stopped only for a second, before I heard her door thud closed and the lock click into place.

Chapter 21

The end of November was sneaking up on me. With everything going on, I almost didn't notice.

But it became increasingly harder to force myself out of bed every morning. Not just because the anniversary of my parents' deaths was fast approaching, but because Wren wasn't there to take my mind off it this time around.

She'd barely said a word to me since our argument. When I entered a room, she left it.

Still, *she* was the one overreacting. She'd been the one to blow a harmless kiss way out of proportion because she—what? Hated McCarthy? I couldn't find it in me to initiate a conversation when she was acting so petty.

When I woke up with a fever, though, I would've liked to ask her for a cold cloth.

Reading 103° F on the thermometer, I sighed my first happy sigh in a while. An excuse not to worry about finals, statistics, my fight with Wren . . . felt good. I threw myself back into the covers and slept on and off for a solid seven hours.

My body ached, I was freezing and sweating, all at the same time, and I could hardly muster enough energy to think about getting up, let alone actually doing it. But I should get some water, at least. Perhaps something to get the fever down? Painkillers, that wet, cold cloth I'd been thinking about?

I pointedly ignored the voice telling me Wren would probably know what to do. And that just a few days ago, she would've gotten me anything I needed. I heaved myself out of bed, wobbled when I stood, swayed when I steered for the closed door, and felt exhausted by the time I reached it. I threw my hair into a high bun, wiped my forehead as if I was about to run a marathon, and opened the door.

I would've screamed if I could've managed it.

There, on the brown leather couch in the middle of the room, sat my tutor. My fake boyfriend. My brother's nemesis. Even without my contacts or glasses, I recognized him, looking as unbothered as ever.

Is this what fever dreams feel like?

If he noticed how awful I looked, he didn't let on. "Ah," he sighed, closing the book out of *Wren's* shelf with a thud. "She's awake." His eyes raked over my silk pajama shorts and the matching top. "Long night?" Sarcasm laced his tone. I thought I might've imagined a flicker of concern cross his features.

"What are you . . . ?" I trailed off, perplexed and overwhelmed and—

"It's Wednesday," he pointed out. He looked at the watch around his wrist, though I had a feeling he knew exactly what time it was. "Three o'clock. An hour past our . . . date. You're really messing my schedule up here." And even then, it took me a few seconds to realize he meant our tutoring session.

God, I'm really out of it.

"Do I look like I could handle an hour of your blabbering right now."

I told myself it was fine. I was sick, and this was what sick people looked like. But in the back of my head, I couldn't help how vulnerable it made me feel. Growing up in the public eye, what I wore mattered, and only became more important after my parents died. People dissected my clothing, trying to read my mood or get a sense of my wellbeing. The message I'd wanted to convey was *I'm fine*.

McCarthy snickered as he stood.

The back of his hand rose to my forehead, and I almost backed away. I didn't want him anywhere near me when I was this sweaty and gross, but I didn't object. I just stood there.

"You're burning up, Pressley," he muttered, eyes narrowing with . . . more concern? Probably not. His hand fell from my forehead to cup my cheek. Gently, quickly. "Seriously burning up," he said as he lowered it.

"What can I say? I'm just that hot, I guess."

"Literally."

"And metaphorically," I added.

"And metaphorically," he repeated. He cleared his throat. "Well, you know what they say? Hot girls let their fake-boyfriends nurse them back to health."

Before I could even begin to object, I was in his arms bridal-style, and before I could object to *that*, he already lowered me onto the couch. McCarthy disappeared into my room without so much as a questioning glance for permission.

When he came back out, he held all three of my throw blankets: the one from my bed, the one hanging over the back of my chair, and the spare one that I wouldn't have found, even if I tried.

"What are you doing here?" I asked again, distracting myself from the fact McCarthy was tucking me in.

A hint of a smile formed on his lips. "You know." *I didn't know.* "Checking whether my only student is skipping my carefully crafted lessons without a good excuse."

I laughed halfheartedly. "So, you just thought you'd break into her apartment?"

"Well." He tried to suppress his grin. "She's also my girlfriend, and I'm a very clingy man." His expression turned serious, the hint of a smile disappearing. "You should really lock your doors when you're home, Pressley. Anyone could've walked in here."

Apparently done with his safety lecture, he asked where I kept the painkillers. I shrugged, deliberately keeping my eyes on the high ceiling. I knew he'd be right there if I were to turn. If I could smell anything, I'd probably be able to detect that minty scent from his gum. Meanwhile, I hadn't even brushed my teeth today. Gross.

McCarthy came back from the bathroom with Tylenol and a glass of water in one hand and a damp washcloth in the other. He almost looked like a knight in shining armor walking over to me.

He sat cross-legged on the green-and-white checkered carpet beside the couch, placing all his findings on the coffee table. "Drink some before you take anything," he ordered gently, handing me the water. Uncharacteristically, I listened. And immediately regretted it.

"Did you just do what I told you? Without arguing?" McCarthy gasped. "Unbelievable. Maybe you should be sick more often."

"I hope this is contagious," I grumbled back, a scowl on my face. McCarthy just plopped the pill into my empty hand.

"I'm immune. My sister gets sick all the time. So, whatever

germs you're spreading—been there, done that. My immune system will persevere." Then he disappeared into the kitchen.

"Sister?" I wondered, because that never made it onto the little fact sheet we'd exchanged at the beginning of this. "I didn't know you had one."

Drawers were opening and closing. "Yeah," he said. "Four of them, actually."

"*Four* sisters?" I felt dumb just repeating every word he said, but I was sick, and I'm sure he understood.

"Diana, Denise, Dakota, Delilah." I was unconcerned with what he was doing in my kitchen. As I closed my eyes, all I focused on was his voice: how softly he spoke, how calming it was.

"Diana's the eldest, just finished grad school. Then, Denise: gap year in Europe and never came back."

"I love Europe," I mumbled, turning on my side.

McCarthy went on. "After Denny, my mother was blessed with *this* fine specimen. I was seven when Dakota was born, and Mom said I wanted her gone immediately. I don't blame myself. She's a pain in the ass even now. Delilah's only twelve." He concluded, right by my side again.

When I opened my eyes, his deep dimple, white teeth, and smooth-shaven face immediately filled my entire field of vision. His lips were spread into a wide smile, one filled with love, adoration, and longing to be back home with his family. I just couldn't look away.

"They sound like they're all much better than you." My voice was barely above a whisper.

He sighed. "They are."

"You sure you'll be fine? With my germs?" He was so close,

there was no way I hadn't fully breathed all of them into his face. Poor guy.

"Is that . . . concern?" His eyes widened, playful shock in his features as he spoke. "Now, who would've thought? Athalia Payton Pressley. Concerned. For me."

I was only focused on the way he'd said my full name. And that I kind of wanted to hear him say it again.

"Never," I said. "I just know men and the flu do not mix well. Always so whiny. As your girlfriend, I don't want to have to deal with that." McCarthy turned to the coffee table, then faced me again with a plate in hand, like a reminder that he was here to take care of *me*, and I shouldn't worry about what might happen to him because of it.

"I'm not hungry." It shot out of me, eyeing the two plain slices of toast suspiciously. I didn't mean to be difficult, but the thought of eating was unbearable enough. Actually eating seemed ten times worse.

"That's too bad. Because you have to eat, Princess."

I shook my head, trying to ignore the nickname that had more of an effect on me each time he used it. My stomach fluttered, my cheeks probably lit up. I was grateful I could blame it on the fever today.

McCarthy sighed. "It'll just get your stomach working a little bit. No strong flavors, no smell," he tried. I shook my head harder.

Balancing the plate in one hand, he reached out slowly, hesitantly tucked a loose strand of brown hair behind my ear. His thumb stroked my cheek. Just once—and there went my stomach again. If the food wouldn't make me feel sick, he was well on his way to doing it himself with his nicknames and lingering touches. "You won't feel sick, I promise."

A promise meant more from him now than it had a few months ago.

Then, the idea of McCarthy nursing me back to health would've sounded like a nightmare. Now, I was quite glad he was here. Secretly.

So, I listened. And I ate, even if it was just a few bites.

He made a joke about my compliance again. I scowled at him. He grinned back. And absolutely no one was around to see us.

When I woke from my prolonged couch nap, McCarthy was gone. My bed had fresh—matching—sheets, the window was open, and a sticky note hung on the vase of McCarthy's flowers, most of them dried out by now.

I knew you liked them, it said. In the corner, he'd doodled a small rose.

Chapter 22

Unfortunately, with my fever dying down I had no excuse to keep me from catching up on the classes I'd missed. Surprisingly, I'd been doing fine for the past hour. Like the model student I *obviously* was, I sat in the living room trying to wrap my head around the material from the last accounting lecture. Really! I was concentrated, focused, and motivated.

Until the doorbell rang, that is. I jumped off the couch, ran toward it, buzzed the door open and didn't even bother to ask who it was. Or cared that I wasn't wearing pants. The massive hoodie I'd found in my closet on a quest for a comfy study outfit covered enough.

All right, maybe I wasn't quite as concentrated and motivated as I thought. But an hour of accounting was enough. For now.

I flung the door open, and my smile didn't even waver when McCarthy stepped out of the elevator. A paper bag dangled from his hand, and his brow wrinkled slightly when he saw me.

"You—?" He seemed confused, and I rolled my eyes behind the round glasses.

"Yes, McCarthy. I'm basically blind. I have four eyes. *I suddenly look so much smarter*," I sighed in defeat. "Let's get it over with." Mockingly, my arms opened wide, bracing for impact.

But instead of hurling insults, mockery and jokes my way,

he positioned his hands on my shoulders to turn me sideways, giving him just enough room to squeeze past me.

"You look adorable," he said, already on his way into the kitchen. "Much less threatening. I could get used to it." Meanwhile, I was trailing after him as if it was his apartment, not mine.

"What are you doing here?" I finally asked as he stopped by the island. "Again."

Triumphantly, he held a brown paper bag up in the air, smile on his lips like he'd just won a trophy. "Thought you might need some fuel," he said. "What with all the catching up you must be doing."

His eyes flicked through the apartment, finding my laptop on the ground from when I'd happily jumped at the first opportunity for distraction. Which was him. "And all the statistics we're about to do."

I grimaced.

"Not to worry." He laughed when he noticed how off-putting the idea was. "I didn't come empty-handed. Does Indian takeout for an hour of statistics sound like a fair trade? You did miss tutoring on Wednesday."

My eyes darted to the paper bag. "Indian?"

That's when I smelled it—the fried goodness of Bhatura bread. McCarthy didn't know it was my favorite; it hadn't even been on my factsheet. Judging by the victorious smile on his lips, it wasn't just a lucky guess, either.

"Is Wren okay?" Panicked, I couldn't even remember the last time I'd seen her. Technically, yes, she was avoiding me. But hypothetically, what did McCarthy have to do to get this information out of her?

His laugh was loud and unapologetic. For a second, it made me forget what I was so worried about. "Wren is fine."

"But you got this from her? Wren Inkwood told *you* about my go-to order? Did you blackmail her? Torture her? What—?"

"She came home when you were sleeping off that fever the other day. I happened to still be around. We talked. No coercion needed and no harm done."

Wren wouldn't step within a ten-foot radius of this guy. If she found him sitting in her living room, she'd walk right back out the door. "You're lying."

"Am not," he muttered. "Scout's honor."

"You're not a scout," I reminded him. "So that means nothing to either of us."

His head fell back when he laughed, the sound rumbling through his chest, before it sent a wave of giddiness through mine. "Fake boyfriend's honor," he amended.

He lifted his hand like he was swearing an oath, and gave a smile I'd never seen before. Sincere, honest, almost boyish. Just for me. I decided to drop it. For now. Instead, I focused on ignoring the tumult in the pit of my stomach, and the urge to find his words kind of cute.

"So how was the game?" *A good distraction.* Though the fact I'd brought up soccer by my own free will concerned me. I guessed anything was better than noticing how nice his hair looked today, how well his clothes fit him.

In response, McCarthy grunted. That smile vanished from his face, and he moved toward the couch. He sat in front of it, rather than on it. I followed suit.

"Could've been better," he said.

While the highs of soccer were high, the lows were all the

lower. Dad used to be in a bad mood for days. Losing anything had been frowned upon when I was growing up, and even the topic made me uncomfortable now.

"Oh," I offered, a little awkwardly. How did one deal with this again?

"Stop," he laughed, waving me off dismissively. "It's fine; happens to the best of us. You don't have to pretend to feel sorry for me." As an afterthought, he added: "Or that you care, at all."

His shoulder bumped mine, and I felt relieved by how casual it was. Though the smile on his lips didn't quite reach his eyes, that changed when he said, "Just be there next time?"

"Why?" I asked, then added, "Apart from the contractual obligation and all that."

McCarthy shrugged, redirecting his attention to fish our orders out of the takeaway bag. The rustling of it was loud enough for me to almost miss his muttered words about *lucky charms* and *winning*. But I didn't.

"Don't lie, you missed this," McCarthy teased. "A-B tests, statistical significances . . ."

I groaned, my head falling back against the couch. Sitting cross-legged, my bare knee almost touched his outspread leg. Eager to start eating, we hadn't moved, and I hadn't even put on pants.

Anyway, I had *not* missed this. If anything, it had kept me in bed a day longer, pretending I was still too sick to start catching up.

"So much." I flashed him a smile that said the opposite and reached for the rest of the Bhatura, ripping off a piece. "I couldn't imagine doing anything more fun with you," I added. And it wasn't supposed to sound like that: kind of sexual, inviting... flirty. *It shouldn't have sounded like that.* I scrambled for another piece of bread.

Did it only sound like that to me?

The daring glance I made as I leaned back caught a glint of amusement in his eyes. I didn't try to look away. It would've cost me a hell of a lot of willpower, and I wanted to save that for when I actually needed it.

With the way the energy in the room shifted, it probably wouldn't take long.

I was sure he'd take the tension right out of our situation with a bad joke or a mean comment that I couldn't be sure he really meant anymore. And I was grateful because it would take my mind off... The Incidents.

From his lips on mine and those strangled sounds of his— *ah, fuck.* I just did it, didn't I?

"I can think of a few things." The words sounded so casual coming out of his mouth, I hadn't fully grasped their meaning until one, two, three seconds ticked by, and he looked my way again. "Can't you?"

This time, my stomach actually flipped. With all the memories of past things, and incidents, lingering touches and random acts of kindness. There was nothing I could do about it.

Trust me, I tried.

I searched his face for even a hint of mockery, but the way his tongue poked the inside of his cheek to suppress a smile didn't seem mocking at all. His gaze wasn't ridiculing in the slightest. It felt genuine, daring, a little teasing, though not in the way I was used to.

Trying to laugh it off didn't work. I was embarrassed by the attempt, which sounded awfully close to a nervous giggle.

"You can?"

The words just slipped out. And *fuck*, if they didn't sound as sexual, inviting, and flirty as those that had gotten me into this predicament, I didn't know what would. My tone naturally adapted that slight drawl—the one I used to get free drinks at bars, or past a bouncer.

McCarthy smirked, slow and dangerous. "Absolutely."

He maneuvered me on top of him, and his hands on my waist brought all the wrong memories back. I sucked in a sharp breath. It took everything in me not to acknowledge the situation I found myself in.

Straddling his lap. Still not wearing pants.

His grip around my waist tightened. I squirmed when his thumb drew circles on my bare hip.

"You know why I'm here," he said.

And I thought *No*. I had absolutely no idea. Not when I was on top of him and he was touching me and I was *enjoying* it. That wasn't how things should be between us.

He was everywhere, all-consuming. If someone asked for my name, the only one that would make it past my lips was his.

All I did know was that I couldn't just feel his hands on my skin or his breath on my lips anymore, but him underneath me, pressed tightly against the waistband of his jeans as I searched for more friction. Just a little more. To soothe that aching need suddenly in every fiber of my being.

His head fell back with a groan, the sound rumbling through his chest and right between my legs. When his eyes fluttered open again, he looked at me like I could give him the entire world.

I expected fireworks and tingling and the heat pooling between my legs to thank me when he seemed to finally close the distance between us. Instead he leaned his forehead against mine, his breath right on my lips, and didn't kiss me.

"'Pearson product-moment correlation'?"

I thought I must've heard him wrong. My breath still stuttered in my throat; I still felt him hard underneath me. So why would he—

"Define it," he said.

"What?"

Instead of explaining, he asked, "You want to kiss me as much as I want to kiss you, right?"

I nodded. *Quickly.*

Was my eagerness embarrassing? Yes, absolutely. Would I regret it tomorrow? Among other things, probably. Did I care? No. *Not at all.*

"Good," he whispered against my lips. "You give me the right answers, and I'll kiss you." He lowered his hands from my waist, skimming my hips and then cupping my ass. He was throbbing underneath me, almost pleading when he said, "And give them to me fast. *Please.*"

My brain was scrambled and my thoughts messed up: I was sure I imagined his words. It was hard to think straight, with his all-consuming presence underneath me, his hands roaming my body and his lips inches from mine. How was I supposed to know anything that way?

His hand trailed down my bare leg and it was instinctual —the way my hips rolled against him. His next breath was sharp. "*Athalia,*" he snapped.

The sound of my name passed through me like a bolt of lightning. "Fast," he reminded me. "*Please.*"

"What was it again? What—I mean—What did you ask?"

God, I was a mess.

"Pearson product-moment correlation."

"Okay." I tried my best to focus. "Okay." I'd gotten that one right the last time. Minutes before his lips had been on mine, his hands on me and his body between my thighs, similarly to how it was now. I groaned, frustrated.

"Pearson product-moment correlation," I repeated. "It measures the direction . . . and strength of association between two variables." I'd never been more eager to get something right.

And it was. I could tell by the way McCarthy placed tender, open-mouthed kisses in the crook of my neck, sucking just enough to make my head fall back with a desperate moan. He brought his lips up to my ear.

"What about the null hypothesis?" he muttered against my skin, his voice just as desperate for me to get it right. "Can you tell me about it, Princess?"

I racked my brain for the answer, ignoring the flashes of him showing up around every corner, and the way my heartbeat picked up at that godforsaken nickname.

"It's a hypothesis." *Duh*, I thought. But McCarthy nodded, and, for emphasis, gave my ass a squeeze. A moan slipped out of me, my hips moved against him, and his breath hitched in sync with mine.

"That's right," he said, encouragingly and sweet. "And what kind?" He kissed my neck again, tongue rolling against my skin.

"It's—" I moaned when he found a particularly sensitive spot on my neck. "It's the one we're trying to disprove," I choked out. "The one that says there's no significance between two variables."

McCarthy bucked his hips upward—his way of telling me I was right again.

His pupils were blown so wide, the brown of his eyes was almost nonexistent. He let his head fall against my chest in exasperation, landing right between my breasts. "And the alternative hypothesis?"

"It's the opposite." It shot out of me. "Of the null hypothesis. So—" I sighed once more. "It says that there *is* a statistical significance."

"Good girl."

It was enough to send another wave of heat between my legs, and it seemed to have the same effect on him. I felt it. His kisses traveled further up my neck—sucking and nibbling my skin—before his face hovered in front of mine, lust and desire and a thousand other things in his eyes.

. "This was by far my worst idea," he breathed out, his voice just above a whisper. "And to think I had so many more questions to ask you." A strangled whine escaped my lips at the prospect.

I wanted him. *Needed him.* There was no other way to explain it. The way his mouth crushed mine probably meant he felt the same way.

It was like we'd each been molded for the other, like we'd been supposed to do this from the moment we met. That's how right it felt.

Panting against my lips, with the sound of his strangled moans when I rocked my hips against his hard cock, I was surprised I noticed anything around me other than him. Somehow,

I was conscious enough to hear the sound of the elevator doors opening outside, though. It could've been the neighbors across the hall, sure, but—

My body tensed enough for McCarthy to bring distance between us. "What's wrong?" Worry flooded his previously hungry eyes, his brows drawing together.

Then, a key rattled in the door. And a second later, I flew off his lap and onto the floor beside him.

We couldn't have looked more suspicious if we'd tried. Wren stood in the doorway, my cheeks burned feverishly, and McCarthy tried to casually cover the obvious bulge in his pants. There was nothing casual about the wince that slipped past his lips when he tried to move.

Wren's eyes darted between us, clearly surprised. She was probably as pleased to see him as she was pleased to see me. So, not at all.

Her expression was as unreadable as always. After a few seconds of silent observation—which was the most attention she'd given me since our argument—Wren moved into the kitchen. Even as she rushed to unpack her groceries, I could feel her eyes burning into me from behind the island.

Act normal, Athalia.

I tried. I *really* tried.

But when I looked back at McCarthy, it seemed almost useless. His tousled hair was painfully obvious, but if Wren had somehow missed that, she probably still clocked how rapidly his chest was rising and falling. I prayed I didn't look half as bad.

Not that he looked *bad*. If anything, this McCarthy was my favorite one so far: flustered, quiet, turned on.

You good? I mouthed, eyes flicking to his little problem.

Although, from what I could tell, it wasn't all that little.

McCarthy grimaced with an exaggerated smile before he mouthed back, *What do you think?* His gaze swept over my body.

"I've been struggling since the second you opened that door in nothing but a hoodie, Athalia." His voice was raspy and low, meant just for me. It was hard to ignore the way my heart fell through the pit of my stomach and between my thighs, beating steadily at the way he uttered *my fucking name*.

"I'm wearing underwear. And socks." The ones I usually wore for early summer tennis games.

McCarthy snorted, rolling his eyes. "Not making it any better."

This was dangerous.

Every fiber of my being pleaded with me to give in. The level of desperation was so unlike me that I was beginning to think Wren's entrance was divine intervention. Sleeping with him wasn't a good idea. We'd known that well before we even kissed.

There was a whole clause dedicated to it in that neatly written up contract of his.

#3 No Sex

Short and sweet. I should stick to it—*we* should.

Chapter 23

McCarthy didn't make following Rule #3 any easier once he got into the habit of showing up at my apartment unannounced. But I couldn't be too mad when I knew his presence would keep me from diving headfirst into finals' revision. "What are you doing here?" I asked.

Instead of answering, McCarthy squeezed past me. I kind of liked how familiar it felt.

"I'm offended. Truly. Can't a fake boyfriend just visit his fake girlfriend, without any ulterior motive?"

"No." I snorted.

"Not when you're supposed to be *oh so busy* on Friday nights." If he thought I'd forgotten about the mysterious plans he had every Friday—which had kept us from scheduling our weekly date on said day—he was dead wrong. "You don't usually have time for me today. Remember?" I teased.

McCarthy shrugged. "I made time."

As if it was no big deal, *making time for me*.

He followed when I headed for my bedroom. Wren and I still hadn't spoken a word since our fight, and McCarthy's presence wouldn't necessarily make things *better* between us, so I didn't want to risk it.

"So." I paused by my bedroom door to let him step past me. "You must have an ulterior motive, then. If you *made time*." I closed the door, threw myself into my chair, and spun around. He took in the desk cluttered with flashcards and notebooks. Against the opposite wall stood my bed, matching sheets courtesy of McCarthy, who'd changed them when I was sick. A pale pink throw hung over its foot. He'd been in here before though, so his gaze didn't linger.

"You got me." His hands raised in mock guilt when he looked back at me. "My ulterior motive is to be the best fake boyfriend you've ever had."

"Seeing as you're my first and only—"

"Do tell me more about being your first and only, Pressley. I'm all ears." I caught a flash of dimple and the way he refused to break eye contact was dizzying. "The kid I usually teach piano to is sick," he amended, too casually for my liking.

Like the though of him with children, patiently teaching them how to play an instrument, wouldn't make even the strongest woman weak in the knees.

"I also thought you might need some distraction. Judging by the state of your desk and the the state of you—"

"—Thanks," I said, head tilting in amused annoyance. If I looked like I hadn't showered in three days and hadn't left my apartment for anything other than lectures for just as long, it was simply because I hadn't.

"My intervention is very much needed. That's not an insult, Athalia. As always, you look perfect. Just exhausted."

"I wouldn't call un-showered and messy *perfect*, but to each their own, I guess."

"I'm not having this debate with you." And apparently that was that, because a second later he asked, "Have you eaten?"

"Haven't had time." I hadn't even had time to think about

food. "Feel like ordering something?" My tone was hopeful.

"Nope." He pushed himself off the door. "Let's cook."

Before I could let him know that we couldn't possibly cook anything with air and water—which were probably the only two things we had in our home—he was heading for the kitchen.

So much for keeping out of Wren's way.

I didn't rush to follow him. He'd catch on to the missing ingredients soon enough. It was only when a joyful, "Perfect!" came from him, that I started to worry.

He must've heard my footsteps. "I'm not going to lie, I expected a little more." His voice was muffled, head still inside the cabinet. Turning, he held a package of pasta in my direction. "But I can work with this." He tossed the cardboard my way.

I couldn't help but comment on the fact he'd already disappeared wrist-deep into our fridge. "I'm glad you're so comfortable here, McCarthy," I said to his back. When he turned around, he presented his infamous dimpled grin.

"Me too."

I tried not to swoon over it, instead sighed with an eye roll—the only way to divert my gaze without looking suspicious. Mumbling a few more words into the depth of the fridge, he turned around with a finality that made me kiss the idea of takeout goodbye. "How does vodka sauce sound?"

"Great. If it's half vodka, half sauce." I blinked up innocently, took pride in the way the corners of his lips quirked.

"Interesting."

When McCarthy finished his tour of every cabinet, the island was crowded with various spices, leftover heavy cream from Wren's baking adventures, an unopened tube of tomato paste (where did that come from?), olive oil, some kind of grated cheese, and a bottle of vodka.

"You don't have fresh garlic or onions, so we've got to improvise," he said, nodding to the spices I didn't even know we owned.

I wandered around the island, coming to a stop on his side of it, curiously eyeing his findings. "I've never even touched a tube of tomato paste, so God knows how that ended up here." My lack of cooking knowledge clearly amused him. But he seemed rather confident around a kitchen, didn't he? "You cook often?"

"As much as necessary. Some people want to be able to care for themselves, Princess." A smug tone played in his words. "Not rely on a delivery guy—*what?*" He interrupted himself with a gasp. Rubbing the back of his head. Where I'd playfully whacked him with a kitchen towel.

I wish I could've enjoyed the feeling a little more.

Instead, my eyes shifted back to the ingredients, going through them once more in the hope it would keep the oncoming wave of guilt at bay. But I felt it coming. Three, two, one—

"*Athalia.*" His voice was suddenly all serious, something soothing in the way he said my name. His thumb hooked underneath my chin to tilt it his way, touch feather-light.

It seemed he was going to say something important, something comforting, something that would keep that oncoming wave away for a while longer—perhaps until the next comment that made me intensely aware of my privilege to the point of . . . discomfort? He cleared his throat. "You *have* boiled water before, right?" He tried hard to keep his lips in a tight line.

I groaned. "Yes, McCarthy. I have boiled water before."

"And cooked pasta?" He sounded a bit more hesitant this

time.

"Yes," I confirmed again. "I have cooked pasta."

"See!" He said like he'd struck gold. "You're better than my sister, then."

"Which one?"

Filling one of the pots with water, he looked over his shoulder with an amused gleam in his eyes. "All of them."

Knowing that despite all his sisters, he seemed to be the one to help his mother cook, that he'd been the one to whip up a quick meal for them when she'd get home late, and that he knew his way around the kitchen, was . . . nice.

"How come?" I wondered.

McCarthy shrugged. "You didn't think my sisters took full advantage of having a brother? A couple of years ago, they didn't want to move out because it meant doing their own chores."

I couldn't help but laugh at the thought of Baby Dylan doing all his sisters laundry, washing their dishes, and cooking for them. McCarthy nudged my shoulder in faked offense.

"That's not funny," he proclaimed, despite the wide smile on his face when he dumped a teaspoon of salt into the water.

"No." I shook my head so quickly that my vision blurred, and my smile was so wide that my cheeks began to hurt. "No, it's not funny at all."

"That's a lot of vodka." I sat on the counter next to the stove, my legs swinging happily in anticipation of the heavenly aroma filling the air.

"You said *half*—"

"In that case," I interrupted, glad my only job was giving useless commentary and driving McCarthy up the wall with it. "It's not enough."

His shoulders slumped, lips parting to let go of a frustrated sigh. "Is this payback for all the times I've been annoying?" He placed the vodka back beside the stove, then casually positioned himself between my legs. Despite my elevated state on the counter, his head still hovered above mine. "If so, I think you're overdoing it a little."

A laugh slipped past my lips. "Oh, am I?"

"I think you are."

"*I* think I'm doing just enough—could probably bump it up a notch."

"*You*," he began, face inching closer to mine ever so slightly, "are a pain in the ass if I've ever met one, Athalia Pressley."

"Funny," I said, not backing down even as he moved to close the gap between us. "I was just thinking the same about you."

He grinned so widely I wanted to squeeze his cheeks grandma-style and admire that dimple for the rest of my life. The way he squinted, the joy in his features and the way his nose crinkled was . . . new.

I swallowed hard, the air suddenly thick. The pasta bubbled happily in the pot beside us, the sauce making the place smell like an Italian restaurant. One of those really good ones on the Lower East Side. But it wasn't the steam making my hands feel clammy, and it wasn't the warmth of the stove either.

It was him.

The way his eyes fell to my lips unapologetically, like he wanted to remember the way they'd felt on his. Like he wasn't desperately trying to forget how well they—*we* fit. It's what I was currently busy with.

But forgetting the way he'd felt below me, forgetting those little sounds he'd make if I were to just bury my hands in his hair now, trail kiss after kiss up his neck, until I found that spot just below his ear seemed impossible. Instead, I remembered that the last time I'd kissed him there, he'd moaned my name before almost taking me on my living room floor.

The possibilities were swimming between us. If I just moved—

A loud hiss interrupted what would've turned inappropriate in a matter of seconds.

The pasta water was boiling over the pot, hissing as it dripped onto the hot stove. McCarthy jumped into action, lowered the heat and took the pot off. He glanced in my direction, and . . . noticed my unwarranted amusement.

"Fuck," I muttered between laughs.

And something about it must've been funny enough for him, too. A second later, we were bent over in synchronized laughter, McCarthy struggling to hold the pot upright in his hands. The focused look on his face as he balanced only made me laugh harder. Which, in turn, made him laugh harder.

It was a vicious cycle. One I participated in gladly.

Despite McCarth almost dropping it, dinner tasted as good as it smelled. And while I was washing my hands in the bathroom, something struck me.

This was a date. Wasn't it?

We'd had plenty of them. One a week for the past month, at least. Sometimes more if there were special events my brother was attending. Though none of them were real, and I wasn't sure if this one was, either.

When you pretended to date someone for as long as we had—when you saw them every day, spent time with them every other, held hands, looked at them lovingly, laughed at their bad jokes—lines began to blur. In this case, even with my contacts in, I couldn't see that line anymore. I couldn't figure out when it had disappeared either.

Was it before or after he'd rewarded me for the right answers with a kiss?

Perhaps the line had gone shaky the second he'd started to appear in my apartment. Where no one was around to witness our acting. Where, even without an audience, he still showed up. I still let him in.

Still deep in thought, I headed back to the kitchen. I was just about to turn the corner when Wren's voice, followed by McCarthy's, brought me to an abrupt stop. What I was perceiving as an animated conversation must've been a passionate argument, right?

I expected the worst when I stepped into their field of vision, though neither of them even noticed my entrance. *Good.* Gave me more time to observe.

Facing each other from opposite corners of the kitchen island, Wren held a bowl of pasta he must've offered her. More importantly, her usual McCarthy scowl was missing. She seemed genuinely interested in what he had to say.

We talked. No coercion needed. No harm done.

Maybe he hadn't lied after all.

"I haven't seen it live yet," McCarthy admitted. Wren immediately interrupted with that giddy tone she only used when discussing one thing. The Lin Manuel Miranda mug on the counter confirmed my suspicion and had probably kicked off the conversation about her favorite musical. I groaned. Internally. After all, I still wanted to eavesdrop.

"Honestly—" She cut herself off with a spoonful of pasta. "It's on a whole other level live! You're really missing out."

"I know." His head fell back in frustration, and the movement was what made him notice me from the corner of his eye. "Athalia. Hey."

Wren stiffened. So did I.

"Anyway..." She scrambled, balancing her cup and bowl in one hand, phone in the other. "Thanks for... this." She raised the pasta in McCarthy's direction clumsily, almost losing a single rigatoni. Our eyes met, and I almost fooled myself into seeing the hint of an apologetic smile on her lips before she passed me without a word, then disappeared in her room.

"Did I just—" My eyes trailed after Wren again, then back to him. "Did you—" I shook my head. "She talked to you. Voluntarily," I added.

"I don't know how voluntary it is when I'm standing in her kitchen, but yes, I guess." He passed me my bowl from the island when I was close enough. "You tried getting along with my best friend. The least I can do is..." Trailing off, he nodded toward her closed door.

Only that it wasn't just McCarthy she had a problem with. This brief encounter was the longest we'd spent in the same room since our fight.

My head fell against his chest with a sigh. "I'm ready for that glass of wine now."

Chapter 24

"I think I've been doing well today."

"Not well enough."

"Well enough to deserve a little credit." Brow raised, I stared McCarthy down across his desk. A break was justified after a correct-answer-streak of seventeen, right?

"I *have* been giving you credit," he pointed out, almost offended that I'd suggest otherwise. "What more do you want me to do? Call you a good girl whenever your answer is correct?"

Tempting.

It looked as though he didn't mean to say that, given our history of . . . Incidents. Immediately on high alert, his attention slipped from my eyes to my lips, then back up to my eyes. Twice. If I hadn't been so focused on him, I might've missed it.

"I don't know." I shrugged. "I'm sure there would be a clause in that contract of yours that forbids it." Never mind that he'd said it before. Just last week.

"Now you're not giving yourself enough credit, Pressley." His eyes gleamed and he shifted in his seat to lean his forearms on the desk. "Most of the rules in there were your suggestions. Including, but not limited to, the one you're so eager to break."

The sound of his chair scraping across the wooden floors sent a chill down my spine, and my heartbeat picked up as he made his way to my side of the desk. Leaning against my side of the desk, his height was as intimidating as it was attractive. I stood in a matter of seconds.

Rolling my shoulders back and fanning my hair out, I cleared my throat. "You didn't have to agree to every single one of my suggestions." I could admit when a comeback was half-assed. My voice hardly carried any of the conviction it usually did.

How could I waste any time thinking of a hilarious comeback when he was right there? Looking at me like that?

His fingers brushed mine, and he interlaced them to pull me closer. "I didn't?"

I stumbled, bracing myself against his chest, before my hands found their place behind his neck. His other hand came up to my cheek, brushing whatever hair was in his way behind my ear; his touch so gentle you'd wonder if we still disliked each other at all.

"I think that's a lie," he whispered. "And I think you know it."

"Careful now, McCarthy," I sighed against him. "You might lose whatever it is that you started." Not long ago. In this exact room. "You're the one who wanted to play, remember? All you have to do is say the words."

McCarthy swallowed thickly, his gaze following my finger as it absentmindedly travelled down his chest, his stomach. His eyes flicked back up to mine.

"Five minutes." They weren't the words I'd expected, but I could work with the way his lips landed on mine, all the gentle touches and lingering looks forgotten. Because the force with which we collided was far from delicate and sweet.

He turned us quickly, effortlessly, helping me get on top of his desk and fitting perfectly between my legs when I spread them. "*Ten minutes*," he corrected himself; so eager, that half of it was mumbled into my skin.

His head dipped somewhere between my neck and shoulder, nibbling, sucking, kissing my skin as if he might never get to do it again. My head fell back with a low moan, hands pressing on the desk behind me. "Ten minutes, and we get back to what we're here to do," he panted before his lips were on mine again.

My restraint snapped. Any thoughts of *can't, shouldn't,* or that contract neither of us seemed to care about anymore left my mind to make more room for him. And how much I wanted this.

His hands fell to my waist, one of them dipping lower, to my thigh, caressing and teasing in little circles. The dark tights I wore were thinner than they should've been in November, though I'd never been happier with my seasonally-inappropriate choice. It felt as though there was no barrier separating my bare skin from his touch at all.

His low groans were enough to make me feel the heat pooling between my legs. Combined with the way his hand inched up my thigh until it disappeared underneath my skirt—I didn't know how I was still sitting upright. It was only when he reached where I needed him most, that he hesitated.

My breath was heavy and I squirmed underneath the missing friction, trying my best not to look too desperate and failing miserably. His eyes flicked to the clock in the room.

"Eight minutes," he muttered when his gaze fell on me again. One brow rose challengingly. "We can do that. Can't we?" Instead of waiting for an answer, his finger brushed across my panties, the motion so unexpected, my already parted lips released a moan that was entirely too loud. "That's all I needed to hear, Princess."

Somersaults were an understatement for what happened in my stomach. The nickname, his hand between my thighs, and the prospect of what was to follow felt electric.

His lips were on mine again a second later, his finger gently—*why was he opting for that* now, *of all times?*—sliding along my covered entrance. Down and back up once before he put a sliver of distance between us again. His fingers were still so teasingly close that I could almost feel them.

"Are you sure about this?" His tone was rough against me, face still close. I'd only have to lean an inch toward him to connect our lips again. It was tempting, but I nodded instead.

"Very sure."

His hand curled around my thigh, fingers trailing along the skin, moving up until they reached the hem of my tights. "I don't want you to regret this," he said in a hush. But I could tell at this point he was trying to reason with himself more than me. And maybe he was right. Maybe it was a bad idea, but I'd be damned if I wasn't determined to see it through now.

"That entirely depends on your performance, doesn't it?" I said as the pad of his thumb dipped between my thighs again. His low laugh was muffled by his lips crashing into mine once more, the vibrations traveling all the way to my stomach.

"I guess it does," he agreed, focusing elsewhere. With his fingers hooking underneath the waistband of my tights, he groaned. "A little help?" he managed to request.

Without thinking of the consequences, I fell back against his desk, hips bucked so he could slide them further down my legs. Books, papers, and whatever other important materials scattered across the table didn't matter. Not to him, not to me.

He slowly slid the fabric down my ass and hips, taking his sweet time with it, watching every minuscule reaction of mine as if he needed to burn the image into his mind.

I sat up as soon as I could, and he let himself be swept up in the fluid motion of our tongues intertwining. Gently, one hand between my thighs, one on my chest, he pushed me back onto his desk. I'd be stupid not to comply and when I did, he smiled sweetly.

He glanced toward the clock. "Close your eyes, Princess." Barely above a whisper, his voice was commanding all the same.

Again, I'd be stupid not to comply.

And despite everything that had happened until this point, despite the fact he'd made me feel better than anyone had managed to do with just a few inappropriate touches, this was where it really started. Where he came alive and devoured me whole.

His hands disappeared under my sweater, scrunching it up with no regard for the fact it cost a fortune. I didn't care either because his finger trailed across my nipple and his lips puckered around it.

And I hadn't expected it. Not his lips around my nipple, not the loud moan that escaped me. He chuckled against my skin, one finger coming up to his mouth when he looked at me. "Remember what I said about these walls?" he asked. "Try to keep quiet for me."

I mouthed a *sorry*, let my head fall to his desk again, and closed my eyes as the next wave of pleasure rolled through me. As his mouth devoted itself to my other nipple, I managed to swallow the sound that crept up my throat. With his body almost entirely on top of mine, I could feel his hard length against my thigh and a small moan slipped from my lips.

But it was harder to stay quiet when his finger began circling my clit over my panties, reaching underneath to tease me just enough, then letting the hem snap back against my skin. He placed his other hand over my mouth, and for a second I wondered why. When he finally hooked his fingers underneath the fabric, pushed it to the side, and made sure it stayed put, I knew.

The sound that came from my lips would've been unavoidable, though now it wasn't more than a muffled whine. His finger circled my clit, the way my own did when I was by myself. His lips still teased my nipples, and my breath was so heavy that I felt I might faint. Still, I kept as quiet as I could, and I guess he could sense my efforts.

"Good girl," he breathed against my exposed skin. His pace didn't waver as he began placing wet kisses down my stomach, along my hips. They moved further down until he spread my legs and buried his head between them. Kiss after kiss, closer to my core, until he hovered right in front of it. Stopping for a moment, his breath against my exposed skin sent shivers down my spine. I had no chance to recover before his tongue provided an entirely different kind of pleasure.

This time, it was my own hand that shot over my mouth. The only sounds in the room were my muted moans, whimpers, and cries as his tongue varied in speed and pressure. And then, when his second hand slid down my thigh, giving no warning before two fingers pumped into me, I was done for.

"God," McCarthy grunted against my clit. The sound was heavenly. "You're so wet for me."

I let my back arch off his desk, waves of pleasure continuing to drive me closer to an orgasm I hadn't expected today. My hands were playing with his hair, tugging at it whenever his fingers found that one spot.

And after a while, they found it *over*, and *over*, and *over* again. "Please don't stop," I murmured. Pleasure was written all over my face as I lifted my head to look at him for the first time. Fuck was it a sight to behold.

It didn't take more than a glance of him between my thighs, his hair a mess and his eyes connecting with mine, for my chest to tighten at the same time as my core did. "Fuck," I hissed, falling back.

"You're gonna come for me, aren't you?" The only answer that made it past my lips was a broken moan, though he got the message. His pace stayed consistent, and I was grateful he was listening to what my body was telling him. *This is good. Don't stop. Just keep going.*

And he did. He did it perfectly.

My teeth bit down on my lower lip as the wave of relief washed over me.

And all with a minute to spare.

No wonder McCarthy was such a frequent topic among girls in party bathrooms.

My eyes slid over to him on the opposite side of his desk, busy reading through the practice quiz he'd made me take, like he hadn't given me the best orgasm of my life twenty minutes ago.

When it seemed like he'd reached the bottom of the last page, my eyes shifted. No need to stroke his ego further. I tried hard to seem just as cool, calm, and collected as he did, but my heart skipped a beat whenever I so much as looked at the wrong parts of him. His lips, his eyes, his fingers—everything reminded me of what he'd done to me on the very desk we were now sitting at. I didn't think I'd ever be able to walk into this office without thinking of McCarthy between my legs.

Life was cruel. Unfair.

I expected him to still be looking at the papers in his hands; instead, I caught him staring at me.

"What?"

McCarthy shook his head in amusement. "Just waiting for you to get back to us." Placing my quiz on the desk, he took the opportunity to halfheartedly sort through the mess my sprawled body had caused earlier. "What is it you're thinking about?"

Based on the tone in his voice, there was no reason for him to ask. He knew.

"You. And how long it's taking you to go through a few answers that are most likely correct." They probably weren't, but my eyes narrowed anyway. "Makes me think you're distracted, McCarthy."

His tongue pressed the inside of his cheek, to keep himself from breaking into a full-on, dimpled grin. "I might be a little preoccupied," he admitted, his gaze sweeping across my body so quickly that I almost missed it.

I asked him the same question he'd asked me. "What is it you're thinking about?"

And he gave me the same answer I'd given him. "You."

I half-expected him to add an *"And how wrong these answers are"* or *"And how you still don't know what you're doing here."*

But he didn't.

Me. Just me.

Now I was the one smiling. If I had dimples, they'd be on full display.

McCarthy cleared his throat. "This is pretty good," he said, practice exam in his hand again. "Still a few kinks to work out, but overall, I expected much, much worse from you."

"I believe a *good girl* is in order."

"Get out of here," he begged with a laugh, head shaking in a way that only made me smile more. "*Please.*"

Chapter 25

Three days until Thanksgiving.

Students and professors were getting ready to leave campus for the long weekend. Lectures had become a burden for every party involved.

And I'd come to terms with the fact that I wouldn't be spending the holiday with Wren this time around. I knew if I asked, she'd take me. No matter the circumstances, she'd be there for me if I needed her. I think.

But Wren was petty, and I was stubborn. So she didn't offer, and I didn't ask.

Maybe a bit of space would be good for us, even. A few days where we wouldn't awkwardly run into each other in the kitchen or tiptoe through the apartment until we reached our rooms to avoid one another.

Space. Friendships didn't need space, did they?

The prospect of a lonely Thanksgiving was scary, though.

Two days until Thanksgiving.

Technically, the anniversary of my parents' death had already passed. The twenty-second was like any other day in November, filled with classes, homework, and finals prep. Seven years ago, though, Thanksgiving had fallen on the twenty-second, so I always associated the holiday with their death. The influx of articles about them at this time of year didn't help. Neither did the Twitter hashtag commemorating Dad or the condolence letter Mom's company sent every year.

This time felt worse.

Maybe—probably—because November was usually the month when Henry still felt most like my twin. We'd never speak about them, but he seemed to hover closer in November. He'd reach out, asking if I'd been okay. We were both still hurting, just coping with the pain differently, so it was easy to forget. November made us remember.

It didn't seem to do that for him this year.

But the fact he'd been more invested in my life since McCarthy was worth it. Right?

One day until Thanksgiving.

I assumed most students had left campus by now. Wren's open door, lights off as if to emphasize her absence, suggested that she had, at least. I tried not to let that bother me. She could've offered and hadn't. Then again, I could've asked—and I didn't do that either.

I hadn't touched my phone since yesterday when the latest article sprung me out of nowhere. Who'd be prepared to see a picture of their dead parents smiling? Stood on the steps of a private jet with Dad looking at Mom and Mom waving at the camera.

Just thinking about it still made my hatred for the press grow. *Hey, let's use the picture of a couple that died in a jet crash where they're standing right in front of one a few years before the accident.*

Vile. But it brought clicks and attention and money. That's what the world revolved around, right?

A sharp knock startled me out of my thoughts, and I emerged from under my blanket. I had no intention of answering whoever was currently abusing the apartment door, but I was curious. Whoever it was *really* wanted to get in here. The knocks became more forceful the longer they went unanswered.

For a moment, I wondered about the likelihood of a reporter or paparazzi attempting to get an exclusive of the billionaires' daughter grieving. I almost laughed at the thought of the public seeing me like this: red, puffy eyes, untamed hair, wearing nothing but an oversized hoodie and underwear from the day before (hey, no judgment—I'm grieving).

But what I heard then was so unexpected, I froze. His voice was so familiar by now, I recognized it even when it was muffled by the walls and doors still separating us.

I scrambled out of my sheets faster than I would on a normal day. The fact I was out of bed at all, instead of hiding under my covers and crying, was huge. Just in case, I patted my cheeks lightly, drying whatever wetness might've stained them otherwise, and opened the door.

Yup, it was McCarthy all right. Wearing casual black suit pants, an oversized, olive sweatshirt, and a black coat.

Something in his expression shifted as his gaze traveled across my features—probably noticing the redness around my nose, how puffy my eyes were.

"Are you still sick?" he asked, his voice . . . quiet, somehow hopeful. When I shook my head slowly, he didn't hesitate.

The six-foot-something giant—the very one who wasn't supposed to be here at all, threw his arms around my body as if he'd been born to do it. His scent engulfed me and his embrace felt tight, warm, protecting. Most of all it was . . . needed. The realization made me tremble.

"Thank you," I muttered into his chest. I wasn't sure if he'd heard me, but I assumed the way his hand came up to play with my hair was a response.

McCarthy took a deep breath, placing his head on top of mine. "I'm so stupid," he breathed out. "I should've been here yesterday. And the day before that. And the day before *that*. I should've—" His hands cupped my face lightly. I hated that my eyes glistened when I looked up at him. "I'm sorry."

I shook my head, the gesture halfhearted. He should be the last person to feel sorry for anything. We didn't even like each other, for God's sake. Still, here he was. Bothering to check up on me before he . . .

I cleared my throat. "So, you're heading home now?" I couldn't figure out the small smile that crept onto his lips, and my eyes narrowed. "What?"

"Come on." His hand slipped into mine so casually, I didn't really notice. He dragged me into my room, and if he was judging the state of it, I couldn't tell. "When was the last time you looked at your phone, Pressley?" That teasing undertone in his voice was back, and I never thought I'd be so glad to hear it. It brought a sense of normalcy, served as a reminder that there were days before and after the grief. It was a distraction from the fact they had died in the first place. And it's exactly what I needed.

"I turned it off when—" The brief high of distraction slipped out from under me. "Just turned it off," I corrected with a shrug, nodding toward the dark screen on my bedside table.

Although I'm sure he could tell there was something off about the statement, he let it be. "That explains why you're neither packed nor dressed. And why you're wearing your glasses." He seemed to think about his statement. "So, get changed and pack." He was silent for a beat, considering. "But leave the glasses on."

Leaving them on was a given with the number of tears spilled this time of year, anyway.

"What?" he asked when I showed no sign of understanding what the hell was going on. "You thought you'd get to fake date me without the awkward meet-the-family Thanksgiving dinner? Where's the fun in that?"

Oh.

Oh no.

"I don't—" I cut myself off. "We shouldn't—"

"I've gotten clear instructions, Pressley," he said firmly, heading for my closet and finding a duffel bag on the top shelf. "And even I hadn't, I'm not leaving you. You owe me, remember?"

Clear instructions?

He turned around, holding the bag out to me. "I'm calling in your debt. You're coming with me."

I was officially lost. Maybe that's why I took the bag from him.

Thirty minutes later—during which I'd packed (threw a random array of clothes into my bag), showered, and got dressed—we were sitting in McCarthy's black Jeep, four-hundred miles between us and Washington D.C. A good mix of road trip appropriate songs played through the car's speakers, and I was just glad to be somewhere that wasn't my deserted apartment.

I'd noticed the Polaroid picture on his dashboard the second I'd gotten in. My wide smile and his wet hair.

"Hey, uh—Thank you," I breathed out. Again.

Why is this man giving me so many damn reasons to be genuinely grateful?

"For all this." As I gestured around the car halfheartedly, my eyes didn't waver from his frame in the driver's seat.

He shrugged, unable to hide the smile that was beginning to tease the corners of his mouth. "Now, if someone would've told me a month ago that you'd be in my car on the way to meet my family, I would've figured it could only be part of some elaborate plan to dump you in the middle of nowhere and see how you'd cope."

My laugh overshadowed the low music coming from the speakers. "Well, I would've figured the only way I'd be in here is unconscious. Now look at me, fully awake and in control of all my actions." Almost all of them. *If I could just get my lips back into a straight line.*

McCarthy snickered in amusement, eyes flickering toward me again. He was quiet only for a beat, then: "Hungry?"

Usually, I was too preoccupied crying, sleeping, or moping to make eating a priority this time of the year. And McCarthy had ambushed me before I'd even made it out of bed. The reminder made my stomach rumble, and it was answer enough. He pulled off the interstate and into the first fast food place he spotted. "You still owe me, remember?" The car slowed.

I did remember. His first text pretending to be a spam number, then inviting himself to be taken out by me.

"Don't know what you're talking about," I pretended, though already searched for my wallet in the bag by my feet.

His hand wrapped around mine, slowly guiding it out of the bag, then snatching my wallet and throwing it onto the backseat.

"Seems you've forgotten your wallet at home," he said like he hadn't just taken it from me. "Shame. What do you want? My treat."

"Surprise me."

When he came back through the swinging doors, he held two bags in one hand and drinks in the other, gesturing wildly for me to open the driver's door. "Never let me make food choices for you again." He complained, dropping the larger of the two bags in my lap. "I feel like I bought the entire menu."

"I can see that." I was already happily rummaging through the results.

"I got you a hot chocolate." He nodded toward one of the cups in the holder. "And thought we could share the strawberry smoothie. Do you like strawberries?" How brow furrowed in light concern (in case I *didn't* like strawberries) and interest (hoping that I *did* like them).

"Yes." My cheeks hurt from smiling and my nose crinkled. "I do like strawberries."

"Good." He nodded, eyes shifting. "Very good."

Falling back into the seat with a handful of fries in my mouth, I sighed contently. Still, I was getting sick and tired of thanking him over, and over, and over again for doing unexpectedly nice things for me *over, and over, and over again.*

"Thank you" slipped past my lips anyway.

Putting the car in reverse, he placed his arm on the back of his seat to glance over his shoulder. His gaze passed over me to the rear window before doubling back as if he couldn't help himself. Then, he winked, and I knew I was in trouble when I didn't even cringe at the gesture. My stomach gave a nervous flutter.

I was moving into fairly dangerous territory, and nothing could stop me.

"And stop being so nice to me," I added as an afterthought. His self-satisfied grin just grew when I took another sip of the smoothie.

"Why?" he asked.

"Because my gratitude is getting to your head, McCarthy."

"And I know where my being nice is getting you." His gaze raked up and down my seated frame. The three seconds he took were the longest he'd allow his eyes to be off the road.

"Where?" I laughed. "Your childhood bedroom?"

"Yeah," he said, amusement still lingering in his tone. "Exactly."

Chapter 26

Entertaining ourselves on the long drive turned into *5 Questions, 10 Seconds*, an impossible game Wren had come up with in our first week together.

I'd been drunk from my first college party, energized off the high of free booze, socializing, and meeting Jason. Not at all tired, I'd found my new roommate in bed with a book in hand, unbothered when I bulldozed through the door, louder than I should have at two in the morning. On a whim, I'd challenged her to 21 Questions, to get to know her better.

Nobody answers 21 questions honestly, she'd explained. Though with five questions in ten seconds, you hardly have time to answer at all, never mind make up a lie. The stress alone made you blurt out the inevitable truth.

It was my turn to ask. "Favorite fruit?"

"Apples."

"Least favorite girlfriend?"

"Ella in Kindergarten."

"Favorite girlfriend?"

"You."

"Why do you hate me?"

"I don't."

"What did you and Wren talk about?"

Another great thing about the game? After getting in the

rhythm, answers just started tumbling out of them.

McCarthy's lips parted, ready to spill. He caught on in the last moment. Grinned. His eyes flicked in my direction, only for a second, head shaking in disbelief.

"That's a low blow, Pressley. Even for you." He wagged his finger at me in amusement, then brought it up to his mouth and pretended to lock it and throw away the key.

I grinned. "Worth a try." I blew a strand of my curtain bangs out of my face, leaning back into the passenger seat. "What did poor Ella do to you?"

I reset the timer on my phone. "Even at our young age, she was a very demanding woman."

"I'm a demanding woman."

McCarthy snickered. "I know." His eyes slid toward the countdown. "Ready?"

I nodded, pressed start, and he fired his first question at me. "Favorite movie?"

"*Moana*."

"First celebrity crush?"

"Young Leo."

"Favorite snack?"

"Sour Patch Kids."

"Why do you need to get back at your brother?"

"Since our parents died—" By the time I'd cut myself off, it was already too late.

It was like we'd been ignoring the elephant in the room, and it finally stepped on us.

I looked at McCarthy like a deer in headlights. I didn't even notice the phone timer buzzing in my lap, until he blindly reached for it and turned it off.

I scoffed, a humorless ghost of a laugh. This drive had been a good distraction from the mess my real life was in. The life that didn't include McCarthy, who took me on road trips, made sure I ate, and was about to introduce me to his whole family over Thanksgiving.

The reminder of dead parents, fucked up sibling dynamics, and crumbling friendships made my mood plummet and my stomach twist with an uncertain dread.

"Is that something you want to talk about?" he asked. "Your parents?"

Until now, I didn't think it was. Not with him, anyway. My eyes shifted, scanning the signs we passed, the trees alongside the road, as I mulled over his question—*his offer.*

I wasn't sure whether I was ready to show him the part of me that wasn't all snappy comebacks and sarcastic jokes. The one that was still broken, would probably always be—a little bit.

"I know it's always helped me," he added thoughtfully, his voice even and calm. "Talking about things, I mean."

And he was right. At least according to my therapist, he was. Stephanie had always insisted that burying my feelings would only make things worse.

Clearly, Henry hadn't listened to her.

"We've still got a long drive ahead of us," McCarthy said, glancing at me. "And I'd love to listen. If that's something you want."

I let out a breath. McCarthy was a good listener; I knew that much. And he *had* offered.

So once the floodgates opened, I told the poor boy everything. More than he probably wanted to know.

"So, your parents both went to HBU?" he asked during

a short pause in my rambling. I nodded. My eyes set on the passing scenery as we steadily approached civilization and left the long, winding highway behind.

"It's where they met," I elaborated. "My dad wrote his thesis at HBU during his semester abroad. They basically begged him to. For the soccer thing. They knew he'd go pro the second he graduated—his parents were adamant that he needed a degree, and HBU wanted his name attached to them. Back then, their soccer team wasn't anything special."

"Because they didn't have me," McCarthy joked, and a reluctant smile accompanied my eye roll.

"Surely," I drawled, exaggerating the word before shifting my gaze outside once more. "I guess they didn't have you, but once Dad agreed to a full ride semester, they had Felix Pressley. He became captain, led them to victory in his senior year, and the rest is history, I guess." The rest being: Felix Pressley becoming a soccer legend by the time he was twenty-three; playing for the British national team until Henry and I were five; then "retiring" to play in the States, where he'd been valued at 70 million dollars.

"And your mom?" Mentioning my mother so casually, I forgot I was grieving her for a second.

That was new. Unfamiliar. Kind of . . . nice. Of him.

I almost thanked him again, just for treating the subject like any other.

"Naomi Yung had a flourishing business by the time she entered her junior year of college," I said, mimicking the thousands of headlines and articles in a booming voice. "First one to focus on deep data instead of just big data, offering applied statistics to—" I cut myself off. McCarthy hadn't asked for a deep dive into my mother's life's work. "She graduated with honors. Her bachelors and her masters. By the time she'd left university, DeepStat had acquired their largest competitor and she was a multimillionaire. Self-made."

"Hold on," McCarthy said. "You're telling me your mom was a . . . statistician?"

"Originally," I said. I knew what he was getting at, so I pointed it out before he could. "Yet here I am," I scoffed, realizing what had been sitting on my chest for so long. "Failing Statistics, of all things. Hating soccer." *And disappointing the only two people I didn't want to disappoint.* "They'd be disappointed if they were here to see, wouldn't they?" I realized how heavily the question hung in the air.

The sound of squeaking brakes interrupted what should've been an awkward silence. My head snapped in his direction. The seatbelt dug into my chest, holding me in place. My eyes, wide, found his.

Did we hit an animal? A *person*? I searched for the reason for his abrupt stop, panic taking over my body, pulse thumping through my skin.

But nothing. Just a dark intersection, entirely empty. The traffic light illuminated the inside of his car in a cool green, turning to harsh red as we sat in silence. Another realization hit: this was the first time I'd let it all out. And it was McCarthy I was letting it out *to*.

If there was one person who shouldn't see me in any of those states (and most definitely not in all of them at the same time), it was McCarthy. Wasn't it?

If that were true, I wondered why his jaw shifted, and his brow creased as he scanned me in the red light. *I'm sorry*, I meant to say. *I didn't mean to unload that on you.* But the words stuck in my throat, and it only got worse when his lips were suddenly on mine, body leaning across the console meant to be separating us.

There was nothing primal or hungry in the way his lips moved against mine. No eagerness to go further, no impatience. Just color rising to my cheeks and stomach flutters as I realized that this was *it*.

That I'd never been kissed so tenderly. So sweetly. So reassuringly.

A kiss had never said so much—more than all the words, in every combination, could ever do.

And when he pulled away, his forehead against mine and his breath a little heavier against the tip of my nose, I wondered if I'd ever recover from this. From him. From the little devil on my shoulder telling me: Dylan McCarthy Williams was *it*.

He opened his eyes, hand still lingering on my cheek as his thumb rubbed feather-light circles. "If I ever hear you say something like that again—" he began, his voice so quiet, I had to concentrate on every word. "You're a once-in-a-lifetime kind of woman, Athalia. You get done what you want to get done, *when* you want to get it done. You don't have to live on your parents' schedule, and you don't live in anyone's shadow. You're your own person. You know that, don't you?"

All I knew was that I didn't know what to say. That he'd rendered me speechless and fucking teary-eyed.

"I'm sorry," I finally got out, sounding less strangled than I felt. "I didn't mean to unload all this on you. I should deal with my own shit before—"

"Shut up." He created another inch of space between us,

his other hand coming up to hold my face. "I'll deal with your shit as much as you'll let me. I want to. Just like I want to hear everything you have to say, everything you want to tell me. Don't ever apologize for that."

Oh God.

I leaned in to kiss him this time.

A little sloppier, more distracted by the taste of his lips and the way he explored me, rather than the funny feeling in the pit of my stomach. His hands moved into my hair. I couldn't help the satisfied sigh that slipped past my lips in the tenth of a second they weren't on his.

The sound drew a low groan out of him that only made me want him more. Closer. *So much closer.* The thought drove me further across the console, heat pooling between my legs as I pushed him back into the driver's seat. I struggled to unbuckle my seatbelt when everything within me just wanted to focus on him.

Teasing my lower lip, biting it gently before my low moan encouraged him to do it harder. Breathing against my parted lips in a way that sent a shiver of need down my spine. Occupying every corner of my conscious mind.

His honey-brown eyes, the dark mess atop his head, that was parted in the middle today, and the way his pink lips would curl into a smirk before eventually breaking into a grin that very rarely revealed his dimple.

A loud honk stopped me in my pursuit of his lap.

My eyes opened as we shot apart. The interior of his car was no longer glowing red, but instead illuminated by the deep green of the traffic light and the insistent headlights of the car behind us.

McCarthy cleared his throat, then struggled to clear his mind enough to shift into first gear. He quickly found his footing again, holding up an apologetic hand to the driver behind us as he got the Jeep rolling with a small squeak of wheels against asphalt.

"You're going to be the death of me," he muttered, glancing my way as he rolled through the residential streets. He seemed familiar with his surroundings now, more comfortable taking his eyes off the road for a second longer to look at me. The teasing tone in his voice told me he was rather pleased about it.

In a lapse of all judgement, I confessed, "I really want you." I sounded almost desperate, my voice breaking as I spoke. And I was shocked to discover I wasn't embarrassed by it at all.

"What?" If only for a second, his flustered state was obvious.

In my hazy mind, he seemed to be around every corner. I was distracted—really, truly distracted for the first time around Thanksgiving. It felt better to think about McCarthy than about my dead parents. So, I leaned into it.

"I really, really want you," I repeated, sounding more casual now. I enjoyed the way he gulped, eyes sliding back to the road, then flicking across my frame again a second later.

"Fuck," he exhaled, shaking his head before it fell back against the headrest. "You can't say shit like that when I'm about to pull into my family's driveway, Athalia." As if on cue, he did.

It's hard to believe we'd been on the road for over six hours when he signaled left, then rolled up to a gate with a family crest at its center. It opened automatically before we'd even come to a halt, allowing McCarthy to drive up the gentle incline.

He stopped in front of four garage doors embedded in a small hill on which the mansion stood, accessible via a prom-worthy staircase. Something I envied and the reason I'd always preferred our summer house in the Hamptons to the New York penthouse we'd grown up in.

The other car standing in front of the closed garage door was a white BMW, specks of dirt sprinkled across its sides and bumper. I wondered which one of his sisters it belonged to.

Were they all here? What about his father? McCarthy hadn't really mentioned him. He hadn't mentioned much about this weekend at all, actually. And I should've probably used the last five minutes of this drive to find out what I was getting into, instead of telling McCarthy how much I wanted to have sex with him. *Jesus.*

The second he turned off the engine and unbuckled his seatbelt, a young girl shot down the stoned staircase and toward the Jeep. *Delilah.*

Any plan to brief me on his family—black-listed topics, names I shouldn't mention, things I should expect—flew out the window. As soon as the man beside me noticed his little sister, his door swung open, and the girl was in his arms within five seconds.

I slid into my coat as soon as the late November air hit me, then closed the door hesitantly. The sound awarded me their attention, and their smiles were so hauntingly similar that there was no doubt about their shared genes.

"Hey," I said, waving at the girl a little awkwardly, nerves suddenly flooding my system. I'd never banked so much on the opinion of a twelve-year-old. God, I hope she liked me, though. I hope they all would.

"Hello." She smiled brightly, approaching me with big, confident strides. Her skin was a little darker than her brother's, her hair curlier and bouncing with each step she took toward me. Without hesitation, she extended her hand for me to shake and offered a smile so bright that every ounce of doubt and worry about this long weekend vanished. "I'm Delilah. So glad to finally meet you."

What McCarthy lacked in politeness and manners, this girl seemed to bring to the table. She gave me a little nod as I shook her hand, and before anyone else had the chance to speak, another unfamiliar voice boomed over the driveway.

"Dylan McCarthy Williams!" An older blonde woman, Mrs. McCarthy, appeared at the top of the stairs, pointing an accusatory finger at her son. She held a pair of oven mitts in one hand and shook her head at the two empty paper bags he was carrying. "You better not have stopped for fast food when I've saved you each a plate of lasagna."

He jogged up the stairs and threw his arms around the woman at least seven inches shorter than him. "How could you accuse me of something so cruel, Ma?" He laughed into the embrace, sneakily handing the bags off to another girl, who'd appeared behind them.

Her dark hair was sleek, and some freckles covered the tan skin across her nose. Comfortable-looking bunny slippers decorated her feet and a fluffy robe hung over her tank top and shorts.

"For me?" she asked, a hint of excitement in her voice at the prospect.

McCarthy nodded, still in his mother's arms and seemingly not planning to move. "Just for you, Dakota. 'Cause you're my favorite." Behind him, Delilah gasped in outrage, while Dakota's smile widened, hastily opening one of the *empty* bags. The smell of our food probably still lingered inside.

Dakota threw the bag at his head. While his sister began complaining, with various insults spilling from her lips and accusatory fingers pointing, his mother's attention slid to me. I tried to smile as casually as I could.

She shook her head in amused disbelief, offering a warm-hearted eye roll at her son's behavior, only to whip him across the back of his head with the oven mitts a second later. My smile turned genuine. He deserved it. Probably.

"So, you beg me to let you bring a girl to Thanksgiving, then skip the introductions?" she asked. I ignored the word *begged* pointedly. I didn't even let myself think of it. "Not *a* girl, Mom," Dakota snickered, wild amusement in her tone. "*The* girl."

Natalie shook her head again. "I cannot believe I raised you." Her tone playful in its accusation.

McCarthy's attention slipped away from his sister—not without throwing a silencing glare her way—but amusement and joy still glimmered in his eyes when they landed on me.

"Nothing's being skipped," he said quickly. "And no one was begging. If I remember correctly, *you* jumped at the opportunity—"

"Because you've been talking about her for—!"

"*Dakota!*" His voice was harsher when he shushed his sister. She leaned against the door frame, watching the situation with obvious amusement. His outburst only made her shrug, and she gave me a wink before she headed back inside.

Clearing his throat, McCarthy overcame the few steps between us. "Sorry about them," he muttered into my hair, the sound traveling into the pit of my stomach where it awoke . . . something. His hand found the small of my back, then gently nudged me inside the house.

"I heard that, young man!" his mom noted from behind us in a sing-song voice, and I couldn't help the muted snort that escaped me. My head shook, craning upward to find him already looking at me.

The tip of his nose was deep red from the cold, cheeks a little lighter. He was smiling—*at me, with me, all of the above.* I didn't know. He just smiled, content and carefree and happy, before he properly introduced me to his mother.

"You should've gotten rid of that Jeep a long time ago, Dylan." Mr. Williams was the spitting image of his son; just that his hair was grey, and his skin was a bit wrinkled and darker. They resembled each other right down to the unamused, lazy tone in their voices.

"Thanks for the input." McCarthy's attention shifted from the lasagna on his plate, though he didn't turn to look at his father, who was sitting on the couch behind him with a newspaper in hand that he wasn't looking up from, either. The similarities in their manners were almost comical. McCarthy gave me a wide, faked smile. "I'll consider it."

His father sighed, head shaking. "You won't," he stated matter-of-factly, as if they'd had this conversation a thousand times before. "At least park it in the garage, so we don't have to look at the godawful thing whenever we leave the house."

As if to sweep the tension out of the air, their older-looking golden retriever rushed into the room. I'd fallen in love with Rose in about two seconds, in which she'd only just managed to jump up my leg. Now, she scurried around the dining table in search of any food that might have fallen off our plates. The way she looked up at me with her big brown eyes made me want to sacrifice my entire meal.

After we'd settled, McCarthy made sure I wouldn't get the chance to excuse myself and hide out to mope some more. Not in a cruel or forceful way—but in less than an hour at his place, I was so involved in conversations that I forgot I should be grieving. I'd learned and understood more about my fake boyfriend in that hour than I had in the entirety of our arrangement.

"*This*," I pointed to the rest of the lasagna on my plate. "Is delicious, Natalie."

She seemed pleased by my words. "I'm sure you would've enjoyed it more if this guy hadn't stopped by some awful fast food place earlier," she said pointedly, then sent a warm smile my way. "But, I'm glad you like it, Athalia."

"It's really good, Mom," he agreed, nodding grandly and trying to keep her eyes off his fork, which was digging into the rest of *my* meal. He didn't succeed, of course.

But Natalie just shook her head once more, hands in the air as if she was giving up. "Good luck," she said as she stood.

"So," Dakota popped into the chair her mother had been in two seconds before. "When are we doing baby photos?" Her question caught me off-guard, though I wasn't about to complain about getting the chance to see embarrassing childhood pictures of McCarthy. So many stories and so much compromising information within my reach.

"As soon as we can, please."

Dakota seemed pleased by my eager reply. McCarthy shot me a look of betrayal, before figuring he shouldn't have expected anything less.

"We're never—" he was cut off by Denise, his Europe-travelling older sister.

"Did someone say baby photos?" She stood behind Dakota's chair, her hands placed on the backrest, excitement lingering in her voice. Her curly hair was in a bun atop her head. "I'm pretty sure Diana still has that video from Aunt Kiki's wedding—" She turned her head toward the living room, the words sounding more like a question as she directed them at their oldest sister, Diana.

"I do!" It came from the couch, and Denise was halfway to her sister by the time she'd finished that sentence.

"His first drop of alcohol," Dakota filled me in quickly.

"When I was *fifteen*," McCarthy added for context. His head landed on the table in playful annoyance. "No baby photos," he groaned. "No dancing videos, either."

"*Dancing videos?*" I was officially intrigued.

Neither of his sisters took him seriously. One last attempt when he said, "*I mean it.*"

"Sure you do," Dakota agreed.

McCarthy glared at his sisters, then pushed away from the dining table. The way his chair scraped across the floor was loud enough for Mr. Williams to shout, "The floors, Dylan! Jesus," from the adjacent living room.

"It's getting exceptionally late, everyone," McCarthy announced loudly. The clock only showed half past ten.

I only just managed to accompany my awkward wave with a "goodnight," before I half-followed and he half-dragged me out of the room and up the stairs.

Chapter 27

I felt like an art critic in a gallery when I looked around his room.

Dark wooden floors, windows cut low. Scattered on the windowsill were a few books and a single plant. The most noticeable feature of the room—apart from the king-sized bed positioned with its headrest against the center of the wall—was the grand piano. There wasn't a speck of dust on the black surface. The leather bench in front of it was placed thoughtfully, allowing for a spectacular view of the backyard when you weren't looking at the ivory keys.

"What?" he asked behind me, amused by my critic-act.

I stepped into the center of the room with my hands crossed behind my back.

"What?" He asked again, voice much closer than before.

I knew if I turned, I'd be staring right at him—his chest—with only a few inches separating us. It was tempting, which was why I continued staring at the few books on the shelf against the wall. "Are you not pleased with your chambers, Princess?" he asked mockingly.

"*My* chambers?" I finally turned to find him just as close as I'd expected. My nose would brush his if he weren't so much taller. Looking up, my eyes narrowed as the question hung in the air between us.

"Well." His head cocked sideways as he shrugged. "Yours for the time being."

My gaze fell on the king-sized bed.

"No—" I shook my head. "No, it's okay. I can sleep in the guest room or on the couch—the floor is fine, too. Really."

"Suddenly so humble. What happened, Pressley?" His lips broke into a smirk, a casual hand brushing a strand of brown behind my ear, before his finger hooked underneath my chin to connect our eyes.

Although I rolled mine at the statement, I answered honestly. "I don't want to take more from you. You're already doing all this—" I gestured around his room to emphasize. "And sacrificing time with your family. I really don't want to intrude any more than I already am." I wish I could turn away from his gaze; humility had never been my strong suit, admitting it even less. But his hand on my cheek wouldn't let me, even if I'd tried.

"*Athalia.*" He dragged my name out playfully, sounding whiny. "I'm not sacrificing anything. You're not intruding." He snickered. "You're not taking from me—I'm giving you the things I want to give you. Willingly. Because I want to."

Fuck. I'm in so much trouble. "And where will you sleep?"

"This is a big house," he said matter-of-factly. "I'll sleep in the guest room."

"*I* can sleep in the guest room."

"I don't want you to."

"I don't want *you* to."

"It's a shame I'm, like, ten inches taller, seventy pounds heavier." I was about to disagree strongly with the ten inches, because it was more like six or seven, when he went on. "Which means you don't stand a chance—"

A surprised squeal ripped out of me. "McCarthy!" I gasped, laughing loudly, suddenly hanging over his shoulder like a sack of flour. Completely and utterly helpless. His hands held me steadily by my waist and thigh, fingers digging into the skin.

Before I really knew what hit me, he maneuvered me onto his bed. Still laughing, squealing, and playfully hitting him on my way down. My fingers clung to the neckline of his pine-green sweater, dragging him with me.

McCarthy's chest rose unsteadily above mine as my laughter slowed. The corners of my lips lowered as our situation dawned on me—him, on top of me, the wide smile I'd caused, and his twinkling eyes not wavering from mine even once.

And I kissed him. Because I didn't know what else to do, and this—laughing and enjoying each other's company, my fluttering stomach—felt more intimate than any physical touch could be. I wasn't used to it, and I wasn't sure if I wanted to be. But *this*—his lips on mine, bodies flush—had become familiar.

Somewhere between fake kisses and statistic books, *he* had become familiar.

I liked the way my body fit his, how we moved against each other so effortlessly. I loved what my touch did to him. And I loved what his did to me.

"I'm going to hate myself for this," he groaned against me, putting an inch of distance between us. The sound that escaped me was pathetic. "But I need to go—"

"Where?" My lips trailed along his neck, placing gentle, open-mouthed kisses along his jawline, feeling his pulse beating against me.

"The guest room," he reminded me, sounding strangled. I emerged from the crook of his neck to look at him, amusement glinting in my eyes.

"You can stay here." The suggestion felt natural. "With me."

McCarthy snorted as he shook his head. "No," he huffed. "I can't."

"Why?"

"*Why?*" His head fell back, repeating the word as if the answer was obvious. "Because you're here."

"And?"

"And." He sighed, wetting his lips. The word lingered as he looked at me with pleading eyes, like it was obvious.

"And?"

"And you're you, Athalia," he finally said. "You're you, and I'm me." His lips moved to my ear, my eyes closing at the proximity before he spoke gently. "And I don't have the willpower it would take to keep me away from you. Because I really, really, *really* want you, too."

It wasn't lost on me that he'd added another *really* to my earlier statement.

His voice had dropped to a whisper, his warm breath tickling my ear with every soft word he murmured. I couldn't take it. The sweet, masculine scent of him, the way I could feel the outline of his body hovering directly above mine—some parts touching, while the most important ones were not. The overwhelming urge to kiss him, needing him to touch me. *Needing to touch him back.*

"So have me." My heartbeat felt louder than the words themselves. For a moment, I wondered if I had said them at all. But then he groaned, and it was confirmation enough. His head fell into the crook of my neck, defeated, done—muttering a "*Fuck*," as he went down.

"You don't know what you do to me, do you?" he said, beginning to place kiss after kiss on my bare skin, working his way up my neck. "I'm trying to be a good person here, and you're making it so fucking difficult." His lips connected with mine again; hungry, ready. And I wished the sensation would've lasted longer than a few seconds. "But not tonight. I'm not sleeping with you when you're grieving. Vulnerable." And with that, he lifted himself up, effortlessly rolling off of his king-sized bed. "Good night, Princess."

I felt my perfectly distracted state slipping further away with each step he took. By the time he reached the door, reality nearly had me in its clutches again. I wanted to scream for him to come back. Instead, I sat there in silence, watching him consider me carefully for another second before turning to leave.

My breath hitched, not quite sure whether his objectively sweet rejection stung more than the fact I was supposed to be grieving in the first place. Or maybe, that it was only his considerateness that had reminded me.

"Dylan?" My whisper was so quiet, I wasn't sure if he'd heard me.

My eyes stung, my throat closed up, and I couldn't keep that sharp intake of breath to myself, either. No air made it past my lips regardless. That's how shallow my breathing had become.

Dying, I thought. *I'm dying*.

Another sharp intake of breath, still shallow and superficial, failing to deliver enough air to my lungs. And somehow, he was right there. Back at my side.

"Athalia," I thought he said. The thrumming of my heartbeat and the sound of my strangled breathing were louder than his voice.

"I'm—" I began, though I could hardly say the word without another sob, another short breath cutting me off. "I'm having—" *a panic attack. I'm having a panic attack*, I wanted to say. *I'm having a panic attack, and I'm sorry. I'm sorry. I'm sorry. I'm sorry. You shouldn't be here for this. I'll be fine.* I couldn't even open my mouth. Just sob after sob after sob, blurry vision, and lack of air.

"I know. Panic attack—I know." His words reeled me back to the present moment. I wasn't sure when his hands had found their way to my shoulders, but compassion was etched into his features. "Your brother used to get them all the time," he murmured, gently moving his fingers against me. I think he kept talking so I'd have something to focus on. "Before tryouts. Before our first games. It's probably why he can't stand me—Hey, focus on my voice, Athalia. You can hear me. You can see me. Right?"

I nodded, the gesture followed by another sob that was cut off by yet another strangled attempt for air. I couldn't really focus on what he'd said—that Henry apparently struggled with the same thing and that McCarthy must've been there to help him through panic attacks as well. That Henry hated him because McCarthy had seen him vulnerable. It wasn't about a stolen jersey number or girlfriend or spot as team captain.

"I—"

But he shook his head quickly.

"No need to explain," McCarthy said quickly. "Deep breath," he instructed. "Just one." He did it first, exhaling loudly and slowly in a way I wish I could. But I tried my best—a wavering, shaky attempt he seemed to appreciate nonetheless.

"Another one." He nodded, did it again. "Focus on me . . .

although I know you hate doing that." The familiarity of his teasing made something in me loosen. I tried to take another breath—less shaky. And another one—less strangled. Until the floodgates opened and air filled my lungs.

"Better?" he asked, and when I nodded faintly, he wrapped himself around me like my favorite blanket. Like he'd never let go.

My chest still rose and fell unevenly, my breathing was still rapid, and my cheeks were still wet. But my face was buried in his neck, my arms slung around his torso, and somehow, I felt okay. Not good, but okay.

"I'm sorry," I finally managed, lifting my head and loosening my grip to look at him. He pulled me back, held me tighter. He did not allow even a sliver of distance between us.

"Don't say that." The way he pleaded took me by surprise. "Please don't say that."

With my rambled "I'm sorry you had to see that" monologue out of the question, I wasn't quite sure what to say. He gently wiped a fresh tear from my cheek, as if it would make a difference.

"I forgot," I said, as if the realization had just occurred again. "I forgot they died. *I forgot*—and when you left, I remembered, and it—God." I lowered my head as I shook it. "How could I forget my parents like that? Now, of all times?" *When Thanksgiving was just around the corner.*

McCarthy considered me for a second before his hand found mine to squeeze. "You're allowed to not be miserable, Athalia. Even today. That doesn't mean you forget about them. That doesn't mean you ever will."

My breath shuddered in my chest.

"But please allow yourself to feel joy. You deserve that. And they wouldn't fault you for it."

Chapter 28

It was past eleven when I woke the next day. I was tempted to stay in bed, forget that yesterday's breakdown happened in front of McCarthy, and try to sleep through this cursed day.

But only for a second.

Maybe I didn't want to be rude after how kind and welcoming McCarthy's family had been yesterday. Maybe I didn't want to come across like a spoiled brat taking it all for granted. Waking up this late probably made me seem like one, regardless. Either way, my decision had absolutely nothing to do with Dylan McCarthy Williams.

No. Nothing at all.

Instead of donning the usual baggy-T-shirt-sweatpants combination I considered my Thanksgiving attire, I actually put in effort. A white collar peeked out from beneath my beige sweater. My brown plaid skirt seemed much shorter than I remembered, now that I'd be wearing it in front of McCarthy's family.

I should've gotten them something—anything—to show my gratitude. And why do I care so much about what they think of me?

Apparently for the same reason I'd showered and done my hair, put a single wave in my curtain bangs, and let the rest of the brown layers fall down my back. I sighed at my reflection in the mirror, green eyes behind round glasses staring back at me.

Maybe I *should* have brought my contacts with me. Then again, my reasoning was solid. I predicted tears on Thanksgiving with the same probability as rain in London, which is why I opted against makeup today, too.

Downstairs, I walked in on McCarthy at the dinner table, playing Monopoly with his sisters. His pained expression spoke for itself, but the few notes of cash laid out in front of him confirmed it. He was losing.

I'd never seen him lose anything.

It was his turn and he was concentrating enough that my arrival went unnoticed. "I have enough to buy this—" he thought aloud, letting the rest of us be part of his process. His finger tapped one of the two dark blue streets. "But then I'm literally left with ten dollars." His groan rang through the room. My lips quirked as I watched.

"What can I say? Capitalism's a bitch, little brother." Denise teased.

Dakota kicked his leg under the table impatiently. "Just buy the damn thing, Dylan. You're holding up the entire game."

"Fuck off," he shot back halfheartedly, but put the notes in the bank, searched for the right card in the stack, and placed a house on his square.

"*You* fuck off."

I made my way toward the five of them, finally drawing his attention. "Good morning, sleepyhead," McCarthy drawled, gesturing to the chair beside him. "We've been up waiting for you to emerge from your coma since eight this morning. Even waited with breakfast."

The smile on my face fell.

I wasn't sure whether to snap at him for *making* them wait or apologize to everyone for *having* to wait. I opted to avoid eye contact and say nothing.

"Oh, come on, Dylan," Diana snickered, hair cut short in a way that screamed 'no-bullshit' the same way her voice did. "Don't be a dick—you've been up for an hour, tops." Before she even finished her sentence, my head swiveled in McCarthy's direction, eyes twitching into a glare.

"Time *is* relative." The wink that accompanied his words made me roll my eyes. McCarthy mouthed a *Sorry*. Noticing my glare, an amused pout formed on his lips. "Old habits die hard," he rasped, head tilting with the hum of his voice.

"Seems like it." His sisters were watching Delilah's next move. By the look of it, she was in the lead, and I took advantage of the distraction.

"Never took you for a risk-taker," I noted casually, nodding at the property he'd bought as if I hadn't just placed my hand on his thigh. As if I wasn't trailing along the muscles underneath his grey sweats.

He tensed under my touch, jaw rigid, and his eyes warily following every single movement of my hand. He cleared his throat, glanced around the table. I dared to inch my hand higher. Higher. And higher again. Until he trapped it underneath his.

"Have some mercy on me, Athalia," he muttered under his breath.

"I don't know what you're talking about," I whispered sweetly, eyes batting. When I stood up to circle behind his chair, he exhaled sharply the moment my hand fell from his leg. I placed my hands on his shoulders instead. "Old habits die hard," I whispered from behind him.

His head fell back playfully as he tried his best to look at me. I raised my brows. "I'll be helping your mom. Good luck, risk-taker." With one last nod in the direction of the gameboard, I strolled into the kitchen.

By three o'clock, I felt bad enough to ask where to find the nearest grocery store. I really should've stopped for chocolate or wine or flowers on the way here. Shown some gratitude. Wasn't that what this stupid day was about in the first place? Nothing could stop me from getting to that store.

Nothing but my turned-off phone. There was no way in hell I was turning it on today. The thought of accidentally stumbling across an article or a rogue condolence text—that came a little late for the actual date, but perfectly timed to make me spiral—was enough to tighten the knot in my stomach.

So, leaving my phone off was a no-brainer.

I had planned to sneak out quickly without anyone noticing, then return with a nice bottle of wine or other treat to make it seem like I had them with me all along. But with my phone temporarily out of order, I couldn't just google the nearest store or use maps to get there. Unfortunately, that only left me with one other option: a tall brunette boy I didn't think I hated anymore.

"Can I use your phone?"

"For what?"

"Just need to check something real quick." My eyes darted through the living room, taking in the way we all sat pressed together on one of the white couches, facing the TV. My voice lowered once more, and I was still following the football game on the screen, hoping that I didn't look suspicious when I whispered, "And take it somewhere. Won't be longer than half an hour." Right? "I think."

"*You think?*" he mocked. "And what is it you need to check, Princess?" He bumped my shoulder with his. We were sitting close enough that he didn't have to move much for that.

"Just—" I shrugged. "Something."

"No." He sounded way too satisfied whenever those words came out of his mouth. Today was no different.

A groan slipped past my lips, and unfortunately the sound wasn't as low as our whispers had been. Every head in the room turned my way.

Synchronized.

"*Dylan,*" his mother whispered harshly before I could even begin to apologize. Her tone adapted that naturally ironic note that always lingered in McCarthy's, too. "For the love of God, stop annoying your *girlfriend*. Please."

My head snapped in his direction at the word, trying not to make the confused, prompting, *please-explain* look on my face too obvious to the rest of them.

"*Mom,*" Dakota playfully whined from the other side of the couch. She shot her mother a scolding look. "She's not his girlfriend. I've told you that a million times already."

"Well, he's treating her like one. What am I supposed to think?" She threw her hands up in confusion. I was just glad the focus was on their bickering, and not on me anymore. The fact that they were arguing about my potential relationship status with their son/brother didn't matter. Did it?

"I told you it's—"

"Yes, yes." Natalie waved her off. "It's complicated, confusing. I don't know what's complicated about the way he looks at—"

"*All right*," McCarthy snapped, clearing his throat to steer my attention away. He hurried me up and away from the couch. Diana and Dakota immediately scooted over to sprawl across the previously occupied space. McCarthy pushed me out of the room before I could pick up any more of the discussion.

"You need to learn to use your inside voice, Pressley," he muttered, coming to a halt in the hallway. "Now, what do you need my phone for?" When I turned around, he was already holding the locked device out to me.

The nearest grocery store open on Thanksgiving was a good twenty-minute drive away. That was how I'd ended up back in McCarthy's Jeep, forced to accept his ride.

"You didn't have to come with me, you know?" I huffed, grabbing a cart as we entered the store. He immediately took it from me. "You should be spending time with your family."

"Oh, so you know how to drive a manual?"

He knew I didn't. I could see it in the smirk growing on his lips and the glint in his eyes. I refocused on the task at hand instead of replying *no, I do not*. "Is there anything else your mom still needs? For dinner?"

"Hop in," he said, completely ignoring my question.

At this point, I was convinced the only reason he'd come along was to make this more difficult for me. He nodded toward the cart. "*Go on*. Don't be a wuss, Pressley."

My brow furrowed. "I can't just—" I gestured into the cart.

"Why not? The store is empty. And even if it wasn't, you don't know anybody here. They don't know you." The challenging undertone in his voice got me. "Now get in the cart."

My annoyed sigh wasn't at all genuine. For some reason, I *wanted* to get in that cart. As soon as he began wheeling me around like his ninety-year-old wife who couldn't walk anymore, I enjoyed it, too.

"All right," I said from my perch. "What can I get your parents, then?"

He hummed while considering. "Mom's always been fond of those little chocolate things."

"Very specific, *thank you*."

He rolled his eyes before they searched the aisles for the *Chocolate* sign. "You won't know them," he said, a teasing smile on his lips when he looked back at me. "They're kind of—" He leaned closer like he was about to share the nuclear codes with me. "Cheap."

"Oh no! My credit card is not designed for purchases under ten dollars. Whatever will we do now?"

"You're annoying." The way he said it was... kind. His voice soft and amused, as if he'd never thought a bad thing about me in his life. Closing my eyes to keep my smile from tearing my face in half, I turned back around as he rolled me toward the little chocolate things his mother loved.

"So?" came his voice from behind, watching me reach for the box of cranberry chocolates he had pointed out. "Do you know them?"

"No," I spat halfheartedly. "But I *could* have known them."

"They don't sell these at Whole Foods," he snickered. "The chances are slim."

"I barely shop at Whole Foods!"

"Because the next one is fifty miles from campus." A laugh

accompanied his words. One I couldn't help but enjoy, no matter how hard I tried not to.

"You know me way too well, McCarthy. How is that?"

"Reading people is one of my many talents." I could tell that *lying* wasn't one of those talents. But I let it go.

Twisting the box of chocolates in my hands absentmindedly, I asked, "What can we get your dad?"

"Nothing at all, if it's up to me." McCarthy attempted to hide the truth behind his words with a joking tone. It didn't work.

"I'm just saying, he'll be there for dinner, then disappear in his office after the table has been cleared. For all I know, he hasn't even noticed that you're here."

I turned in the cart to face him completely, considering the shift in his attitude. "You never mention him," I began carefully, but McCarthy shrugged again, inspecting the aisles instead of looking at me.

"Well," he sighed. Shrugged again. "Nothing worthy of mentioning. He's basically as absent as yours—" He caught himself a little too late, eyes widening.

"I'm *so* sorry—" It shot out of him. "It's just, he's been basically absent since he realized I'm more capable of kicking a ball than throwing one. He tries to pay for shit, I guess, but—not that that's equal to your—You—I'm really sorry."

Somehow, I didn't care much at all about what had slipped out. I liked how he spoke about my parents so casually, even if he'd mentioned what I was trying hard to forget.

"So, he'd rather have you play football?"

"Or work in a bank. *Do something respectable*." he said, clearly relieved I wasn't holding his words against him. "Anyways, there's no need to get him anything."

"All right," I conceded, not wanting to push it. "But how else will I get your *entire* family to love me?"

McCarthy considered me for a long moment. "Don't you worry," he said. "You're well on your way to be invited back for Christmas . . . and Easter, for all I can tell."

"I really like them. Your family, I mean."

"Good." I could hear the smile on his face. "Because it's all *Athalia this*, *Athalia that*. I wouldn't know how to break the news if you didn't."

I chuckled, finding the thought objectively sweet. "Just like you, then."

Silence.

"No doubt about it."

Chapter 29

Growing up in a four-person household—with usually only three of us eating because Dad was out of town, state, or country—I was used to leftovers, especially around Thanksgiving. Mom would give the chef the following weekend off, and we'd live exclusively off turkey, mashed potatoes, and cranberry sauce for three days.

Glancing across the table that definitely wouldn't have any leftovers at the end of the meal, I was shocked to realize it was the first time today that I'd truly thought of my parents. Usually, my mind would be filled with nothing but memories: that one time Mom caved and got us fast food on Christmas Eve or Dad winning the season and flying us out to Disney World to celebrate for an entire weekend. Those happy memories were rare, but not because I'd had a terrible childhood.

More so because the bad overrode the good so quickly, it was barely a year after their death before all I thought about when I heard my parents' names was the plane wreckage, the headlines announcing their deaths, and the way my aunt broke down on the phone, before having to tell us her sister had died.

Goddamn it. Hadn't this been about distraction?

I snapped out of it with a shake of my body, tearing my eyes away from the few pieces of turkey left. The conversation around me was still animated, so at least my mental absence went unnoticed.

I wondered if they knew about my parents—why I was here. How much had McCarthy told them?

I turned toward him, startling when I found his eyes on me already. *So much for going unnoticed.*

"Someone's jumpy today." He grinned, brows raised.

"Oh my God," I muttered, letting out the breath I'd held in. "Don't just sit there and *stare* at me," I hissed in a whisper. "You scared the living daylights out of me."

"By . . . looking at you?" The grin was audible in his voice, and I didn't have to look at him to know it was probably heavenly.

"Yes," I snapped. "By looking at me with those big, beautiful eyes, and not saying a damn word—" My mouth shut abruptly, stopping my rambling before it could get worse.

I did just say that out loud, didn't I?

It was a matter of seconds before he confirmed my fear. "Big and beautiful." He hummed beside me, clearly pleased by the slip-up. "I was about to suggest you should lay off the wine for the night," he said. "But if it's going to be the reason for more compliments . . ." His voice trailed off.

I scowled, finally sending a glare his way. "It was half a glass."

More than that had seemed too dangerous to try around strangers, especially when I wanted them to like me. A lot. It was only after we'd moved into the living room, while watching Dakota (tipsy) debate Denise (flat-out drunk) on the significance of Taylor Swift's entire discography, that I realized just how much.

"So your parents let her drink," I whispered to McCarthy as I nodded at the glass of wine in Dakota's hand. He was sitting next to me, but I was fully focused on his sisters' argument.

"Are you kidding me?" Dakota's eyes narrowed at her older sister. "Denise, how could you disregard 'Would've, Could've, Should've'? 'Give me back my girlhood, it was mine first?' she sang, off key. "Seriously?"

I snorted, finally turning away from them when Denise sighed, "You're sixteen, Dakota. You don't know what you're talking about."

McCarthy nodded when I looked at him. "Only when she's around Mom. And nothing hard. Just beer, wine . . . that kind of stuff. Makes it much less appealing once you're off to college, I can tell you that much," he added.

I couldn't look away from the smile that tugged at the corners of his lips. I don't think I wanted to. "I love them," I admitted, fully turning to face him. "I can't help it."

Another laugh. "I'm sure they love you, too."

"You think?"

"I know."

I think something broken and shriveled-up inside of me was healing around them. Something that wasn't used to big families, drama-free gatherings, and arguing Taylor Swift's top ten songs. When was the last time I'd been around something like that?

The thought should've been sad—I expected it to be, at least—but I smiled brightly, stomach fluttering when McCarthy matched it. *God*, he was a great distraction.

McCarthy could distract me just by talking about the goddamn weather. Anything beyond that—his hands on me, lips on mine, bodies pressed against each other's—would probably leave me feeling blissful for the rest of the fucking week. No matter which one it was.

The thought alone sparked something in me. A little fire that, if I wasn't careful, would turn into an inferno so quickly that I wouldn't even notice at first. As soon as I remembered the way he felt against me, the way he sounded, I couldn't stop. I still had a contract to break. A game to win.

"Dylan?"

He straightened, as if electrocuted by my voice and the way those five letters sounded coming from my mouth.

"Hm?" he asked, blinking down at me, probably trying not to let his eyes wander to the hand I'd just placed on his thigh.

"Wine makes me sleepy," I lied, holding eye contact.

"Does it?" His lip quirked. "Even just half a glass? Two hours ago?"

I nodded. "It's white wine," I explained, like that made all the difference. When I leaned in for the final blow, my mouth right by his ear, goose bumps formed across his neck. His head turned to confirm the rest of his family was still occupied, but that only made it easier to brush my lips across his skin.

I placed a single kiss below his ear. He sucked in a breath. "You know where to find me," I murmured. "If you change your mind about that contract you want to honor so badly."

It was past midnight, and I was greeted with a chorus of "sleep well" from McCarthy's siblings as I headed upstairs.

I couldn't help the victorious smirk when I heard him say "Excuse me," less than a minute later.

"Going to bed?" I asked from the top of the staircase he was climbing. "Seems like a silly coincidence, doesn't it?"

He jumped two stairs at a time until he stood on the step below me. I still had to look up. "Let's call it that. A silly coincidence."

"I've got another one." I shifted closer, rested my hands against his chest. His breath faltered as my fingertips slid up his body, then behind his neck, my arms crossing.

"Oh yeah?" he rasped.

The words flushed my cheeks with heat, and something deep in my stomach twisted before uncoiling in relief as I finally overcame the hair's breadth between us. I swallowed his sigh of similar relief when his lips pressed against mine, eager and curious.

"What's the other coincidence?" he asked, between one kiss and the next, moving us away from the staircase. My back flattened against the wall behind me.

"A room down the hall, with a bed so big—" Before I finished my sentence, I tugged him back down to me by the collar of his shirt. Even with his lips back on mine and my legs wobbling with need, we made it to that room in what felt like a heartbeat.

We only separated once the piano bench dug into the back of my legs. I stumbled onto it.

My eyes lifted up . . . and up and up, until they connected with his.

"I'm—" He cut himself off, like the past few minutes were as much of a blur to him as they were to me, and he wasn't quite sure how we'd ended up in this position.

Almost level with his crotch, I couldn't help slipping a finger below the waistband of his pants. Just lingering. "Did you change your mind?" I asked, embarrassingly hopeful. "About the contract? About honoring it?"

A bolt of realization flashed across his features.

"I want you to know this," he said firmly, crouching down to my level. "I might've started this little game, but I never claimed I'd win. I never said you couldn't get me to lose, just by looking at me for a little too long. There's nothing—" He overcame his hesitance by taking my face in his hands, holding me gently.

"Fuck that contract," he said. "There's nothing I want more than to touch you, to feel you again. My head between your thighs, your body underneath mine—" He exhaled a strong breath, his hand behind my neck, fingers disappearing into my hair. "God, to hear you moan my fucking name." His head shook as our eyes connected, lust undeniable in his gaze. "Every time I'm in my office, I can't help but think of you. It's taken a toll on my productivity."

My breath caught in my throat when he trailed his other hand along my skin. Like he was carving me from marble, he followed every contour, dragging his thumb across my lips. His fingers continued down my neck, slipping under my top, touch so feather light as he circled my collar bones that goose bumps were inevitable. "So, I don't think you understand how much I want you, Athalia."

"You can have me," I promised, fueled by nothing but my own need and the way his hand had dropped to my bare thigh, right below the hem of my skirt. "If I can have you, then you can have me. I *want* you to have me."

"You have me. Jesus Christ, Athalia. You've *had* me. I'm at your mercy. Putty in your fucking hands—"

I didn't let him finish his sentence.

With the first swipe of his tongue, he took every rational thought from my mind. Replacing it with the sensation of his fingers dancing up my leg, his breath against my lips and his words replayed in my head over and over and over again.

McCarthy dropped to his knees, shuffling between my legs. I reveled at the contact. He groaned when the heel of my foot pushed him closer.

His hand inched up the hem of my skirt. Breathing heavily, he asked, "Can I—?" I barely managed a nod, a broken moan, before I felt the pad of his thumb against my clit, nothing but a flimsy piece of fabric separating my skin from his.

"Fuck." He held my eyes with his. "You don't know how much I've missed those little sounds." I was trying my best to contain them, to keep quiet the way I had in his office. But he dragged his thumb down my entrance, then pushed it underneath my panties, and I couldn't help myself. "That's what I'm talking about," he hummed against my skin. "There you go, Princess."

His gentle encouragement was entirely contrary to the way he pushed my panties to one side. His fingers hovered right where I needed him most. "This all right?"

"More than," was all I managed. "Please—" *Do something*, I wanted to say. But his finger pushed inside me before I could, and he stifled a groan when he realized how wet I was for him.

I failed at keeping quiet, but I was hoping the walls were thick. One glance at least confirmed we'd managed to close the door in the heat of whatever got us here. McCarthy got back to his feet, keeping his fingers still, bent over my body on the piano bench. Our gazes held for one, two, three seconds, and I squirmed underneath his touch.

Anticipation thrummed beneath my skin, my stomach tightening with every moment he refused to move his fingers. I held my breath. Just when I was about to combust, when

I thought the anticipation would honest to God kill me, he curled his middle and ring fingers buried inside me. And began moving.

It almost killed me just the same.

His pace steadied, whispered encouragements making it through the haze. "I love seeing you like this," he groaned. "You look so beautiful when you're about to come for me."

And I was about to, wasn't I? Five minutes in a room with Dylan McCarthy Williams and I was ready to burst at the seams for him. He seemed to interpret every twitch of my body, every sound from my mouth perfectly.

His thumb stroked my clit, moving in sync with the fingers still pushing in and out of me. My head fell back, and my eyes found his. The way he looked down at me, one hand bracing on the bench, the other occupied with getting me closer to what I knew would be an amazing orgasm, pushed me over the edge. I lost all sense of up and down. The world spun and my arms scrambled for purchase behind me. I remembered a little too late it would be the piano my hand grasped onto. "Dylan—"

I came in sync with the deep, rich sound of my arm pounding against the keys.

My other hand pulled McCarthy back to my lips, and he happily kissed me through the ebbing waves. My fingers twitched with the last one, hitting another random key before slipping off the piano.

"That was—" I was still trying to catch my breath when he agreed.

"Yeah." He planted a kiss against the top of my head. "Are you—?"

"Yeah." I nodded, but I didn't think I could stand yet. I could barely lift my head to look up. Awe swam in his eyes, and I couldn't help my chest tightening at the way he looked at me.

His dark hair was tousled, nothing left of the way he'd parted it in the middle this morning. His cheeks were flushed and his chest rose and fell almost as heavily as mine. I played with one of the closed buttons of his shirt. My eyes trailed to where he was straining against his pants. "Do you want me to—?"

McCarthy caught my hand in his. "Don't." He swallowed thickly. "One touch and you're gonna make me ruin these pants."

I laughed when I looked back up, but there wasn't a hint of humor in his features. "I mean it." He brought my hand to his lips, kissed each finger slowly. "Whenever I think about your hands on me, it definitely lasts longer than five seconds. Let me keep it that way." Placing his lips on the back of my hand, his eyes lifted. "Please?"

"Okay." I nodded, trying to ignore the blush on my cheeks. Watching as he straightened back up to his six foot two with me, I couldn't help but say, "I don't want to ask more of you—"

"—Please do."

Out of pure selfishness, just because I wanted to see what he'd look like sleeping next to me, I asked, "Will you stay with me tonight?"

Unlike last night, he did.

Chapter 30

It had been worth it. Hearing his even breaths before I fell asleep, and pretending not to wake when he brushed a strand of hair out of my face the next morning. His touch lingered before he tiptoed out of his room as dawn was just breaking.

His casual smiles and usual jokes would suggest last night never happened. The way our fingers brushed when no one else was looking showed me he hadn't forgotten, though. I certainly wouldn't.

There's nothing I want more than to touch you, to feel you. My head between your thighs. Hearing you moan my fucking name.

So, yeah. I noticed how snug the white long-sleeve fit around his biceps. And how perky his butt looked as he carried our bags to his Jeep.

Sue me.

As he loaded our luggage into the back of the car, I leaned against the passenger side. The sun was out for the first time in a while, and though it was still cold—seeing-your-breath kind of cold—the sun made it bearable. I squinted, watching the McCarthy Williams' trot out of their house one after the other, a smile on my face when Natalie was the first to embrace me.

"It was lovely meeting you, Athalia. *Really.*" She squeezed me tightly, and I delightedly returned the gesture. "Such a change of pace from the troublemakers I usually have around." She gave all five of her children a playfully scolding look, and while complaints rained from their mouths, a laugh escaped mine.

"Thank you for having me," I said softly. "It means a lot. More than you can probably imagine." I sighed. "I'll extend the same courtesy to you guys. Promise." With that, she walked the few steps over to her son while I said goodbye to the rest of his family.

Diana leaned against the car beside me with a loud sigh. Facing the sun, she squinted a little as she smiled, and I swear the warmth it radiated was similar. "So," she said, eyes shooting to her brother just once, very quickly. "I'm glad he finally had the balls to do this."

"Do what?" I hope I wasn't missing some big, obvious thing that'd make me look stupid for not connecting the dots. But Diana just smiled.

"You know," she said, then gestured back and forth between Dylan and me. I don't think I knew. "This thing. With you. And him. God knows he's been wanting to ask you o—"

"Great!" Dylan clapped his hands together, cutting his sister off and throwing an arm around her. I almost groaned at his interruption. "Goodbye, Didi." The grin on his face told me he knew exactly what he was doing. "Always a pleasure."

Diana rolled her eyes, but she slung her arms around him anyway. "I guess that's your sign to leave," she snickered, a knowing brow raised.

"It is indeed." Opening the passenger door, he looked at me expectantly when I didn't immediately jump into the vehicle. After a nod in its direction, I slipped inside. He gave everyone another hug—his mother's was a bit longer—and then jogged around the car to get inside.

"*You—*" I grumbled as soon as he pulled out of the driveway, pointing an accusatory finger his way. "You always interrupt my most interesting conversations. Do you know that?"

His sheepish smile was noticeable even though he was concentrating on the road. "I might."

This time, in the safety of his car, I let that frustrated groan out. "So, what was she about to say, then?"

"Who?"

"Your sister."

"Which one?"

Another groan. "*Diana.*"

"Oh." His eyes darted to me again, coming to a halt at a stop sign. "No idea." He shifted into first gear and got us rolling again.

"You're the worst." I glared to up the dramatics. "Seriously."

He grimaced. "I'm about to make it so much worse, Princess. I'm sorry."

"What?" I asked carefully.

"How does Statistics for the rest of the drive sound to you?"

My face fell, body deflating. "No."

The self-satisfaction was prominent in his smile and the amount of confidence in his one-word answer. "Yes."

"I'm just going to get some gas." Turning right to pull into the station, Dylan took the opportunity to let his gaze wander my way. An hour of Statistics later, I could use the break. "Take that time to think of the correct answer."

"Fuck you—"

But my insult was cut off by his door closing. I groaned

loudly, all alone in his car. After the hell I'd just been through, it was a well-earned release. Unfortunately, halfway through the unnecessarily long, frustration-filled sound, the passenger door swung open, and I was so startled that my groan turned into a horrified squeal. A horror-movie worthy scream.

I wished I had his mother's oven mitts to whack across his head. My hand still on my heart, I could feel it nearly bursting. "Dylan!"

At some point during the weekend, his first name had become common enough to slip out. He had become familiar enough to laugh or cry with. He was more than just a tutor, reluctant ally, or fake boyfriend.

His grin was wide, and sweet, and irresistible. All dimples, zero shame.

Forearm resting against the top of his car, he leaned down to eye level, then pointed a finger at me. "And do *not* google the answer." My door shut again.

This time, I watched his every move until he disappeared into the gas station to pay. As soon as his silhouette disappeared behind the sliding glass, I made use of his little piece of friendly advice. I hadn't even considered googling anything. Honestly, I'd forgotten I owned a phone over the last few days. His reminder was much appreciated.

Until my missed messages began flooding in.

The *dings* cut themselves off—that's how many were coming in. And although I turned the sound off as soon as I could, the vibrations were enough of an indicator of how fucked I'd be going through them all.

Maybe I'd just get a new number, instead.

With my stomach churning, phone still vibrating, and

messages continuing to pop up in the notifications bar, I went to do what Dylan had told me not to. Unfortunately, I didn't get quite that far.

> **HENRY, Wednesday, 9:22 PM**
> \> are u home?
> \> could you just open the door please?
> \> your lights are off.
> \> could you just open the door?
> \> i'm staying over the holidays. if you need anything lmk
> \> please?
> \> Athalia?

They all came in, one after the other. I didn't know what compelled me to click on the banner notification, but a second later I was staring at a string of grey text messages, missed call notifications and my brother's name on top of the chat.

> **HENRY, Thursday, 9:09 AM**
> \> are you okay?
> \> do you need me to come over?
> \> i will

> **HENRY, Thursday, 9:45 AM**
> \> i know i fucked up but can you just open the door?
> \> i heard you and wren had a falling out
> \> and i don't want you to be alone today
> \> are you okay?

> your neighbor let me in. i'm waiting in front of
your door if you need me
> not that you need me for anything but
> yeah

HENRY, Thursday, 4:01 PM
> i'm getting worried.

Followed by a string of missed calls. Followed by:

HENRY, Thursday, 7:30 PM
> seriously just let me know you want space and
I'll back off
> but you're not saying anything and i'm freaking
out a little here
> athalia?

HENRY, Thursday, 11:11 PM
> i'm thankful for you, little sister

That final message felt like a punch to the gut. My eyes welled with tears, fueled by guilt, more guilt, and then some.

Feeling guilty hadn't been on my fight-with-Henry bingo card. But how could I not?

I'd just . . . left him. My twin brother, who'd gone through the same kind of traumatic loss, felt as awful as I did every year but just hid it better. And he wasn't just grieving—albeit in that if-I-don't-acknowledge-something-it-doesn't-exist kind of way of his—he'd also been worried sick.

About *me*.

The worst thing? That, somehow, this was what I'd wanted from this whole McCarthy nonsense, right? His attention—seeing that he cared. The chat bubbles on my phone indicated that I'd gotten exactly that, and I still didn't feel any better. Worse, probably.

Mindlessly, I scrolled through the dozens of unanswered texts from distant relatives, old acquaintances, and friends. My finger stopped at Wren's contact picture, hovering and tempted to click it. I had already messed with my mood anyway, hadn't I? Fuck it.

To my surprise—and I felt kind of douche-y for expecting her to care as much as Henry had—our last normal messages smiled at me brightly. There were only two new texts underneath them.

> **WREN, Thursday, 10:20 AM**
> > if he fucks this up i'll murder him, but can't help thinking of u today and hope he doesn't fuck it up (although I'd love to murder him)
> > got some things to explain, talk when we're home

She knew. The realization punched me in the gut.

We talked. No coercion needed, no harm done.

Was this what they had talked about that day? Asking him whether he'd take care of me when she couldn't—*wouldn't*?

I didn't think I'd ever felt as loved and humiliated at the same time. Didn't think I had ever hated and appreciated a gesture more. I didn't even know whether to be angry or grateful, to scream or laugh, or cry.

Fortunately, that decision was made for me when Dylan jogged out of the gas station with a plastic bag in hand. As quickly as I could, I slipped my phone back into the bag, and leaned into my seat, trying to give a genuine looking smile. I blinked the wetness out of my eyes, sniffed to get it out of my system. *Distraction, distraction, distraction,* I told myself. By now, I knew McCarthy was a good one.

The boy slipped into the seat beside me, slamming the door shut. "It's freezing out there," he complained with a shiver, throwing the bag into my lap and rubbing his hands together as if he couldn't just turn the car—and therefore the heating—on.

"Like your soul," I sighed, kind of mindlessly.

"Wow." His hand flew up to his chest, clasping his heart as if it were aching. The playfully pained expression made me smile. "What happened in the past five minutes that has made me the subject of your harsh criticism, Pressley? Seriously," he pressed. "I'm hurt."

Another laugh rattled out of me. I think I realized right then that he wasn't just a great distraction when we were trying not to have sex with each other and half-failing; he was a great distraction, *period.* "And to think I got you Sour Patch Kids—I should probably return them while we're still here." He nodded at the bag in my lap with a teasing smile he tried to suppress. He started the car.

The way he made me laugh so effortlessly took me by surprise. There were many things I thought might come out of this agreement: my brother's affection, the feeling of sweet revenge. A dead body. But, I didn't expect genuine enjoyment to be one of them. Even my occasional lapse-of-judgement-attraction, or the urge to kiss him whenever his dimple showed, was less shocking than that.

"So." My head twisted in his direction when he spoke.

"*So*," I mirrored, eyes narrowing in suspicion.

"Do you have an answer for me?"

I blinked. *Did I miss something?*

"For my statistical problem," he added in explanation.

"Now I remember why I called your soul cold," I grumbled, crossing my arms. "You've been torturing me for an hour, Dylan. Can't I just enjoy the rest of our little road trip?"

"You're *enjoying* our little road trip?" The question felt like a trap, so I just groaned and slumped back into my seat.

"I'm *trying* to." If my eyes weren't closed, I'd have rolled them to distract myself from the same realization I had just a few moments ago: I was enjoying this. Not just the road trip, not just the distraction, but his company. Him.

"And I'm trying to help you pass Statistics, Princess." This time, I could tell the nickname was back to being an insult. However, my stomach, and the way it fluttered, did not interpret it that way. At all. "So, let's not give up now, alright?" His voice had adopted a soft, reassuring tone. Almost a murmur. The hopeful look in his eyes when they flicked my way was all it took.

With a defeated sigh, I turned back to the road ahead. "Like I said," I teased under my breath. "*Soulless.*"

He seemed to take that as a sign that I was on board, because he adjusted in his seat happily and I could feel his smile from my seat.

"You *have* been getting better," he reminded.

Another word of encouragement or praise, just another word in that silky smooth tone of his, and it would get significantly harder for me to keep my head clear. In fact, it was already filling with how much I enjoyed being around him.

I tried to steer away from that as best as I could.

"Well, I'd hope so," I joked. Tried to joke. I wasn't very convinced it landed, until the corners of his mouth twitched. "You'd make an exceptionally shitty teacher otherwise."

"Or the problem could be an exceptionally shitty student."

I couldn't help but laugh. Then I couldn't seem to stop. When the sound of his laughter joined mine, it was like the floodgates opened, and every sound from him was funnier than the last.

My belly hurt, my cheeks ached, and it was probably the most physical activity I'd done in a while. That's how I felt, at least: exhausted, but energized. Happy, carefree. Distracted.

I was still smiling when our laughter died out. "Touché," I said, eyes on him. "I guess the probability of your hypothesis is much more likely."

And he almost looked impressed.

Chapter 31

Who'd have thought that after being trapped in a car with Dylan McCarthy Williams for hours on end, the part I would dread most would be arriving at our destination?

> got some things to explain, talk when we're home

The reminder of Wren's message made me unbuckle my seatbelt uncharacteristically slowly and slip into my coat even slower. I redid my bun twice and adjusted my glasses at least a dozen times.

Dylan had hopped out of the car as soon as we'd stopped in front of the brick complex, grabbing my bag from the trunk. It seemed he hadn't even noticed my hesitancy until he swung the duffel bag over his shoulder and saw I was still in the same spot he'd left me in.

In the rearview mirror, I could see him scanning me intently with narrow eyes.

"Don't try to psychoanalyze me," I warned as soon as he swung open the passenger door.

"I wouldn't think of it," he swore with a laugh that said otherwise, playfully bowing and gesturing for me to finally get out of the Jeep. "Just trying to figure out what about my car is so inviting that you can't seem to get out of it. Or is it just me you don't want to leave behind?" he added. I made a point of ignoring him.

Getting out anyway, I couldn't help but glance up at the building's top floor. Although you couldn't see through the windows, the soft light coming from them was enough to make my stomach turn a second time. My attention fell back to him.

"Wren's probably home," I said, trying not to sound nervous about it. "You can give me that," I nodded at my bag over his shoulder. "There's no need to add fuel to the fire."

"Athalia," Dylan sighed in response, moving toward the entrance of my building as if I hadn't just said he shouldn't. I slammed the door of his Jeep shut and hurried after him. "Don't you remember? She and I are *this* tight now?" He crossed two fingers. "There is no fire to add fuel to."

I pushed past him with a single humorless laugh. "You can give me my bag," I repeated as I unlocked the door. After pushing it open, I turned back with an expectant look. He walked past me.

I groaned and ran after him once more, but he'd already pushed the button for the elevator by the time I caught up. Coming to a stop beside him, both of us waiting for the doors to pop open, I shook my head.

"You are *by far* the most annoying person I have ever come across." The hint of his grin in my periphery told me my eyes should stay on the metal doors ahead if I wanted to remain firm in my stance. "I just want you to know that."

"There's, like, three pairs of shoes, four hoodies, jeans, sweatpants, shirts, dresses, and God knows what else in here. If you think I'm letting you carry a bag that weighs as much as you do, I'm insulted."

My mind was running overtime to check the accuracy of his list. I double-checked. Triple-checked. How—?

"I helped you pack. Remember?"

"You didn't help me pack," I reminded him. "You watched me pack." And I didn't think he had actually watched, never mind paid any attention to it.

He waved me off. "Same thing." Finally, he let the bag drop from his shoulder, catching it in his hand just as we reached the top floor.

But it wasn't the same thing. Packing and watching. Paying attention and not paying attention to the little things. It was like night and day. Did he not understand that? Or did he just try not to?

"Give Wren my regards." My duffel bag stood in the hallway, ready to be slid across the few feet to my apartment—*if* it was as heavy as he made it out to be.

When he stepped back into the elevator to allow its doors to close, I just felt really grateful. For everything.

For taking me in over Thanksgiving. For letting me sleep in his bed. For kissing me. For not having sex with me when I was clearly just trying to find distraction from my grief. For buying me my favorite snacks. For driving me home. For not insisting on coming in. For respecting my decision—my boundaries.

The doors slid shut, our eyes still connected when those two words escaped my lips once more. Words I'd said countless times before.

"Thank you." Although I only whispered them, the way I caught his lip twitching and his head beginning to tip before the doors closed between us, I could tell he'd heard me.

I exhaled a long, deep breath, one that was meant to prepare me for whatever waited behind my front door. A few likely scenarios loomed.

1. Wren could still be ignoring me.
2. Wren could be baking again.
3. Wren could . . . apologize.

I wasn't prepared for any of those options.

The door to her room was closed. I should've felt relieved not to find the kitchen filled with baking utensils, muffins, and cupcakes, but I was a bit disappointed.

I didn't know what I expected after her text. *Need to talk.* What did that even mean?

Perhaps instead of the apology I'd hoped for, she'd tell me she couldn't take it anymore and move out? Oh God.

That thought kicked my anxiety into overdrive; my heart started beating twice as fast, and my palms began to sweat. I let my bag slide to the ground. Until now, I'd been convinced this argument was just a rough patch in our everlasting friendship—one we'd overcome and laugh about in a few years.

Now, though, with the seed of her moving out planted in my mind, that didn't feel so certain.

"Athalia."

I startled when her voice pulled me from my thoughts, jerking around to face her. I didn't know what she saw on my face, but it made her hesitant smile fall at once.

"Are you moving out?" I couldn't hold back the question at all. If she was, I had a right to know as soon as she made that decision, right? As her roommate, as her best friend. Or something like that.

"What?" Her brow furrowed deeply as she pushed herself off the doorframe she'd been leaning against.

"You said we needed to talk," I reminded her. "If we were dating, I would've assumed that text meant that you're breaking up with me. Moving out seems like the equivalent here." The words sounded more rational as they formed on my tongue; in reality, the thought had just popped into my head and was so scary, my overthinking made me stick with it.

She shook her head. Quickly. "What?" she said again. Perhaps it didn't sound rational at all. "I'm not moving out—of course not." Before I could even take a relieved breath, the confusion in her features was overtaken by something else. "Do you want me to?"

"No." I did not want Wren to move out. That much was certain.

"Okay." She nodded, relaxing. "Good."

Unsure what to do or say next, my eyes shifted, roaming the apartment as if I hadn't already been living here for over a year. My arms swung by my side. I blew light raspberries when it stayed quiet for a few seconds too long to be comfortable.

This didn't just feel awkward to me, did it?

"So." I cleared my throat in an attempt to fill the silence, and Wren mirrored my gesture, nodding.

"So," she repeated, dragging it out to keep from going quiet again. "Uh—" I didn't think I'd heard her stammer once in the years I'd known her. And I didn't know if that put me at ease or scared the shit out of me.

"I'm just going to unpack—"

"I'm sorry—"

We spoke at the same time, cutting each other off.

"Oh, yeah," she quickly agreed, gesturing to my bag with a nervous laugh. "Go unpack, I—"

But there was no way. Not after she'd just blurted out those magic words. I didn't even *want* to unpack. It was by far the worst thing about going on a trip.

"No, no." I waved her off. "Go on. I've got time."

Wren nodded, her short hair moving lightly. Then she sighed loudly. "How was your . . . trip?" The question sounded innocent enough, though I saw right through it.

"The trip you organized for me?" I wondered, hoping my suspicions were right. Although it caught her off guard, she nodded.

"Was that a mistake?" Concern riddled her tone, her features—her entire presence was nerves and anxiety.

"No." My answer was deliberately calm, cool, and collected—glad to report I was starting to find my footing again, and I was ready to hear the explanation that was clearly needed. "I had a good time."

She nodded, seeming both pleased and disturbed by the statement. Given my history with Dylan, I was neither surprised nor offended.

"Did he mess up?"

I couldn't suppress the amused twitch of my lip, remembering her text vividly. "So that you can kill him?"

"Yes."

"No."

A relieved puff of air and likely some disappointment that she wouldn't get to beat him up. She was more sure of her words as she slumped against the sofa's armrest, hands driving across her face in frustration.

"I'm sorry." She groaned. "God, I'm so, so sorry. You have no idea." As if just now realizing the weight of her actions, she groaned once more.

The next time our eyes met, the regret in hers almost tore me to pieces, too.

"I overreacted, acted like a jerk, and then almost left you by yourself over Thanksgiving—" She shook her head so roughly, it cut off her words. "And all over fucking McCarthy. It's not even my business what you do. *Who* you do. I guess I just didn't expect it, you know? We hate that guy. I thought we did." She stopped herself, eyes widening. "Or I did. I guess you never really had a reason, apart from the whole Henry thing. He hates McCarthy, so you do, too. But that's not *really* a reason, is it?" Her gaze lifted from the floor, brown eyes taking me in as I leaned against the kitchen counter, playing with one of the paper takeout menus absentmindedly.

"Did you?" I asked carefully. "Have a reason?"

I'd never really questioned Wren's dislike for the guy. How much Henry hated him primed me to simply accept that McCarthy was the worst person to walk the campus.

"Not really," she admitted. "I mean, I thought I did. Once Henry mentioned how McCarthy was so obviously into you, that's all I saw whenever he happened to be in the same room. And I assumed you hated him just as much as your brother. I guess I kind of convinced myself of that, so I wouldn't—"

Wren swallowed, hesitating, eyes shifting again. "Just because that way, I didn't have any reason to be jealous, I guess."

The other shoe dropped.

Just that it wasn't a shoe, but a bomb—nuclear and deadly,

and the impact destroyed everything in its vicinity.

"You like him." That's why she hadn't liked my revenge plan, why she didn't want me to fake-date him, and why she'd freaked out when she found out that we'd kissed.

And as an oblivious idiot, I hadn't realized I was basically dating my best friend's crush. "I had no idea," I confessed as the realization settled in.

"Seriously?"

The tone in her voice made me risk a glance at her. Double-taking when I . . . found an amused smile on her lips? Her pierced brow raised. "I do not like McCarthy." She actually shuddered at the thought. "God, no."

"But you said you were jealous." Why else would she be— "Oh."

Oh.

Oh, Jesus.

"Wait—" But she didn't.

"*Listen,*" she began, avoiding my gaze. "I swore to myself I wouldn't tell you any of this until I was over this—*over you.* And I am," she added. "When you said that thing about the jealous girlfriend—" Guilt twisted my gut inside out. "It's the first time I noticed how much this stupid crush was affecting our friendship. I didn't want to lose you, but in order to get over this, I couldn't just—"

She shook her head, defeat in the sound of her sigh. "I wanted to apologize an hour after I'd stormed off. But I thought . . . If I could just have some time. You know? A few days, maybe a week. But then it'd been *weeks*, Thanksgiving around the corner, and I just missed you *more*. I didn't want to leave you, I swear—"

She exhaled loudly, eyes finally finding me. I wasn't sure what she saw in my face. I, for once, couldn't form a coherent sentence. My mind was too much of a mess for a task so challenging.

Had it been obvious? Had I just been too focused on myself to notice my best friend developing feelings for me? How ironic that I accused my brother of being too selfish to notice anyone else around him, when I clearly wasn't any better.

I still felt too confused, too dumb, too guilty to give an acceptable answer. Like, *Hey, don't worry about it. You can't choose that type of stuff, and I'm flattered.* Or *Thank you for telling me.* Or: *Oh my God, I had no idea. I'm so sorry for being an oblivious asshole who's been telling you all about the bad sex with her ex-boyfriend.*

I felt the worst about that. Every time I'd talked to her about my love life. My ex-boyfriends. *Sex.*

Her voice drew me back to reality. The one in which she'd gotten over me, apparently. Otherwise, we wouldn't be having this conversation. That's what she'd said, right? "But if you would've come home with me, I'd have been back to square one, I think. Even with—I wasn't sure—" she stuttered.

"With what?"

Wren swallowed, and I think she was . . . blushing? I wasn't entirely sure because I didn't know she was capable of that. But her cheeks were as red as the HBU logo.

"I met someone," she blurted. "I think."

"You *think*?"

She slid from the armrest she'd sat against and onto the couch, and I followed her lead, getting comfortable for what could very well become a long conversation. One I looked forward to. But Wren shook her head with a laugh. "Later. I'm trying to apologize right now, you nosy ass. The list is so long. First of all, I've been a dick for the past few weeks. Maybe it makes more sense now that you . . . know, but that doesn't excuse how childish it was. Moving on: Thanksgiving—"

I didn't like the way my stomach clenched just at the mention of Thanksgiving, which was the only reason I interrupted her apology.

"You needed your space," I said quickly. You can't get over someone when you live with them, especially not if you also bring them home over the holidays.

"I needed my space, but I still could've handled this whole thing so. Much. Better. Instead of just up and leaving without so much as a note. Fuck, this is so bad." Her eyes jumped back to me, almost panicked. "I really am sorry. So, *so* sorry. I don't know what came over me."

"Well." I cleared my throat, giving her a gentle smile. The serious distress radiating off her made me unnecessarily nervous. "You did leave me with McCarthy, didn't you? So that's . . . certainly something." Hearing the hint of amusement in my voice, she gave a small smile.

"He behaved?" she wondered, and the choice of words made a single laugh fly out of me.

I shrugged. "Too much."

"Good." She hummed, then looked back at me. "I think?"

"I'm not so sure."

"At least," she mused. "He's not as bad for you as I initially thought."

Maybe. Maybe not. I didn't really want to think more about that statement, because if Dylan was good for me, where would that leave us? With a whole lot of shit to figure out. "So you met someone."

Yeah, okay, the change of topic wasn't smooth at all—but Wren was blushing again, and it threw her off enough not to notice my bad attempt.

She cleared her throat. "Everything was so weird between us, you know? I felt bad because my stupid feelings were ruining our friendship and—"

"—*I* felt bad because I thought I was ruining our friendship."

"I really missed you." There was a pause, a long look that said *I'm sorry* even though, I realized, she had nothing to apologize for. "Everything felt so lonely. Dinner. Walking to class. Studying. It seems unfair to say, but Laila was just . . . there."

"Laila!" I gasped. Mike's cousin. Long blonde hair, the sweetest voice, the kindest blue eyes.

Wren shushed me with an amused glare. "I told her, like, the second time we hung out. About our fight. About my feelings. Isn't that absurd?" Usually, it took Wren at least twelve business months to open up. "But she listened. She got it. She said, *I've been there. It sucks.* She helped me sort through the mess in my head until we weren't talking about you anymore, but the book she last read and my favorite foods and when we'd see each other again."

I couldn't explain the pressure behind my eyes. Guilt, maybe, for not having noticed sooner? Causing her enough pain that she had to distance herself? Or perhaps I was just happy she'd found someone that made her smile the way she was now—absentmindedly and beyond her control.

I didn't want to think about the guy who made *me* smile like that, but I did.

"It took me weeks to realize Laila saying she could relate meant that she liked girls. That she could like me. That when she looked at me, laughed at me *not* laughing, called and texted, it could be more than just pity and worry for a new friend." Also unlike Wren—who was usually putting two and two together before it could even turn into four.

"So now you're . . . ?"

"Dating. I guess." Wren shrugged. "No labels. I don't want to be, like, too much—"

I gasped again. "Wren Inkwood! Is that you, overthinking? I never thought I'd see the day!"

She bumped my shoulder hard, but I could see the smile on her face and I could feel the one on mine, threatening to tear my cheeks in half.

The doorbell rang before I could ask more questions. So many of them. Wren hopped off the couch with the agility of a top athlete, probably just glad she could escape my cross-examination, then buzzed the downstairs entrance open, not even asking who it was.

"Expecting anyone?"

"Not unless Prem's taking orders telepathically now. I was about to order when I saw you pull up . . . Yes, I was watching the street from our window like a creep. Do not comment on it."

I only managed to ask one of the questions still swirling in my head. Undoubtedly, it was the most important one. "Are we good, Wren? Seriously and honestly good?"

"If you can forgive me?"

I laughed at the absurdity of her words. If I could forgive *what*? Having a crush on her best friend? Taking the time she needed to get over it? Making sure I wouldn't be alone over

Thanksgiving?

I nodded. "Of course."

Wren smiled, relief written all over her when she opened the door. My face fell at who she revealed.

Henry's frame filled the doorway, and his eyes found mine in a heartbeat. He didn't wait to be asked in, pushing past Wren with an infuriating sense of purpose.

"Henry—" stuttered out of me, immediately on high alert. I stood up.

He seethed as he made his way over, stopping only a foot in front of me. "One day I think I might kill you, Athalia." With the way he sounded, I wouldn't doubt it.

The icy cold of his voice made an uneasy feeling crawl down my neck, and the gleam in his usually warm green eyes only made it worse.

"You're just sitting around. Enjoying a nice conversation with your friend. Probably waiting for takeout. Or about to order some?" His eyes scanned the room to check whether his guess was correct. I wondered how he always *just knew*. "While your brother thinks you're lying in a ditch somewhere!"

I flinched when his voice turned into a roar, sounding angrier than I'd ever heard. "I've called the police twice now. Crying on the fucking line about how my sister's been kidnapped. And here you are." Henry's eyes snapped back to mine. The ache in my chest doubled.

I'd felt bad reading his texts earlier, but this was something else entirely.

There was a different kind of vulnerability in his words, his voice. The way he looked at me suggested that there had never been any malice between us until *I* decided to leave without telling him—as if he hadn't been ignoring me for the past seven years, and this was the first time he seemed to care at all.

He didn't let me get a word in. Just kept ranting and rambling and getting as much off his chest as he'd shared with me since their deaths.

"Getting out of McCarthy's fucking car, of all things."

I wondered if he'd just so happened to be looking out of his window across the street. Or if he'd been watching my building, hoping I'd come back. And I wondered just how much worse that made the situation for him—me getting out of Dylan's car.

My chest rose and fell heavily; I was unsure what to do, what to say. I just stood there, dumbfounded and guilt ridden.

"And you're fine." Again, he gestured to me, faking joy in his voice before his head snapped to Wren. "She's fine." He nodded in my direction when he looked at her, as if he had to confirm it to himself.

"You could've texted Wren to check on me." I think I short-circuited again when those words shot out of my mouth. I wouldn't otherwise be dumb enough to accuse him of not doing enough when I was clearly in the wrong. But the way Wren looked at him—like she was about to physically fight the guy, despite their glaring height difference—I was sure I'd wake up to a kitchen full of cakes and muffins. I had enough to sort out with my brother as it was, I didn't need the two of them getting into it too.

Henry's attention landed on me again. His brows rose. "You don't think I did?" At this point, he sounded fucking defeated. And I think hearing that hurt more than any word he'd said.

Because Henry Parker Pressley didn't give up—his ego wouldn't let him. He didn't get defeated, and he most certainly didn't cry on the phone to anyone. The realization that I'd been the cause of both stung. Terribly. Trying to shove those thoughts to the furthest corner of my mind, my eyes fell on Wren again. If he'd texted her, why wouldn't she just tell him where I was?

She shrugged nonchalantly, eyes pointedly on me. "If you're angry with him, so am I. Doesn't matter if we're fighting or not."

Henry groaned.

"This whole thing has taken twenty years off my life," he muttered, rubbing his face before he looked at me again. He hesitated for a moment.

When he moved, I half expected him to tackle me the way he had when we'd been younger. I did not expect his arms around my body, squeezing harder than he should. "Please don't ever do that again," he muttered, anger replaced by desperation.

The same desperation that made him cling to the hug like a toddler. "*Please.*" His breath came unevenly. I felt his chest rise and fall rapidly when I leaned into him. And I nodded, unable to say anything—not quite sure if I wanted to.

It had been seven years since I'd been in my brother's arms like that. When he wasn't mysteriously drunk, trying to annoy me or playing around. His last serious hug had been right after we'd found out about their deaths and right before he shut me out.

Chapter 32

Wren gave us the privacy needed for the inevitable. Henry's ankle rested across his knee, bouncing as he sank further into our brown leather couch.

"I called Stephanie."

His words caught me off guard. There were a lot of things I expected from this conversation, but not our therapist's name coming out of his mouth. As I watched him trace the sofa's stitching, one leg still restlessly moving, he seemed nervous enough for the both of us.

I tried to keep my expression blank because I wasn't sure what would play on my face otherwise. Surprise about the admission? Compassion for how hard this conversation was going to be for him? Relief because we were finally having it?

So, my face said nothing. Neither did I.

And the words began tumbling out of him.

"About what happened, why I—" He took a deep breath, closed his eyes like he was trying to recite something he'd studied over and over again. "Why I feel the need to control your life whenever I lose some control over mine." The words rushed out of him so quickly that I was almost tempted to make him say it again. His hand drove through his hair, and he sighed again. "I just want what's best for you, and sometimes I forget that's not always what's best for me, too."

Rain splattered against the windows and I tried not to break at the first sign of affection from him.

"Did Stephanie help you figure that one out?" I wondered, barely keeping my voice even. "You know, it shouldn't take a professional who charges two hundred dollars an hour to be able to see that."

His dry laugh filled the space around us. "I know," he said. "I know. And I'm sorry. I'm so sorry, Lia—" His voice broke, and he didn't even bother masking the slip-up.

I'm sorry.

I repeated the words in my head, over and over again. My eyes stung.

But there was no feeling of accomplishment. I thought his apology was what I'd been aiming for. I wanted him to realize he fucked up. I wanted him to care. He seemed to be doing both now, yet I didn't feel any closer to him.

"Would you say something?" Desperation edged into his tone.

"For what?"

He looked puzzled. "What?"

"What are you sorry for, Henry?"

"Lia—" He wanted to argue, but the look on my face stopped him. With a resigned sigh, he continued, "For overstepping. For sending that email. I apologize for everything. Why are you . . . laughing?"

"You really think I did this entire thing because you sent Shaw an email you shouldn't have? Was I pissed? Of course. You overstepped. Massively. And you should work on that, but—" I shook my head. "This thing, dating McCarthy—it was the first time you actually seemed to care. We never talked about anything but school and grades until you stormed into my apartment with those statistic notes." I was almost embarrassed to admit it. "And when you thought there was more between us... you *cared*. I've been wanting you to care since they died."

He blinked at me, and I could tell he didn't know what to say.

But I was on a roll. "I'm sorry for leaving without telling you. I never wanted to worry you like that. But you cannot blame me for wanting my brother back. Even if it means we're fighting, at least we're doing *something*. At least you thought about me, fucking talked to me."

Seven years of suppressed feelings flooded out of me. The dam that had kept my cheeks dry broke when my brother's eyes started to glisten and his teeth dug into his bottom lip to keep it from quivering.

For the second time that night, and for the second time in seven years, I found myself in Henry's arms. He squeezed me so hard, it felt like he was making up for the fact that it had been so long.

"Fuck," he breathed against the top of my head. "Fuck, Lia—"

"I felt so alone, you know? And you just kept moving further and further away. Until you were way out of reach."

He swallowed hard, and he exhaled loudly. "I'm so sorry," he whispered. "I never wanted you to feel alone. I just wanted to give you space. I didn't want to keep you from making your own choices unless absolutely necessary. Like I would've wanted—" He cut himself off like he'd remembered something. "But I guess what I think is best for me isn't necessarily what you think is best for you."

I smiled against his chest, sniffled. "I really love Stephanie."

"Maybe she's worth those two-hundred dollars an hour, huh?"

"Maybe she is," I agreed. "What made you go back to her?"

"I really didn't know what to do about you. I just wanted the opinion of someone who didn't hate McCarthy as much as I do. And with the whole Hamptons thing—"

"What Hamptons thing?"

His gaze cut to mine. I saw the way he cursed himself for letting the word slip. When he didn't say anything, I repeated myself. "What Hamptons thing, Henry?"

This time, he cursed out loud. "I didn't mean to tell you."

"We *just* talked about that—"

"I know, I know." His hands shot up. "I'm sorry. I didn't want to tell you about the summer house because I didn't want you to worry. I've got it under control."

My stomach plummeted a thousand miles. "The summer house?"

His face twisted into a grimace, probably because he noted the concern in my voice. "They were going to tear it down."

I blinked at him.

The summer house? *Our* summer house? With its beautiful marble hallways and white sandstone columns? The rose garden and tiled pool in the backyard? The one where we'd spent every summer since we'd moved to New York?

I'd cried for days when our parents sold it, eyes on a different property in the neighborhood. Before they were able to buy that one, and well before we could make new memories there, they died.

And now someone was going to tear it down?

"What do you mean?" I asked. "You've *got it under control.*

What does that mean?"

"It means I talked to Aunt Claire." My face soured at the mention. He was back to tracing the couch's stitching. "And it's basically ours."

"Ours?"

Henry shrugged. "Ours. Theirs. *The Pressley residence*," he joked before his face turned serious. "It's our family's again. We've got it back."

I didn't remember the last time I'd heard those words. *Our family.*

"I didn't want you to worry. I know how much you love that place, and with all those memories attached to it . . . I wasn't sure if the sale was gonna go through until a few days ago. It's kind of the reason I've been on edge recently—losing that last part of our childhood not marred by death and grief. For a while, it felt like there was nothing I could do about that."

Which, for a control freak like Henry, must've been almost unbearable. "I couldn't stomach the thought of telling you, either." His eyes flicked up to me. "And I'm not saying any of that to make myself look better."

I was glad for the humor in his voice, the way his lips turned into a sheepish smile. "Although, you've got to admit . . ." He trailed off.

I slapped his arm halfheartedly. "Shut up."

He was right, though. What would make him look better, if not this? The fact he'd bought a piece of our childhood, *cared* enough about our childhood to do so—or at least nudged our aunt and uncle to. I didn't think he cared half as much about that place as I did, but alas.

It's where Henry and I had learned how to swim, right

before he'd learned how long he could dunk my head underwater without drowning me. Where I'd purposefully kicked at least a dozen soccer balls into the bushes when he wasn't looking. Where we'd fall asleep in Mom's arms every night during the one week she took off work each summer. Where Dad had taught Henry how to rainbow flick. I remembered that, because it was the first time I'd seen Dad laugh since his team lost that season.

"Oh God." The alarm in his voice caught me off guard. "Are you crying?" Concern filled his eyes. Henry could barely handle his own emotions, I wasn't sure what he'd plan on doing with mine. "I haven't seen you cry in . . ."

"Seven years." The realization dimmed his features, and I blinked heavily to keep the few stray tears at bay.

He sighed. His chest heaved. "I really am sorry," he repeated.

And I believed him.

Chapter 33

Henry's apology came with a string of attachments I did not expect.

Firstly, another hug. Third time's the charm, right?

I didn't mind that as much as the thought of Dylan, and the way my chest tightened at what this whole conversation with Henry meant for us. That there was no need for an *us* anymore.

I should be celebrating my victory: I got Henry to *apologize*. I wasn't forced to date Dylan anymore.

My life could go back to normal.

It had to go back to normal.

In an effort to stabilize our relationship, my brother's first good deed was to give me Dylan's address . . . very, very reluctantly.

And he'd barely been out the door before I slipped into the one pair of black boots I didn't have to unlace to get in and out of, and the first coat I saw— neither matching the rest of my outfit. Then I shouted a goodbye to Wren and left. I didn't even bring an umbrella.

I rehearsed what I'd say to him on the way.

Just came by to say we can stop pretending to like each other now. Henry apologized, so we can end this whole thing and go our separate ways. Thanks for two great orgasms. Sorry I won't get to return them! I really would've liked to.

"Athalia?"

My heart pounded in my chest as I stood on the porch of the house he shared with two of his teammates, Blake and Caden. Soaked to the bones, wet hair stringy against my face, I blinked up at him. "Dylan," I breathed.

Apparently, I hadn't rehearsed well enough. My mind was blank—white room with nothing inside. Nothing but him. And the grey sweatpants hanging low on his waist, V disappearing in them. Plus, the fact he wasn't wearing a shirt.

There was a definite scent of toothpaste lingering between us.

I shivered, not sure whether it was due to the sight of him or the wet clothes clinging to me like glue.

"*Jesus.*" He ushered me inside the house and closed the door behind us. "Did you *walk* here, Athalia?" He peeled me out of my wet coat, and the gesture made me realize I didn't plan to stay long—

"Henry apologized," I blurted.

McCarthy stilled, like he knew what it meant. Then, he hung my coat on the rack and said, "Didn't know he had it in him."

I dripped onto his floors. My boots left size-seven prints of mud and water in his entrance, and I was pretty sure I stood in a puddle that had formed inside of them. The look he threw over his shoulder still heated every part of my body.

I needed to end this. *Now.*

Well on my way to developing pneumonia, I shouldn't be feeling warm and fuzzy. I'd gotten everything I wanted out of our arrangement, but I still wanted him.

"Which means we can . . ." But I chickened out, trailed off.

He turned to face me fully. "Yes." Then he went down on

his knees and forced the air right out of my lungs. Dylan got to work on the laces of my left boot, taking his time when I could've easily wiggled out of them. Despite not finishing my sentence, I knew he understood when he said, "It seems that's what it means."

His fingers curled around my calf, and my pulse skyrocketed. I felt his touch scorch me through the thick denim of my jeans. He gently guided one foot out of my boot and then repeated the same thing with the other. I gasped softly when his finger grazed my bare skin while untying it.

Rising back up to his full height, he leaned out of the front door to dump the water on his porch, then set my boots below the heater behind me. The only sound, when he stood right in front of me again, was my heart beating a thousand miles a minute.

"And what about it?" he asked.

What about the apology?

At the very least, there was the fact there was no need for any kind of relationship between us at all. I had gotten what I wanted, and Dylan had never wanted anything out of this in the first place. *Not really.*

So there was no point in pretending anymore.

I could've easily brought it all up. I could've said: *Look, McCarthy, you don't have to hang out with me anymore. No more fake dating necessary! This is a good thing. Yay!*

I didn't.

"Hm?" The deep hum in his voice was all I needed to solidify a decision I'd unconsciously made somewhere between orgasm number one and two. Somewhere between that time he'd call me 'good girl' and when he'd calmed me after a panic attack.

I shook my head. "Nothing."

I kissed Dylan as if I hadn't been about to fake break up with him. And he kissed me back as if there was nothing fake about this arrangement at all.

His lips moved against mine longingly, only reinforcing the fear that I'd made the wrong decision by not ending this when I had the chance. One more step and I'd be falling off the metaphorical cliff in my head. The point of no return edged closer with every swirl of his tongue against mine.

Pulling back, he said, "You're dripping." He laughed against my lips, voice low and hushed.

"So get me out of these."

His laughter died out, and something else entirely took over his expression. He didn't hesitate to press his lips to mine again, groaning.

"Jump," he mumbled against me, and my legs wrapped around his waist effortlessly. He didn't seem to care about my wet clothes against his bare skin, although he shivered at first contact. His hands cupping my ass, he moved, and a soft, muted moan escaped me when his lips trailed along my neck. If he was leaving a trail of dark bruises all over me, I'd worry about it later. Makeup existed for that very reason.

His brown hair fell into his face when he pulled back, eyes dark and devious. "My room's upstairs," he informed me, as if I cared, then moved toward what I assumed was the staircase.

I didn't check. When my eyes weren't closed because I was kissing him, I focused on the way his brows drew together when I rubbed against his hard length, how he stifled a moan when I trailed a finger down his bare chest.

A squeal ripped through my throat when he almost lost

balance halfway up the stairs, and I slipped out of his arms for my own safety.

"Not a word about that," he grumbled before I had the chance to say anything, though a sly smirk played on his lips. The long corridor we ended up in showed two doors on each side, and McCarthy's hand slipped into mine before he dragged me into the second on the right.

I didn't have much time to look around. Vaguely made out a closet opposite his bed and a desk right by the door before his lips were back on mine, and our combined efforts shifted us toward his bed. It was made up with blue sheets, the two pillows fluffed.

A gust of air escaped my lips as my body fell onto the soft mattress. My stomach twisted when he turned on the light at his bedside table and I saw him hovering over me. "I need to see you," Dylan reasoned, as if there was no way around it.

The light was dim, barely enough to make out his prominent jawline, the cheekbones, brown hair that seemed almost midnight black.

Neither of us cared that my wet clothes soaked his sheets.

His hair flopped over his forehead, and his silver necklace dangled between us. His breath was heavy and his eyes dark. We looked at each other for just a second too long for this to be strictly physical. Seeing him like this, gazing at me like that, there was no way.

Get it together, Athalia.

Instead of backing out like I probably should have, I pulled him back down on top of me, and we were kissing again.

My hands were buried in his hair, reminding me once more that 3-in-1 shampoo could never achieve this level of softness.

I pulled at it playfully, a grin on my lips, and he bit down on my lower one, coercing soft whimpers out of me.

"Hey." He pushed away from me. "This wasn't my plan. This isn't why I agreed to help you out," he said, searching my reaction carefully. It was hard to concentrate on anything other than how easy it would be to connect them with his again. "You know that, right?"

I nodded, then asked teasingly, "You want to stop, then?"

Given what was pressing against the inside of my thigh, I knew he didn't.

"God, no."

His lips crashed to mine, hands beginning to roam my body.

I quickly followed suit. It had been all about me in his office, then on the piano bench. And it was a crime I hadn't gotten the chance to feel much of him yet. With my fingers gliding along his toned stomach, tracing every ab underneath my fingertips, I felt like I'd robbed myself of an unknown pleasure. That feeling only intensified when his breath became heavier the further down my fingers trailed.

I'd never appreciated sweatpants as much as I did when I could feel his length through them. He groaned at the friction, and the sound traveled right between my legs. His hand slipped underneath my tight, long-sleeved top, his touch sending goose bumps across my skin. Sneakily, as his hands travelled up and up and up, the hem of it followed. I wanted to get rid of it right then and there.

Not because it was cold and wet, only because I wanted his touch everywhere: no barriers.

Sitting up at once, my chest heaving, I pulled it over my head. Well, *tried to*, until my elbow hit something hard in the process. I faltered, registering a stream of curses coming from Dylan's lips.

No, no, no.

My eyes widened, head still buried in the fabric as I scrambled to pull it over my head. Throwing it to the side carelessly, I was greeted by McCarthy rubbing his chin, trying to soothe the pain my elbow seemed to have caused.

"Fuck, I'm *so* sorry," I said, feeling my cheeks grow red as I tried to see how bad it was. "Are you okay?" My hand gently cupped his cheek to make him face me. Worry filled my eyes when they met his.

Dylan, clearly amused, shook his head. "Even now you'll take any and every opportunity to knock me out, huh?" he joked, eyes still locked with mine before he noticed the missing piece of clothing. He watched my chest rising and falling. His gaze lingered, and I suddenly felt the need to grab a pillow and hide behind it.

I'd never been particularly self-conscious about my looks. And while a B-cup had its perks, when my boobs were being scrutinized like they were a painting in the Louvre—and by the one guy in whom I had yet to find a physical flaw—I wouldn't have minded a cup size bigger. Or two.

"Yeah," he mumbled, just as I was about to break the short silence between us. "I'm definitely okay." The encounter with my elbow seemed instantly forgotten.

"You're staring," I pointed out, an eyebrow raised and a smile I couldn't suppress on my lips.

"I guess I am." There wasn't a hint of embarrassment or shame in his voice before his lips crashed onto mine again. He kissed my jaw, trailed his lips further down my neck and chest.

Making his way down my body, he merely grazed one nipple before he moved on, leaving a trail of sloppy kisses all the way down to my wet jeans.

His eyes jumped to mine, head tilting as his hand lingered over the zipper, waiting for my approval to continue. I just nodded, not sure I'd be able to form a coherent sentence.

"Use your words, Princess," he teased, placing another kiss right above my waistband, making me squirm underneath him.

"Take them off," I told him. "Please."

Almost completely exposed, I pulled him back up to my face. I couldn't help but stare at how the muscles in his arms moved when his hands trailed along my body, how they shifted underneath his skin. How his defined torso raised and fell heavily, in sync with his breathing.

"God," I breathed out. "I hope you're bad at this." My confession was met with a low laugh, and it only reinforced my words. "Really, *really* bad."

You came here to break up with him, I reminded myself. But I could still do that after, couldn't I? Watching as he slid out of his sweatpants, reminded again of the bulge straining against his boxer briefs, I decided getting this out of my system would be good.

This primal, hungry need for him.

"I'll try my best." His eyes jumped to mine. "Just for you."

"Will you?"

"No." He managed to slip that in just before our lips connected again, and my hands enjoyed exploring his defined back enough that I didn't care. When that last piece of fabric came off, and he rolled the condom he'd found in the nightstand down his length, that fear was only replaced by factual knowledge.

Whatever happened next wouldn't be bad.

He stroked himself once. *Not at all.*

Good sex. Just really good sex. That's all it was. Two grown adults getting it out of their system before going their separate ways. Purely physical attraction fizzing between us. That's all there was to it.

I don't think I believed it for a second.

"Look at me," he murmured, and my gaze returned to his, eyes a little wider than they were before. His fingers hooked underneath my panties, teasing down and back up my wet folds. My breath grew heavier, lids threatening to fall shut every time he pushed between me a little more, never fully.

"Athalia." His voice was dark and heavy, and my eyes opened fully again. "Look at me, Princess," he muttered. I tried my best to oblige, though when he slid the last piece of fabric down my legs in one skillful motion, I couldn't help but throw my head back with a satisfied sigh.

"Hey." I could feel him align with my entrance. "Look away, and I'll stop."

"Is that a threat?" My eyes narrowed at him, though the teasing tone in my voice was obvious enough to make his lips curl into a smirk. I moved against his cock, and I got a deep sound of satisfaction in return.

"It absolutely is."

Whatever I meant to retort, I forgot as soon as he pushed into me. My head fell back, though my eyes stayed on him. I made sure of it, just in case he'd follow through on his threat.

With every inch he added, his breathing deepened until a low, unapologetic moan escaped his lips when he was inside me fully. Just feeling him, feeling myself adjust around him, made me a writhing mess underneath him.

"*Shhh,*" he whispered, eyes fluttering shut only for a second. "I know, Love. I know." A kiss to my forehead, and I shuddered at the touch.

His first thrust was hesitant, slow. As if he didn't want to miss a single sensation as he explored me. His eyes connected with mine again, an unspoken question lingering in their depths that I answered with another moan.

This was fine—more than fine.

So, he moved again, settling into a steady rhythm. The room filled with sounds we were both trying our best to suppress... unsuccessfully.

"Athalia," he said. "You're a dream." He was edging me closer to relief with every snap of his hips against me, every rasp of his voice. "You don't know how often you've been in mine."

When his hand trailed across my nipples, down my stomach and between my legs, I was done for. "Fuck," he groaned, slowing down, becoming sloppier. "You feel so good." Every sound he couldn't seem to suppress traveled right between my legs. Clinging to him like he was my lifeline, I moved my hips against his.

"I think—" But before I could finish my sentence, he reached where I needed him most, and I cut myself off with another moan. And he kept finding that spot over, and over, and over again until I felt ready to combust.

"What is it?" he whispered, not altering his pace now that he knew I was close. "Talk to me."

Between heavy breaths I forced out, "I'm—oh God—"

He buried his face in my neck. "Sorry, just me."

My face contorted into a laugh, and a moan, and the edge of relief. "I'm gonna—"

My orgasm flooded through me somewhat unexpectedly, twitching and pulsing underneath him enough to get him to his own.

Peppering my skin with kisses, he rolled onto the other side of his bed. I shuddered with every touch, still panting.

For a moment, we were quiet.

"Bad enough?" The amusement in his voice was masked by his still ragged breathing. We both kept our gazes locked on the ceiling, and my eyes narrowed, even though I wasn't looking at him.

"Awful."

"Yeah?" The shuffling sound from beside me indicated he'd turned his head toward me, and I mirrored his gesture, just happy I hadn't been first. I found a smile and messy hair: a deadly combination. Just as deadly as the fact that it hadn't been bad enough. In fact, it hadn't been bad at all.

"Just terrible." I insisted, watching his lip twitch with a laugh he was desperately trying to hold back. "So bad, I can't even put it into words—" I shrieked. Propped up against his headboard, Dylan pulled me on top of him, hands curling around my hips to steady me.

"Good," he said, pressing a short, casual kiss to my lips. "Never again, then?"

"Well . . . Maybe once or twice."

"Once or twice?" he confirmed.

I rolled my eyes playfully as if it hadn't been my idea in the first place. "If you *insist*."

"All right." He placed another kiss onto my lips, short and

sweet. "Once or twice it is." And another one. This one longer as he turned us onto our sides, guiding us into the position we'd eventually fall asleep in.

Involuntarily.

Because if this was as casual and physical-only as I had wanted it to be, I should've left. Really, I should've broken up with him before I'd even gotten myself into this mess. Because there was absolutely nothing casual about short kisses and falling asleep next to each other.

Chapter 34

However, there was something very casual about waking up in an empty bed the morning after. Nothing said "this isn't a serious relationship" like reaching for the person that's supposed to be lying next to you, only to find their spot cold and empty.

I should have been ecstatic about it. Better to find out Dylan had changed his mind about me now than after I'd replayed that thing he did with his fingers or the way he'd moaned my name when he came.

Why wasn't I ecstatic about this?

Turning with a grumble, I opened my eyes to the empty side of his bed. The covers were neatly pulled back, the imprint of his head still on the pillow. That's when I noticed the hot pink sticky note stuck to the headboard, and my stomach twisted.

Sticky notes didn't say casual to me, my physical-only side complained.

Sticky notes didn't say casual to me! my why-wasn't-I-ecstatic-about-this side cheered.

I got up embarrassingly quickly, then ripped the pink paper off the headboard.

Had to leave for Harvard game. By the time you're up, I'll probably be done. Text me. We can go celebrate.

In the corner, he'd drawn a rose identical to the ones he'd been terrorizing me with just weeks ago. *Fuck just physical.*

According to the huge smile on my face, one side had won so long ago that denial had become my trusted companion. I let that admission simmer for a moment. Took a deep breath in and out. Thought about it. Thought about him. Thought about him some more. Took a deeper breath and scrambled out of his bed, away from his smell entangled in the sheets.

I'd fallen off that cliff a while ago.

ME, Saturday, 11:25 AM
> how well did being cocky serve you? did you win or is this going to be a defeat-lunch?
> either way I'm down

I didn't know why I had expected an immediate response, but when it didn't come, I didn't like the disappointment settling in. I took my time getting dressed, deliberately keeping my phone out of reach. It wouldn't hold out much longer with its ten percent battery, anyway.

My jeans were no longer on the floor. Hanging across the heater under the window, they weren't wet anymore either. But Dylan must not have had the time to search for my shirt because when I found it half hidden under his bed, it was still damp. I cringed at the touch.

A few minutes later, I was wearing Dylan's grey HBU hoodie and a pair of fuzzy socks from the back of a drawer.

I tiptoed down the corridor and staircase before I realized both of his roommates were on the soccer team, and there was no need to be quiet. Something swelled in my chest at the thought that he'd trusted me enough to leave me here by myself.

Three hours later, I was back in full denial mode. Square one: Dylan McCarthy Williams was despicable. Just the worst. I had never liked him, would never like him, and last night was as big a mistake as asking him to be my fake boyfriend in the first place.

He hadn't replied to my texts, if you couldn't tell.

I hunched over a textbook at our kitchen counter. Wren was on the other side, trying to decide what food to order. There were at least twenty menus spread across the island.

I read the exact same sentence for the fourth time, and my head slumped onto the open book with a groan.

"What?" Wren asked, brows furrowed.

"Nothing."

My response wasn't very convincing because a moment later, she asked again. "What is it?"

"You're going to laugh at me."

A beat of silence passed as she tried to figure me out. She was usually great at that, so her lighthearted answer didn't surprise me.

"I probably will," she agreed, and I raised my head from the textbook to glare at her. "But tell me anyway; maybe there's wisdom behind the joke I'll make."

I hesitated before the word "McCarthy," slipped out. And I wasn't surprised when her brow furrowed. I wouldn't have understood what I'd said if I hadn't been thinking about him (and my unanswered texts) for the past few hours, either.

"What?" she confirmed that I'd spoken too quietly. Maybe it's better that way.

"McCarthy," I breathed out, slower and with more conviction behind my words. "It's McCarthy—*God*, this is embarrassing."

When my eyes slid to her again, they narrowed.

Wren's goofy grin was rare; it revealed her white teeth, crinkled her nose, and narrowed her eyes, not in annoyance but laughter. "*What?*" I practically hissed, prompting an amused snort.

"Nothing." Her hands flew up in mock surrender, then she changed her mind. "I'm just wondering if you even know his first name at this point." The incredulous look on my face made her continue. "Well," she began. "You've been dating for months. You've been hooking up, too, I assume. Do you moan his last—"

I cut her off so quickly that I would've stumbled over any word that wasn't: "Wren!" Hushing and blushing; loudly, hysterically. "We have *not* been 'dating for months.'" I put air quotes around the words.

"What do you call hanging out every day and going on actual *planned* dates, like, once a week, then?" She raised her eyebrows as if she knew she had won right then and there. But I wasn't giving up that easily.

"*Fake* dating."

"Your orgasms are fake, too, then?"

I grabbed the dish towel I had been fidgeting with and threw it at her, hurling it right into her face and knocking a few takeout menus off the counter in the process.

"Stop," I whined. "Why is it so weird to talk about him like that? We love talking shit about men. It's like our favorite hobby." I pouted.

Her smile softened and her head tilted in that *I'm-going-to-be-a-good-friend-now* way. Like when she'd pulled an all-nighter to help me study for my last final or when she had to tell me my ex-boyfriend was cheating on me. She'd sat me down, put an arm around me, her head on my shoulder before she did. She was looking at me the way she had back then, too.

"Because you like him." I had only come to terms with the fact this morning—and had since done a 180 on the idea. I also wasn't sure how I felt discussing my apparent feelings with Wren—or, more accurately, how she felt discussing them with me. After last night . . .

I shook my head. "We don't—" I started, then reconsidered. "If you're not comfortable, we don't have to talk about it. Him. Really—"

She slapped me upside the head. "Athalia Payton Pressley," she said. "Don't make this weird. Don't you dare! I got over it, now you have to. And if we're not discussing dirty details in a week, you've failed. So for now, let's settle on your feelings. *You like him.*"

Any lingering reservations dissolved. Things might feel awkward for a while longer, but she was right, I did have to get over it. *Wren was still my best friend. Last night really hadn't changed much between us.*

I glanced at my phone in resignation. "He hasn't even texted me back, and—" My eyes widened, and Wren gave me a knowing look. "Oh my God," I gasped. "That was pathetic. I'm pathetic, aren't I?"

And to top it all off, as if it was an instinct I couldn't fight off, even if I'd wanted to (which I didn't), I jumped for my phone the second it vibrated on the counter next to me. Hope fizzed in the pit of my stomach when I turned it over.

"LinkedIn." I slid my phone back across the counter.

"Oh my." She sighed, smile back on her lips as she shook

her head sympathetically. "You've got it bad, haven't you?" Her tone was as teasing as it was genuine, her smile as amused as it was comforting.

"I wish I had another dish towel." But I didn't disagree. "I don't want to have it bad." I concluded, looking at her as if she had the power to extract my feelings, bottle them up, and make them look pretty on a shelf.

"Been there, done that," she joked. There was no bitterness in her voice, but I felt guilty regardless.

"Look." She cleared her throat, trying her best to steer clear of any awkwardness. "I may not be McCarthy's biggest fan," she admitted, nudging me toward the living room. I grabbed my phone from the counter, just in case. It earned me an eye roll. "And if it turns out he has no reason to ghost you, I will personally kick his ass." I let myself sink into the couch cushions with a deep sigh. "But until then . . ." Wren trailed off as if it were hard enough to give him the benefit of the doubt.

I dropped my head onto her shoulder in defeat. "I think I hate him," I lied.

"We can pretend you do," Wren's voice adapted a comforting lull. "What do you hate most about him?"

We'd spent so much time together, and yet all I could think of was one thing.

"That he doesn't know how to use his phone." I sounded like a pouty child, and I didn't care one bit. Neither did Wren.

"For me, it's the ego," she said. "But not knowing how to use his phone is a close second."

"How close?"

"*Very close.*"

"Good." My lips twisted into a smile, and I adjusted my head on her shoulder for more comfort. Right then, I was just glad we were here together, glad she stuck around, and really glad she was still my best friend.

"Fuck him, right?" I asked, eyes darting down to the name McCarthy shining brightly on my screen. "I shouldn't answer," I said more confidently. Immediately, that crumbled, and I sent her another look. "Right?"

The green and red call buttons were equally enticing.

"Well," Wren began. "I'd love to hear him beg for forgiveness." One point for green. "On the other hand, he needs to know you're not constantly available for him." Two points for red because it was a much more compelling argument.

But my distress only grew when the phone had been ringing long enough that it would stop any second. Short-circuiting—as I did when it came to McCarthy—I picked up.

"Look who finally remembered they had a phone," I drawled sarcastically. Wren gave me a thumbs-up.

"Athalia."

My stomach dropped when Dylan wasn't on the other end. I held the phone away from my ear to read the contact name again. *McCarthy* was written in bold, big letters underneath the seconds of the call ticking by: nine, ten, eleven. "Hello?"

I quickly brought it back to my ear. "Yes?" I said, unsure where the lump in my throat came from. "Who's this?" Wren gave me a strange look as I held her gaze.

"It's Blake—"

"Blake!" I repeated, a little too cheery. Wren's brows drew together just like mine had. "Is this your way of asking for my number?" A fake laugh accompanied my attempt at a joke, and it fell on deaf ears.

Blake cleared his throat at the other end of the line, as if preparing for a speech in front of thousands of people. "Listen, uh—" he stammered, and I knew if we were having this conversation face to face, he'd be avoiding my gaze. But we weren't, and so I kept my eyes on my best friend for some kind of comfort. "It's Dylan," he said.

My head spun, immediately jumping to death. Car crash, heart attack, a rough foul that caused a broken neck. The possibilities were endless, and my breath picked up.

"What about Dylan?" My voice was surprisingly neutral considering the wave of panic that had just crashed over me. I think the hand in the pocket of McCarthy's hoodie was shaking. The one holding the phone was not.

Wren looked concerned and the entire situation felt all too familiar.

Flashbacks of Aunt Claire on the phone, eyes continuing to flicker back and forth between my brother and me as she tried to comprehend her sister's sudden death. She had probably felt similar to how I did now, my mind immediately jumping to the worst case scenario.

"We're in the hospital, he's—" Blake hesitated, and I didn't mean to jump at that cue. The word kind of just slipped out.

"Dead."

Wren shot in my direction so fast, I was surprised she didn't fall over her own feet. Concern riddled her features as she leaned closer to the phone I pressed tightly against my ear.

"What?" His breath hitched. "No, no—*God, no.* It's nothing like that." I exhaled for the first time since hearing his voice.

"He's pretty bruised up, a couple of broken ribs, the hospital gave him . . . *something*—"

Not dead, but pretty bruised up with a couple broken ribs, in so much pain the hospital had to give him *something*. It didn't sound like a reason to celebrate. "Which one?"

Blake stuttered on the other line. "Which—?" he repeated. "Which drugs?" He cleared his throat. "I don't know; I could probably ask." He was moving around, maybe scouring the hospital corridors for a nurse or doctor. I shook my head even though he couldn't see it.

"Hospital." I interrupted his search, and he paused on the other end. "Which hospital?"

"Oh. Saint Francis Memorial—"

The line went dead because I'd killed it, already halfway through the apartment, throwing on sneakers and a coat, grabbing my car keys.

"What on earth do you think you're doing?" I was mid-departure when Wren's voice boomed through the space. She had put on shoes too and was heading for the coatrack. She snatched the car keys out of my hand, grabbed her own, and without waiting for a reply, stepped through the door I had opened for myself. When I closed it behind me, she finally asked, "Where are we going?"

I don't know why, but I laughed. Maybe it was the nerves, the adrenaline coursing through my veins. Maybe the endless adoration I had for the girl beside me. I sighed, and it felt as though my entire face twitched back to reality. "Saint Francis Memorial."

Wren's brows drew up slightly, her eye twitched once, and her lips curled in concern and worry. For me or Dylan? I didn't know.

Her pace picked up, though she said nothing. I could tell she wanted to stop right there to comfort me, but she knew the last thing I needed was to slow down. So, we power-walked to her car while she typed the address of the hospital into her maps app.

As she drove, I filled Wren in on the broken ribs, the bruises, and the drugs.

"*But*," I added. "Not dead." I tried to sound hopeful. But how low was the bar if not dead was supposed to be encouraging?

"God," I exhaled, my body slumping back into the seat. "I'm an asshole." Wren's eyes jumped from the road onto me for a second, and I took that as a sign to go on. "I was annoyed the guy wasn't answering a stupid text when he was probably on his way to the fucking hospital."

It had been similar with my parents. Henry and I had been upset about their spontaneous Thanksgiving trip idea, which hadn't included their children. We'd been dumped with one of the sitters our parents relied on, sitting in the living room overlooking New York City.

"I hope it rains," Henry had said. "I hope the food is bad," I had countered. Hours after they should've arrived, hours without the usual "made it" text or call, we'd kept going. "I hope the mosquitos are vicious this time of the year," Henry had said. "I hope the water is cold," I had said.

By then, they were already dead.

"You're not an asshole." Wren snapped me out of my thoughts.

"I am! Even *you* gave him the benefit of the doubt." I didn't even realize the severity of that until now. "Oh my God," I gasped again. "Even you—"

"Athalia," she snapped. "Would you stop guilt-tripping yourself over something you had no control over or knowledge of?"

My mouth opened to disagree, though her sharp glare silenced me. For the remainder of the short drive, my legs bounced in the passenger seat as I struggled not to go on and on about how much of a selfish asshole I was. By the time we'd parked the car and walked inside, the only thing I could think of was Dylan.

The presence of an entire soccer team in the hospital lobby not only indicated we'd found the right place, but also that the accident couldn't have been too long ago. That, or his team just loved him so much, they were still here hours later. They were probably hoping he'd get discharged today, but from what Blake said, I doubted Dylan would spend his night anywhere other than a hospital room. Some players sat with their heads down, others had offered their spot to the few elderly people among the hospital crowd. My brother stood in the farthest corner there was, his arms crossed in front of his chest, staring at his feet, one of which was propped against the wall behind him.

Later, I thought. Instead, I scanned the place for Blake.

I spun around at least three times, pushing myself up on my tiptoes to catch a glance of his dark skin and short hair. Nothing. Just rows of vaguely familiar faces noticing me, then falling into whispered conversations like little girls who weren't sure if they'd just walked past a celebrity.

If they knew why I was here, couldn't one of them just point me in the right direction? The right room? The right floor?

"Room 219, second floor."

I hurled toward my answered prayer. And stared back at

Wren. "How do you know?"

Her head tilted lightly, turning me toward the receptionist. "I *asked*," she said, giving the blonde, middle-aged woman a light wave. "And the nice lady told me." The nice lady smiled back at us, then nodded.

"But you hate talking to strangers."

Wren was the introvert to my extrovert. When there were reservations to make, customer service lines to call, or questions to ask, she sent me to handle them. Since it was the only thing I could do for her—the only way she seemingly benefited from our friendship—I did so gladly.

Wren asking the receptionist (*anything*, never mind where we'd find McCarthy) was to me what premium *Hamilton* tickets were to her.

I love you! I mouthed, watching her make her way over to Henry as I pressed the button to the second floor. Six times.

Chapter 35

222, 221, 220—I came to an abrupt halt, seeing Room 219 before spotting Blake on one of the hallway chairs.

"Oh," I stuttered, for God knows what reason. "Hey." My gaze drifted back to the closed door of the room, only vaguely aware that Blake had settled in beside me.

"I didn't think you'd actually come," was the first thing he said to me. "Now I feel bad for not thinking you'd actually come."

Some of the tension in the air evaporated. "Does this make me pass your background check, then?" I asked. My eyes only flickered toward him to make sure he got the reference to our conversation in the bar. The amused smile on his lips told me he did. It felt like an eternity ago.

"Athalia." He chuckled softly. "You passed that so long ago, you shouldn't even be thinking about it anymore." Then, he gestured to the door. "I didn't tell him you were coming."

"Seeing as you didn't think I was, that makes sense."

"Sorry again."

I think he was waiting for me to go in. I think I was, too. Three times I'd been just about to make the first step, and three times I'd changed my mind, then only swayed lightly in the direction of the door.

Blake cleared his throat again. "By the way, the drugs are

kind of... intense." He seemed almost amused. "Which is why I'm out here, and not getting my ear chewed off in there. He can't seem to shut the fuck up."

And then I just stopped thinking, stopped overthinking, really, and grabbed the handle, even though I was completely unprepared for what would meet me inside.

I think I held my breath until my eyes fell on Dylan. He looked... not all that bad.

. There was a fat bruise on his cheek, but no sign of a broken rib, although, admittedly, I wasn't sure what signs of a broken rib I could have picked up on.

"Oh God." My eyes snapped back to his, concern furrowing my brow. "I'm dead," he said. "I've gone to heaven?" After a long pause, he offered a corrective; "Or hell."

"You think I'd get into heaven?" I huffed, amusement mixing with relief as I stepped toward him. It was so easy—slipping into sarcasm and irony and jokes, even when the situation didn't call for it.

He smiled, wide and loopy, his head rolling to the side to follow my every move until I stood right beside him.

"Fuck no," he snorted. "If anything, you're the reason I'm down here now." He reached out his hand to interlace his fingers with mine, smiling up at me as if he'd just declared his love, instead of calling me a demon that landed him in hell.

"Ouch." But I wasn't the least bit offended. "How are you?"

"Don't lie—" he started, drowsily amused. "You were always hoping I got injured one way or another. This is just a delayed manifestation of that." His smile was teasing.

"That's—" *outrageous, awful... true.* "Not true," Was what I settled for. Dylan snorted.

"You cheered every time I got fouled or missed a shot."

God. I had, hadn't I?

My eyes narrowed. "Did Henry tell you that?"

"No one told me that," he stated matter-of-factly. "I saw—" He cut himself off, debating whether to go on. "When you picked your brother up from practice the first time, I asked what your name was, and he told me to fuck off. Since then, watching you is all I've been doing." He shook his head. "Thinking about you, too. Noticing you. When I walk into a room, it's second nature to look for you. It's no different when I'm on the field. I look through the stands until I do or don't see you. I didn't even know why."

I wondered how much of that his sober self would have admitted. But he seemed content with his words, a lazy grin on his lips at the memory.

"Well . . ." I shrugged, trying to ignore the guilt gnawing at every fiber of my being. "Wren might've rubbed off on me. You should've seen how excited she was when she told me about that time you got punched in the face."

His face lit up at the memory, strangely enough. "Oh!" He swooned, head falling to one side as he squeezed my hand. "You should've seen how I defended your honor!"

The haze of the memory or the number of drugs meant he didn't pick up on the confusion lacing my features until I asked, "What?"

He startled. "What?"

"*My* honor?"

"Yes, yes," he rushed out. "That's what I just said—" He cut himself off, brows drawing together in confusion again. "I'm speaking, right? My lips are moving? Words are coming out of them?"

I snorted. "Yes, McCarthy. Words are coming out of you. They just don't make any sense. What does my honor have to do with you getting knocked out?"

"I did *not* get knocked out," he asserted, offended by the accusation. "Took it like a champ to get Baker—" I assumed that was the puncher. "A red card after he couldn't stop running his mouth."

The memory alone seemed to rile him up enough as he went on. "*'Pressley, where's your hot sister?' 'Pressley, mind giving her my number?' Pressley, your sister* this, *your sister* that. And Jesus Christ, I *needed* him to shut up. Your brother did, too. He was about ready to knock him out, by the looks of it. But it was only halftime, and we couldn't afford Henry off the field. So, I stepped up. Pissed Baker off enough to take a swing at me."

He was full-on grinning now, lost in the memory. Entirely ignoring (or too high to notice) the stunned expression on my face. Speechless. *Again.* I cleared my throat, tried to swallow the swelling adoration I felt for him. I couldn't deal with what his words did to me right now.

"How are you?" I asked.

He patted the side of his bed, prompting me to sit with a sigh. "Like a 200-pound, 6'4 Harvard guy tackled me." His head fell back into the oversized pillow, but his eyes stayed on me. "Go on," he urged. "Ask me what happened."

I couldn't suppress the smile when I did. "What happened?"

"A 200-pound, 6'4 Harvard guy tackled me." He seemed pleased. "Which landed me on such a heavy load of drugs, I'm still not sure you're actually here."

"And what if I am?"

"Then I'd be very happy about that."

"If I weren't?"

"I'd need to talk to my therapist about why I'm hallucinating the girl I'm supposed to hate into my hospital room."

Supposed to.

My stomach turned, twisted, then released, all in the span of a few seconds. I felt giddy and nervous, and I hadn't felt like that since I'd bought my first really expensive bag. An actual giggle escaped my lips before I managed to catch it.

"Probably because you've had the best sex of your life with her," I suggested thoughtfully, proud of the laugh that hurled out of him, only to feel guilty when he flinched in pain. "Sorry," I managed to say. "Seeing how funny I am, this is going to be hard." He laughed again, flinched again.

"See?" I said sheepishly, and Dylan waved me off with the hand that wasn't still hold mine.

"I heard she had a terrible time," he said, a brow raised. "Awful, if I remember correctly."

"She might've been . . . exaggerating."

"Is that why she's here?"

"Perhaps." I shrugged. "Or perhaps she feels bad for thinking you were ghosting her when you were actually in the hospital." The confession kind of just slipped out. "And trust me—" I hurried on. "She feels *so* bad, she promises to actually help you the next time you're cooking. She'll even do it all by herself if you want her to."

Dylan managed to suppress a laugh, skipping the part where he hissed in pain. "You're so romantic," he said sarcastically. "It's what I love most about you."

I probably should've been more apprehensive about a loaded

statement like that. What I love most about you tended to entail there was any love at all. It usually went: I love you, but what I love most about you is *(blank)*.

And maybe if he'd spelled it out, made it a big deal, maybe then it would've freaked me out. Though, honestly, in hindsight, I think we had both said "I love you" to each other in our own ways that day in the hospital. Maybe that's why I hadn't felt nervous. Just happy. Content. Grateful.

I held his hand a little tighter in mine. "Can you say that again when you're not high as a kite?"

Dylan grinned when he nodded enthusiastically. "Sure I can," he boasted. "I'll say it until you don't want to hear it anymore."

"And that's a promise?" I asked, as amused as I was curious.

"A threat." He winked very wonkily, and I blamed it on the drugs. Again.

My head tilted lightly. "That's one hell of a commitment, Dylan."

His lips split wider at his name on my lips. Then, he shrugged.

"Well," he began. "I'm a pretty reliable guy, Athalia."

Chapter 36

"It's my broken ribs."

"You cannot blame everything on your broken ribs." My brows rose along with the corners of my mouth, and I shook my head as I continued to sneak curious glances at his screen. "Not when it's nearly been a month."

"When I took this exam—" He waved his phone around, though the motion was too quick for me to read what it said on the screen. "I was out of the hospital for a week. And it's *showing*."

"So show me!" I whined, rolling from my side of the bed over to his, where he sat propped against the headboard.

We had woken up to emails about our Statistics II grades being posted. Today was the end of Shaw's two-week period to post them, so it wasn't unexpected. Still, I had about a million better things to do in the morning. Like, not think about Statistics and the possibility of failing a class, especially not the one my mother's legacy had been built upon.

"No."

In one quick movement, I straddled his lap, face hovering right in front of his with a grin. "Please?" I pressed a quick kiss on his nose, then his cheek, then his chin. Dylan huffed.

"That's not fair," he muttered under his breath, managing to catch my face in his hands before I could press a kiss to his lips and seal the deal.

"I'll show you mine if you show me yours," he said, and I groaned, dramatically falling off his lap before snuggling against his side.

"I don't know mine."

"You haven't checked?"

"No."

An incredulous look spread across his features when I craned my neck up to look at him. "What?" I huffed. "I'm not particularly fond of ruining my day. It *just* started." The humor in my voice fell on deaf ears.

"You don't think you failed, do you?" Dylan sat up straighter now, turned to me with his serious-face on full display.

I hadn't thought about how my fear of failing might affect him.

Would it be insulting? After the hours he'd poured into making sure I wouldn't fail, was thinking I had ungrateful? My mouth stayed shut, gaze steering clear of his, as I took in the white flower patterns on my white bedding. *Beautiful stitching.*

"Athalia."

My eyes snapped back to his, Serious-Dylan still in control of the conversation. I shrugged.

"Maybe," I muttered to myself. He heard me anyway.

"You were so confident after that exam," he reminded.

"It's called post-final euphoria," I explained. "You know? When you're done with all your exams, and you finally feel like you have a life again."

He looked me dead in the eyes and said, "No." And it reminded me of all the reasons we shouldn't have worked so well for the past few weeks. He was a workaholic at the ripe age of twenty-three. I probably hadn't thought about work for longer than a total of ten minutes of my life.

He was always busy. I was mostly bored.

College, grades, and graduating were his purpose. I was still trying to find mine.

He took life so seriously. I . . . didn't.

It was a weird whirlwind of mismatches that somehow just . . . matched. When I'd been ready to throw in the towel and drop out—which happened at least three times a week during finals—Dylan was there to keep me grounded.

When he'd get lost in his head, overworked himself, or forgot to sleep, I was there to drag him into bed and sentence him to an eight-hour sleep.

"Come on." He nudged my side gently, brows rising when my eyes slid back to him. "I know you want to." Then he wiggled his eyebrows, causing my lips to break into a grin before I could bury my head in the pillows. Two groans escaped me.

The first one acknowledged how little I wanted to look. The second one acknowledged I would have to eventually. So why not now?

"If I'm in a bad mood the entire ride to D.C.," I warned as I sat up, reaching for my phone on the nightstand. "That's on you, and I'll never let you forget."

One more glance at him made me turn my screen slightly, and a muffled complaint slipped past his lips. "Just let me check first," I muttered, suddenly tenser than I'd like to admit. I typed in the login for the account, keeping myself from visibly shaking as the page loaded.

I swallowed thickly, my eyes fixed on the screen with equal parts anticipation and dread.

"And?" Dylan nudged, but I simply raised a hand, watching the spinning wheel on the screen. My heart sank when it disappeared and made way for the grading system.

And there it was.

There it was.

There. It. Was.

My sense of disbelief was almost entirely overshadowed by relief, gratitude, joy.

My gaze snapped to Dylan, letting my phone fall into my lap. A wide smile spread across my face.

"Thank you!" I screeched, wishing I could jump him without the possibility of breaking a rib again. "Thank you. Thank you. Thank you."

"See?" he whispered into my hair. "Nothing to worry about."

He said that without having seen my grade. Whether I had barely passed with a C or aced the exam with an A seemed to be none of his concern. Whatever grade I was content with, he'd be proud of, too.

"You really showed Shaw, didn't you?"

"Technically . . ." My head lifted from his chest, a smirk on my lips as I looked at him. "I showed you, too." His quirked brow made me go on. "You thought I was a hopeless case. You even told Shaw I was!"

His face softened as he remembered. "I would never do that."

"But you told me—"

"Athalia," he sighed deeply. "There wasn't a second in all this where I didn't believe in you."

I think my heart just got bigger simply to let more of him in.

"I knew how smart you were before you ever stepped

foot into my office, and there wasn't a doubt in my mind you wouldn't thrive, with a little guidance and the right . . . motivation."

"So you lied to me? About the Shaw thing?"

"Of course I did." And his honesty—how unapologetic he was about it—was so relieving.

"What else?" I wondered, my head tilting in curiosity and amusement alike. "Did you lie about, I mean."

He thought for a second, then looked back at me. Shrugged. "Hating you."

"Hating me?"

"Probably even just disliking you a little bit. But I lied to myself about that for longer."

The realization of that settled. I wished I could say the same back, have this be our full-circle moment, where we'd realize we had both been undyingly in love with each other from the moment we had laid eyes on the other.

Not that we'd said "I love you." Those three words slipped out so soon in my previous relationships; in this one, I wanted to savor them until I'd burst if I didn't tell him. And I think none of his relationships had lasted long enough to even consider it. In a way, this was uncharted territory for both of us.

And maybe that made it easier.

Refraining from saying the words didn't mean we weren't still making it known every single day. Every time he carried me to bed after I fell asleep on the couch, every bad joke he laughed at, every meal he cooked when I suggested takeout said *I love you* all over again.

I just smiled at his words, my nose crinkling. "I knew you've always been obsessed with me," I joked, lightheartedness replacing the silence his admission had left behind. Dylan's eyes rolled in that incredibly endearing way before he pressed a kiss on my forehead and hurled himself out of bed.

"God," he sighed as he stretched, giving me an incredible view of his body in nothing but boxer briefs. The bruising across his ribs had gone down and the pale blue left behind was much less menacing. "I forget how much of a pain in the ass you are sometimes."

Which was just another one of the million ways of saying "I love you" he had adopted.

I love you too, Dylan McCarthy Williams.

Epilogue

"Ten minutes, people!" somebody shouted over the music. The rest of the crowd erupted into cheers. Hands, and possibly bodies, were thrown in the air as the numbers on the projector screen began counting down.

The hand holding my cocktail glass shot upward, and if I weren't as euphoric as I was, perhaps I would've cared more about some of the sticky liquid spilling onto my dress.

But I was euphoric, and I didn't care. My glass clinked with Wren's water midair and I made a point of looking her in the eyes to avoid bad luck. Then, I repeated the procedure with Laila, the "extremely casual" date Wren brought to the annual Pressley New Year's Eve party.

The only difference from the past few years was the absence of views from the top of a New York City skyscraper, which had been replaced by idyllic gardens and rosebushes in the Hamptons. Additionally, instead of one McCarthy Williams getting invited (reluctantly), six of them got (enthusiastic) invitations.

I twirled in place to look for my one, though seeing through the dense crowd proved to be far more difficult than anticipated. With an excusing glance toward Wren, one she rightfully understood as *I'll be right back*, I wove through dancing bodies, sharing smiles and laughs with vaguely familiar strangers as I pushed past them.

I spotted my brother leaning against the bar in the back, a drunken, wary look on his face. If I just followed his gaze... bingo. My McCarthy stood with the rest of them, having formed a casual circle from which only the youngest of his family members was missing. Even his dad showed a relatively pleased expression.

By the time my gaze shifted back to my brother, his attention had already drifted. Henry had always been a people-watcher, more so than a mingler, though I was surprised by who I found at the other end of his gaze.

"You invited Paula," I said by way of greeting, watching her curly hair bounce with the sway of her hips, in tune with the music. "Are you guys better?"

"No," he grunted, though his eyes stayed on her. "I also invited her friends. I invited most people I've spoken to. This has nothing to do with Paula, specifically—" He caught himself rambling and immediately shut it off.

I nodded. "Classic. You invited her friends to make it seem less like you wanted to see her—"

"I didn't want—"

"They didn't hook up, by the way. Her and Dylan," I blurted out, and I felt Henry's eyes on me for the first time. "And you never told me that you thought that just because you saw them *hug*. Are you twelve?"

Henry blinked one, two, three times, which he probably needed to compute the information. His mask of nonchalance barely slipped out of place, but the fact that it had at all told me the revelation changed things. Hopefully for the better.

Now that the summer house debacle had been fixed, the MLS draft was over, and Henry had a professional contract lined up, maybe he'd have more time for other things in his life. Relationships that weren't familial or professional.

"Dylan." He hummed disapprovingly. Like his first name tasted sour on his tongue. At the mention, Henry's eyes slid back to him across the room. "Still wondering if we really had to invite all six of them," he said drily. "I know you're taking advantage of my guilty conscience. And I still can't seem to do anything about it. You ask, I say yes."

"Don't worry, I just have that effect on people." I winked. "I do appreciate you trying. With him."

Henry snickered, clearly overcoming something before he asked, "So you guys are . . . what? Dating?" He winced, like the thought caused him physical pain. "You'd think after what you put me through the past few months, I'd be used to the thought by now."

Clearly, he was not.

"I don't know," I admitted, eyes trailing back to Dylan at the other end of the room. He spotted me at the same time, smiled, and started in our direction, right as someone in the crowd announced, "Five minutes!"

Loud cheers erupted through the room. Henry leaned toward me to make sure I'd hear him over the noise. "For the record," he said. "If he hurts you, I'll kill him myself."

I think that was as much of an approval as I'd get from Henry.

"You said you'd be nice," I pointed out before Dylan could make it to us. Henry's hands shot up in defense, almost offended at the accusation. "Even Wren liked having him at *Hamilton*."

Henry shook his head dismissively. "You know how she gets about *Hamilton*," he pointed out. "That's not a fair comparison."

Maybe not. "Still—"

"I haven't said anything," he grunted back.

"It's the *way* you said it."

"Said what?"

"If he hurts me." I tried my best to mirror his tone and attitude. Henry snorted. "It's like you're expecting it."

"I said it perfectly normally, Athalia. The way any brother would."

I groaned, turning toward him with an accusatory finger lifted. "You did *not*—"

Strong arms wrapped around me from behind, effectively cutting me off. "You most definitely did not," Dylan chimed in, his eyes on my brother. I didn't need to see the smug grin on his face to know it was there.

It was Henry's turn to groan in annoyance, glaring at the man behind me. "You don't even know what we're talking about," he pointed out, eyes shifting as I felt Dylan's lips against my cheek, kissing it once.

"I don't need to." He stepped around me casually, and it was like second nature to lean into him. "There's few times you do *anything*, at all—"

"McCarthy," Henry snapped, eyes flicking to Dylan's arm around my shoulder. "I swear to God if you don't—"

"Henry!" I glared at him. "*Behave.* Don't laugh—you too, Dylan." I finally turned, just in time to see the smug expression slip from his face. "We've talked about this." The reminder was met with an eye roll, but it made a smile find its way to my brother's face.

"*Yes, Dylan.* You've talked about this," Henry gloated, though another one of my glares finally shut him up.

I sighed, faking a swoon. "I just love that you guys get along so well." My fake smile turned into a scowl—maybe a pout—and Dylan gave me another kiss on the forehead before interlacing our hands.

"Come with me," he said simply, and by the time I followed, I wasn't paying attention to how he tipped his head toward my brother or how Henry mirrored the gesture in a silent goodbye.

Dylan gently guided me after him. Given the way he navigated through the house with such ease, one would think he spent most of his summers here. Perhaps it was easy because he had no true destination in mind. He led me around corners, through corridors, until the music was mere background noise, and the only light was the moon, shining through the large balcony window.

"Since the first guests arrived, all I've wanted to do was steal you away." He twirled me around once before pulling me to his chest. "You look so pretty tonight."

"And you decided to do that right now? Two minutes before midnight?" My gaze was as incredulous as it was adoring. "You really thought that was the best time to steal me away, Dylan?"

He nodded proudly, taking a few steps back to lean against the wall, pulling me along with him. His head fell back. "God," he muttered. "I love it when you call me that," he said, his eyes returning to me. "Have I ever mentioned how much I love it?"

I grinned so widely my cheeks hurt. "It *is* your name," I pointed out.

He shook his head quickly. "I don't love it because it's my name," he protested. "I love it because you're saying it."

It was another one of those moments. *I love you too.*

In the distance, people began to count down. "*Ten! Nine! Eight!*" they chanted from the main room in unison. "*Seven!*

Six! Five!"

Dylan's smile was subtle, his head tilting slightly, when his hand moved from my waist to cup my cheek.

"*Four! Three! Two!*"

"Can I kiss you?" he asked against my lips, a sliver of air all that separated us. Instead of answering, I just did. Pressed my lips to his lightly and lovingly, missing all the heat that usually played into this part of our night.

I love you too, Dylan McCarthy Williams.

"First of January," he whispered against my lips, reminding me of that contract for the first time since we broke it. "How does it feel to be officially on the market again?" He failed to hide his dimpled grin.

"So." I pressed a kiss to his lips. "*So.*" Another kiss. "Lonely." And another one.

He hummed against my mouth, nodding in mocked understanding as he caught my lip between his. "Yes," he sighed, a groan bubbling in his throat. "Me too." He looked at me. "Such a coincidence—both of us single and lonely at the same time." His tongue flicked over his lips. "Isn't it?"

"*Such* a coincidence," I agreed, nodding grandly. "Whatever can we do about it?"

He laced our hands together and kissed me. The fireworks lit up the hallway. They matched what was happening in my stomach, and the moment could've been perfect for many reasons, but I could only think of one . . .

1. I loved him.

I was in love with him.

Our kiss faded into deep smiles, hovering against the others, his forehead pressed to mine. A light note of champagne lingered on his breath when he sighed against me.

And, like he could read my mind, he said, "I love you too, Athalia."

Acknowledgments

The last time I said "Thank you for reading what I wrote" (in a much longer and sentimental way) was over three years ago, on a website where, arguably, too many people to truly wrap my head around . . . read something I wrote. LESSONS IN FAKING wouldn't exist if it weren't for you, so you deserve my first big fat thank you. For every sweet comment, message and your encouragement over the years. I honestly don't know where I'd be without you.

Now, onto the truckload of people I'm also immensely thankful for. From drafting to publishing: I'm glad I wasn't alone at any step of the way.

Thank you to my wonderful editor, Katharina, for every 'What if we focus more on this?' that turned this book into what it is today. You're a genius.

Thank you, Domi, for figuratively holding my hand throughout this entire thing since you first read the earliest of early drafts. I would've probably combusted if you hadn't been there to receive every thought I ever had, in a string of twenty-five texts.

My mum cried when I officially announced this book, which, in turn, made me cry and had us sending crying-selfies back and forth for a solid thirty minutes. Thank you for being my biggest supporter (and also for picking up every single one of my five calls a day): I love you.

Last but not least (because Google said this shouldn't be longer than one page and I'm not quite sure what I'm doing yet) thank you to every single person who allowed me to chew their ear off about this before I could officially do so to everyone else on social media. Thank you for every encouraging "That's so cool!," tearful "I'm so proud of you!" or sarcastically loving "I'll be your biggest fan!" If you find yourself in this category and aren't quite sure if I'm really thinking about you while writing this: I am. Thank you, from the bottom of my heart!

To say publishing this book feels like a dream would be an understatement. And if it *is* a dream, please don't pinch me.

Thank you. Thank you. Thank you.

uncorrected proof

Content Warning

This book contains the following content:
   Mention of parents' death, plane crash, loss, grief

uncorrected proof

uncorrected proof